THE TYWI ESTUARY KILLINGS

THE CARMARTHEN CRIME SERIES BOOK 2

JOHN NICHOLL

Boldwood

First published in 2018. This edition first published in Great Britain in 2022 by Boldwood Books Ltd.

Cover Design by Head Design

Cover Photography: Shutterstock

A CIP catalogue record for this book is available from the British Library.

Paperback ISBN 978-1-80426-309-9

Large Print ISBN 978-1-80426-308-2

Hardback ISBN 978-1-80426-310-5

Ebook ISBN 978-1-80426-307-5

Kindle ISBN 978-1-80426-306-8

Audio CD ISBN 978-1-80426-315-0

MP3 CD ISBN 978-1-80426-314-3

Digital audio download ISBN 978-1-80426-311-2

Boldwood Books Ltd
23 Bowerdean Street
London SW6 3TN
www.boldwoodbooks.com

To Laura, Ben, and Edward, I'm proud of you all.

1

9 OCTOBER 1982

Detective Sergeant Gareth Gravel sat back in the driver's seat of his West Wales Police Mondeo and stared at the Smith family's front door for almost five minutes before finally exiting the vehicle. Delivering bad news was never easy. He'd seriously considered delegating the task to one of the force's new-fangled touchy-feely family liaison officers for a time, but he'd eventually decided that it was something he had to do himself. He was a DS now, and rank carried responsibilities as well as privileges. It was his case, his failure, and like it or not, he had to man up, say his piece and face the inevitable shitstorm coming his way. Best get it over with and get out of there just as fast as his size tens could carry him.

Grav, as he was known by all in the force, took one last drag on his cigar before throwing the glowing butt to the ground and grinding it into the gutter with the heel of a shoe that was badly in need of polish. Come on, Grav my boy, let's get this done. He'd be in the rugby club with a pint of Best Bitter in one hand and a set of darts in the other before he knew it.

A small part of him was hoping he wouldn't receive an answer as he walked down the concrete driveway, approached the front door and knocked with gradually increasing force. But, all too soon, a naked bulb bathed the hall in a depressing yellow hue and a man in his mid-thirties, who he immediately recognised as David Smith, stood facing him.

'Can I come in for a chat, Mr Smith?'

Smith gripped the doorframe to either side of him. 'Any news?'

'Can we speak inside, Mr Smith? There are things we need to discuss.'

'Just say it, man. We're sick of waiting.'

'I'd rather not do this on the doorstep, if that's all right with you?'

Smith lowered his arms, turned without reply and hurried towards the lounge, where his wife was shuffling from one foot to the other as if the floor was too cold to stand on.

'Sergeant Gravel's finally got some news for us, Jan.'

Janice Smith forced a less-than-convincing smile, oblivious to her involuntary dance. 'Can I get you a cup of something, Sergeant? You look as if you could do with it.'

'I'm all right, thanks, love. Kind of you to offer.'

'You're sure? It's no trouble.'

Grav took a seat in a convenient armchair and thought for a moment that she may start weeping. 'Oh, go on then, you've talked me into it. I'll have a mug of tea with plenty of sugar.'

'And a biscuit?'

'Thanks, love, it's appreciated. Chocolate if you've got one.'

'One mug of sweet tea and a nice Bourbon coming up. Anything for you, Dai?'

He shook his head. 'I'm good, thanks, Jan.'

David Smith waited for his wife to leave the room before moving to the very edge of the settee. 'Right, what the hell's all this about? This isn't a social visit. That's blatantly bloody obvious to all of us. Why drag it out?'

'Is Rebecca in the house?'

Smith frowned, the hairs on the back of his neck standing to attention. 'Why ask about Becca? Hasn't she been through enough for one short lifetime?'

'I just don't want her overhearing our conversation.'

Smith swallowed hard. 'That's one thing you don't have to worry about. She's staying with Jan's mum and dad for a couple of days. They've got a caravan on the Pembrokeshire coast near Amroth. There's a heated pool. We thought it might take her mind off things. God knows she could do with it.'

'Okay, that's good to know. Small mercies and all that. Do you want me to hang on for the missus to rejoin us before kicking off?'

Smith shook his head. 'No, just crack on. I can bring her up to speed when you're gone. I'm not sure she can take much more of this shit anyway. She's on antidepressants as it is.'

'Okay, if that's how you want to play it. We've finally got a decision from the Crown Prosecution Service.'

Smith hung his head. 'So, come on. What's the verdict?'

'It's not good news.'

'Oh, for fuck's sake!'

'The CPS don't think there's sufficient evidence to prosecute Sheridan. It's not going to court.'

Smith slumped back in his chair. 'But, the video interviews. She told that police officer and social worker *everything* that happened to her. All of it! She went into graphic detail, just as *you* said she'd have to. She relived all those terrible events to give *you* the evidence you said you needed. Can you imagine what that was like? For her? For us as her parents? She's suffered flashbacks, nightmares, and she's wetting the bed again almost every night. She's nearly seven for fuck's sake. Regression, that's what her social worker called it. Feeling like shit when she shouldn't have a care in the world is probably a more accurate description from what I've seen. And now you're telling me she went through all that for nothing. Is that what you're telling me?'

'I'm sorry, Mr Smith, I truly am. We did all we could. I promise you. But, it's not like the good old days when the police decided whether or not to bring a suspect to court. It's down to the Crown Prosecution Service these days. And they just don't feel they've got enough to secure a successful prosecution, despite the evidence provided by your daughter. That's how they work. They have to think there's a good chance of success before going ahead. I don't agree with them, for what it's worth. I think any half-decent jury would see she's telling the truth, but the decision's made. I've tried. I've pulled out all the stops. There's nothing more I can do.'

A single tear ran down Smith's right cheek and found a home on his collar. 'Well, that's just not good enough. You gave us the distinct impression that Sheridan would be locked up for a long, long time. Surely you can persuade them to change their minds. Let a jury decide. That's all I'm asking.'

'I'm sorry, I've done everything I can. There's no point in me feeding you some bullshit version of events to make you feel a little better. It's not going to happen, whatever else I say or do... unless we can come up with more credible evidence. Something solid that corroborates your daughter's allegations. A game changer.'

'And are you likely to?'

Grav shook his head, wishing he had a different, more optimistic reply to offer. But he had to tell it like it was. The man deserved the truth. However unwelcome. However unpalatable. 'I can't see it happening.'

Smith was on his feet now, his voice raised and reverberating with raw emotion. 'He touched her. He made her touch him. My little girl. It went on for months. She's six years old, for fuck's sake. The dirty bastard violated her, and you're telling me he's going to get away with it! How the hell am I supposed to tell Jan? It'll break her heart.'

Grav looked on, temporarily lost for words as the father disintegrated in front of him.

* * *

'Refreshments coming up. Here you go boys...' Janice stopped and stared. 'What is it, Dai? What's happened?'

'I'll uh... I'll tell you later.'

'Dai?'

He opened his mouth as if to speak, but then closed it again, unable to find the words.

Janice shrieked, dropped the tray to the floor, turned away from the two men and ran upstairs to Rebecca's bedroom, where she clutched a soft toy to her chest and closed the door against the world.

'Did you see the state she's in?'

'Yeah, I'm sorry.'

'You've let us down, Sergeant. You've let me down. You've let the missus down, and worst of all, you've let Rebecca down. You do realise that, don't you? This is real life, not some fucking game.'

Grav reached out and placed a hand on one of Smith's broad shoulders, reluctantly choosing to ig-nore the wailing coming from the first floor. 'I gave Sheridan a seriously hard time, if you know what I'm saying. We kept him at the station for as long as the law allowed, but he just sat there in total silence with a smirk on his ugly face, refusing to answer a single question for hour after hour.'

Smith pulled away, his face contorting as he choked back his tears. 'You're telling me you did your best. You're telling me you pulled out all the stops.

But it wasn't good enough. It wasn't nearly good enough.'

'No, it wasn't. Not even close.'

'So how'd it go so horribly wrong?'

'Sheridan's one clever bastard. He knew there was no unequivocal forensic evidence; he knew his wife had given him alibis for some of the relevant dates and he knew the only witness was a six-year-old little girl. He believed he had a good chance of walking away if he kept his mouth tight shut, and he was right. The bastard knew exactly what he was doing.'

'So he's free to get on with his life as if he did nothing at all?'

'Look, Dai, I'd slice the cunt's balls off if it were up to me. But, yeah, that's the crux of it. In the eyes of the law, he's an innocent man.'

David Smith screwed up his face and spat his words. 'I'll tear the dirty bastard apart if I see him.'

'And I wouldn't blame you, Dai. Honestly, I wouldn't. I'd want to do much the same thing myself in your place. But Janice needs you here. Rebecca needs you here. What good would you be to them banged up in prison for fuck knows how long?'

'There's no justice in this world.'

'Sometimes there is and sometimes there isn't. That's the truth of it. I'll put the word out within the force. Sheridan will slip up. His kind always do. We'll nail him for something in the end.'

Smith followed as Grav rushed towards the front door. 'That's the best you've got? You'll get him one day?'

'Now might be a good time to go and see that wife of yours. You've both got to find a way of putting this behind you, Dai. Leave Sheridan to me. I've seen it before. If you don't, it'll destroy you.'

2

2 DECEMBER 1999 – SEVENTEEN YEARS
LATER

Twenty-three-year-old Rebecca Smith made the
most of her opportunity for a lie-in before finally
switching off her alarm, throwing back her single
quilt and jumping out of bed with an easy enthusiasm she hadn't felt in quite some time. The one advantage of living alone, she reminded herself, was
being your own boss in your own home. Or at least
as far as both the past and current circumstances
allowed.

Rebecca made a quick bathroom visit before
pulling on a thick woollen cardigan against the
morning frost and heading downstairs to prepare
breakfast. It felt good to be alone with her thoughts,

good to have some time to herself, and best of all to have a new target in mind. Such things gave purpose to her lonely existence and made life worth living. She hadn't self-harmed even once since putting her plans into action. No cuts, no bruises and no thoughts of suicide. That spoke for itself. She was inspired. Driven. Happiness was perhaps something of an exaggeration, but mild contentment was a reasonable description of her current state of mind. As long as she focused. As long as she prevented her mind wandering and didn't let that smug bastard into her head even for a single second.

She stood at the kitchen table and noticed that her hand was trembling slightly as she dropped a generous portion of cereal into a porcelain bowl. She added chilled soya milk from the small counter fridge and a light sprinkling of local honey she considered a justifiable treat, while waiting for the kettle to come to the boil. Why did the frigging thing always take so long when you were watching it?

Rebecca glanced at her laptop charging on a nearby countertop and briefly considered checking to see if her latest target had sent any further messages. But she quickly decided it could wait for another hour or so. Let the bastard sweat. Don't seem too keen. That was best. It wasn't as if he were going anywhere. Perhaps give her mum a ring after breakfast instead. It had been a while and duty must. She had to be the good daughter whatever the pressures of life.

* * *

The phone rang and rang for what seemed like an age, but was in reality a little over a minute, before Janice Smith finally said, 'Hello,' in a breathless voice that sounded as if she'd just completed a marathon.

Oh, Mum. Poor Mum. She sounded older and more exhausted by the day. Stress could do that to a girl. 'Hi, Mum, it's Becca. Are you okay? You sound a little out of breath.'

Janice took a blue plastic asthma inhaler from her corduroy flares and inhaled two urgent puffs before stuffing it back in a front pocket. 'Hi, Becca, I'm fine, thanks. I was upstairs seeing to Dad as usual. But, more to the point, how are you on this fine morning?'

She was putting on a brave face again. She'd

been doing it for seventeen years. Why would she change now? 'How's Dad doing? I keep meaning to call, but work's been hectic.'

'It's good to hear your voice again. How's that wonderful boyfriend of yours? Didn't you say he's a barrister?'

What a gullible woman. Or did it suit her mum to believe? Perhaps it was a positive choice of sorts. A coping mechanism. Truth and lies became one as required.

'Are you still there, Becca? The phone seems to be playing up again.'

'He's away at the moment, working on a high-profile case in London. You may have seen it on the news.'

'Not that big murder case involving the actor?'

She'd fallen for it hook, line and sinker. Swallowed every deceptive word. 'Yes, that's the one. Paul's a QC now. The youngest in the country.'

'Well, that's marvellous. You've fallen on your feet with that one.'

'So, how's Dad?'

She paused before replying, fidgeting with her cuff. 'Much the same, to be honest. That last stroke did a lot of damage. He can't really do very much at all for himself any more. I know you're busy with that important job of yours, but we haven't seen you for months. He'd love to see you again.'

Rebecca threw her half-empty cup at the nearest wall, smashing it into what seemed a hundred jagged pieces.

'What was that, Rebecca? It sounded like a window breaking.'

Focus, Becca, focus. It would all be over soon enough. 'I'm good, Mum. I just dropped a cup, that's all. There's nothing to worry about... you were telling me about Dad. Are the council carers still coming to the house?'

'Oh, yes, four times every day. They don't stay for nearly long enough, but they do their best with the time they're allocated. I couldn't do without them, to be honest. That's the truth of it. Shit happens. I've just had to get used to it.'

'All that misery because one dirty perverted bastard did what he did. He's still haunting us like a brooding, malicious, spiteful spirit. He blew our lives apart. We were pulverised. Dragged through a mincer. Me, you and Dad. None of us were ever the same again. He's a dark shadow that hangs over our very existence.'

Janice Smith closed her eyes tight shut. 'Oh, not this again. The dark mantra of your fragile soul. You've got to learn to put all that behind you, Becca. Like that nice social worker said all those years ago. Do you remember? Dad's life is over. That's the brutal reality. And mine's not much better. But yours is just beginning. You've got a great job, a lovely home and that wonderful boyfriend you've told me all about. Try to concentrate on the good things in life and look to the future. That's my advice. Sometimes memories are our enemies rather than our friends. Sometimes the past is best forgotten.'

Blah de blah de blah. Easier said than done. And at least she was doing something about it. Something positive. Something meaningful. Not wallowing in her guilt and sorrow like *they* were.

'Hello, Becca, are you still there? The phone keeps going dead on me.'

'Sheridan's still with us. He's like a foul odour that we can't wash away, however hard we try.'

Janice Smith administered two further urgent puffs of her bronchodilator, and sank to the floor as her chest tightened, tighter, tighter and tighter, as if squeezed by an invisible vice as she gasped for breath. 'Can't we t-talk about s-something d-different for a change? Please, c-cariad! I just c-can't take any more of this.' She was panting hard now, like an overheated dog in need of water. 'T-tell me about that j-job of yours. You're s-such a clever girl.'

'I've been promoted again.'

'Oh, well done. That's w-wonderful to h-hear. You're doing so v-very well for yourself. Tell m-me all about it.'

'It's always the same. Anything to cheer up your unhappy existence.'

'I'm just taking an interest, that's all. There's no n-need to be cruel.'

'I'm still at Police Headquarters. Computers. But I'm a supervisor now. It means more money and my own office.'

'Congratulations, you d-deserve it after all your hard work at that university. So what exactly d-do you do with those computers of yours?'

Rebecca held the handset out in front of her and glared at it before speaking again. 'I haven't got time to explain all that now. It's complicated. There's things I need to get on with. Things demanding my attention. I'll ring again in a week or two.'

Janice's breathing was calmer now. The vice released to some extent as she began to relax. 'I'm so pleased you're doing so well. I'll tell Dad all about it. You're a credit to us... I love you, Becca.'

Rebecca broke into a smile that lit up her face. 'And I love you too, Mum. Give my best to Dad.'

'I will. It'll cheer him up a bit.'

Duty done and time to go. Where was that laptop? The bastard would be champing at the bit by now. 'Bye for now, Mum. Speak soon.'

'Bye, Becca. Look after yourself. I love you.'

3

Grav sat opposite Dr Susan Gibson, the force's consultant psychologist of choice, and pondered why the hands of the wall clock above her head were moving so very slowly. Didn't time fly when you were enjoying yourself. If he could speed them up and get out of there, he'd be a very happy man. 'Are we nearly done, Doc? I've got work to get on with. Criminals didn't arrest themselves the last time I looked.'

She looked him in the eye and smiled. 'You've got to love a trier. You know you've got to finish the ten sessions. You know this is the last one. Be patient, man. We've just got to complete the final evaluation and I can write a report for the chief superintendent. You're going to have to be satisfied with that.'

The DI took a gulp of his coffee and grinned. 'Well, thank fuck for that. As much as I enjoy your good looks and sparkling personality, I'll be glad to get this over with. You told me to be honest, so there you go. I can't be more honest than that.'

'Always the comedian. Always a brave face. A common survival tactic among high-risk, high-stress occupations like yours. You're not kidding anyone. I've seen it all before more times than I care to count.'

'Is it really that obvious?'

'Look, Grav, I suggest you swallow that well-practised male macho pride of yours for a minute or two and tell me if you've found the process useful in any way. The answers in the most recent questionnaires you completed for me suggest you're making progress, although there's still some way to go before you're truly on top of things.'

'You think?'

'Yes, one hundred per cent. DS Rankin's death hit you hard. It was the final blow that knocked you off your feet. The straw that finally broke the camel's

back, to use the predictable cliché. You've already acknowledged that more than once. Don't go doing a
U-turn on me at this late stage in the proceedings.
That wouldn't do either of us any favours, especially
you.'

Grav reached both hands out wide in front of
him and held them there for a moment. 'Yeah, I
was knocked off track for a time. But, surely that's
normal. We were close mates as well as colleagues.
I miss him. I'm not ashamed to admit it. You knew
him yourself. He was a great bloke. One of the
best.'

'Knocked off track? That's got to be the under-
statement of the year. You struck a fellow officer. You
hit him to the floor in front of witnesses. You were
lucky not to be prosecuted. You know that as well as
I do.'

Grav drained his mug, savouring the intense
sweetness at the bottom. 'Trevor Simpson? He's got
the sort of face you want to punch. Surely you're not
going to hold that against me?'

She fumbled with her notes on the coffee table in
front of her. 'You've got to take this seriously if you're
going to stay in the job. I like you. I want to help. But

you've got to cooperate to that end. Sometimes you're your own worst enemy.'

His lips pressed together and for a moment it looked as if he might cry.

'Come on now, Grav, you have to admit that you weren't coping. You have to acknowledge that things are getting a little easier now. You're more your old self again, yes?'

'Yeah, okay, I was struggling. I'll put my hands up to that. But post-traumatic stress? Come on, really? Isn't that a bit over the top? I thought that was something suffered by combat soldiers.'

'Another coffee?'

He checked the clock again and smiled thinly as she refilled his mug. 'Thanks, love, it's appreciated.'

'We've had this conversation more than once. It's time for you to accept reality once and for all. Denial isn't helpful. Not at this late stage of the process. You had *all* the symptoms we've discussed over the weeks. Ding, ding! Does that lot ring a bell? You're still suffering from some of them to varying degrees.'

'Okay, enough said, point taken.'

'You were faced with Heather's bowel cancer and untimely death. You two were childhood sweethearts. You were together for a very long time by anyone's standards. That's more than most people could cope with right there. And then you had a series of particularly demanding cases. You're not immune to emotional and psychological distress, despite the tough-guy image you choose to portray to the world. You're flesh and blood just like the rest of us mortals. You can't tell me you weren't affected.'

'Okay, the organised abuse case took a heavy emotional toll on the investigating officers, me included. We're talking about young kids. Some still in nappies, for fuck's sake. The offences were horrendous. What the hell's wrong with those people?'

'Then came the discovery of five young women's bodies in a local wood.'

Grav flinched as the memory stung and festered. 'Thanks for the reminder.'

'And then, just when you thought things couldn't get any worse, came Clive's death. Not just his death, but the very nature of his death. Suicide hits loved ones right in the gut. Friends, relatives. It's visceral. Brutal. Almost impossible to bear.'

He raised a hand to his face as his eyes filled with

tears. 'Thanks for all the help, Doc. Do any of your patients ever come back for another appointment?'

She smiled, but the expression left her face as quickly as it appeared. 'You've been through a great deal. You're human, just like the rest of us. And you care, however much you like to hide your feelings with a joke or a sharp word. That makes it harder. A lot harder. It's not one single event that caused the PTSD. It was an accumulation of factors, one after another. A series of blows no less real than what you inflicted on DI Simpson... and down you went, Grav. Down you went.' She paused momentarily and held her hands together as if in prayer as he shifted his gaze to the wall. 'Now, *please* tell me you understand. Tell me you're taking this on board. I need to hear you say it.'

He closed his eyes and bit the inside of his lower lip hard, tasting blood. 'Okay, I accept things haven't been easy. Things got on top of me. But I'm over it. You've said that yourself. I'm back on track.'

She shook her head slowly and blew the air from her mouth with a perceivable high-pitched sound. 'Don't put words in my mouth, Grav. I've decided to recommend you stay in the force despite my misgivings, God help me. But you're *far* from over it. Unwelcome memories have a frustrating habit of rearing up, sinking their teeth in and clinging on like limpets. All I've done is give you coping strategies to help you shake them off. You *badly* need that three-week holiday we were talking about. That's not optional, by the way. I'll be making that crystal clear in my report. Go and visit that son of yours. And I want a postcard so I know you're actually there. Put yourself first for once in your life. Do you hear what I'm saying to you?'

The DI held his hands high above his head as if surrendering at gunpoint. 'Okay, okay, you've got me. I get the message. You don't want to come with me, do you? I'm sure I could fit you in my suitcase if I tried hard enough.'

'Here we go again. Back to the comic side. Your usual fallback position when the direction of the discussion challenges or unnerves you even in the slightest.'

'So, is that a yes?'

'I'd love to, but I don't think my husband would be too chuffed. He's kind of possessive.'

'Yeah, yeah, any excuse. If I looked like Robert Redford, you'd be all over it.'

She laughed, handed him two A4 sheets of typed paper, and sighed theatrically. 'Now, concentrate, get those filled in for one final time, and I'll leave you in peace to get on with your life. How does that sound?'

Grav reached out and squeezed her hand before sitting back and beginning to tick various boxes less than enthusiastically. 'No, seriously, I'm grateful, love. Talking has been useful. I didn't think it would be, but it has been. I'm coping. And you'll be glad to hear that the holiday's booked and paid for. Hold on, Barbados, here I come.'

4

Rebecca perched on the edge of her single bed with her computer resting on her lap, tip tapping the keys with a rapidly moving red-painted fingernail. She adjusted her reading glasses with her free hand, stared at the screen, and shook her head as multiple beads of sweat formed on her brow despite the winter chill. The filthy bastard was typing again... brace yourself, Becca. Oh, for fuck's sake. It was more of the same. Gross! No surprises there. He was nothing if not predictable. They all were. As transparent as polished glass. What else would he write? What else would he have to say for himself? It was always manipulative. Always with his ultimate goal in mind. That was why the slimeball was online in the first place. That was why he trawled the internet night and day in search of suitable prey. Tip tap, tip tap. Tap away, you misguided miscreant, you slug, you rodent, you societal curse. I know exactly what you are and I'm coming after you like a steam train. Okay, give him time, Becca, give him time. If you gave them enough rope... his fantasies were becoming ever more extreme. His desires more perverse. And he was gaining confidence now. More sure of himself. Revealing his true nature like never before. He was telling her what he'd like to do to her. He was telling her what he'd like her to do to him in familiar graphic detail. And he promised generous gifts. Of course he did. Favours. Anything her little heart desired, if she entertained his proposals and satisfied his longings. The cost was unimportant. The expense of little, if any, consequence. It was up to her. Just choose. That's all she had to do. Designer clothes, trainers, a new mobile, the very latest top-of-the-range computer, and a pony. Even a frigging pony! He was playing his best cards now. And he really believed he was winning. He thought he was approaching the endgame. He could smell it, taste it, almost touch it. This middle-aged husband and father who believed he'd been exchanging daily messages with a ten-year-old schoolgirl for almost six weeks. The outwardly respectable man who'd gradually upped the ante and sent her photos of his flabby milk-white naked body with his face carefully hidden. Always hidden. If she agreed to meet, he'd give her anything she wanted. As long as she told no one. As long as it remained their special secret, he'd give her the world. Of course he would. He'd give her the frigging world.

She took a slow deep breath, in through her nose, and blew the air from pursed lips with a barely audible whistle. He was hooked. The slippery bastard was well and truly hooked. She had him. It was just a matter of time. If he thought he was grooming her, he was *very* sadly mistaken. Ha! Who was hunting who now? Predator had become quarry. Okay, her childhood abuser had avoided prosecution. He hadn't paid a suitably high price despite her disclosures. Despite her determined protestations to any trusted adult who was willing to listen. He'd got away with destroying her childhood innocence. He'd damaged her and he'd damaged her family. But this one would pay. Oh yes, the sick bastard would pay. It was time to pounce. Time to sink in her claws. She was a roaring lioness now, not the cowering mouse of the long gone past. It was time to drive home her advantage and reel the bastard in.

She glanced at the latest sexual selfie appearing before her, adjusted her long dyed brown fringe with trembling fingers, swallowed hard, resisted the impulse to vomit, and spat tiny globules of warm saliva at the screen before typing again:

Wow!!!! youll give me a pony. Youll realy give me a pony?
Of course I will, my dear. And I'll teach you to ride it.
will you????
Yes, I promise. But only if we meet. Only if it's our special secret.
Wen can I have it?
After we meet. After we've had some fun together.
Realy????
I promised, didn't I? I always keep my promises.
Can I choos the ponys name????
Yes, of course you can, my dear. But, where do you

live? I need to know where you live. I can't buy you
the pony until I know where you live.

She pictured him sitting at his computer, sweaty,
naked, and masturbating like his life depended on it.
Make him wait, Becca. Make the bastard wait. He's
gagging for it. Ready for plucking. She counted
slowly to ten before typing again:

Carmarthen I live in Carmarthen on the concil estate
neer the park
Ah, that's good. I don't live very far away from you.
And I know the perfect place for the pony to live. But,
it has to be our secret. Just like I said. You can't tell
anyone. Not a single one. Not your parents, nor
friends, not your teacher, nobody. That's very, very
important. You do understand that, don't you?

She paused again with her finger hovering over
the keyboard, eyes narrowing, but only for five seconds this time:

yer I understand but were would we meet?
I'm a music teacher. Tell your mum and dad that you

want piano lessons. I'll give you my name and contact number. You can tell them that one of your
friends told you all about me. Tell them she said what
a nice man I am. Tell them she said what a great
teacher I am. That should do it. Parents like that sort
of thing. It'll be like a game. Our game. Just yours
and mine.

She flinched as events took an unexpected turn.
Think, Becca, think. That wouldn't do. It wouldn't do
at all. She wouldn't be able to prepare properly.
There'd be too many potential pitfalls. Too many
risks.

You could come to my house

This time it was his turn to pause before responding:

We have to be alone when we meet. That's very, very
important. I thought you understood that. I thought
you wanted the pony.

Rebecca grinned. The bastard was very close to

panic. It couldn't be more obvious. He was anxious. Desperate. He'd agree to almost anything she suggested. She was right on track. Back in control.

My mum and dad are going away for the week end. its there aniversary or somthing. Im staying at a frends house on our estate but you could come round to the house on friday before I go
It has to be after dark. That's important. It has to be dark and you have to be alone.
I could mesage you when my mum and dad go. I could tell them I want to finish my homework before going to Kates. they wouldnt mind they trust me. its only a few doors away
That's good. You're a very clever girl. Now, I just need your address. That's all, just your address.
She typed the address, minus postcode in the interests of authenticity, and sent it with the press of a key.
Thank you, my dear. I've got it. You really are a very good girl. I'll see you on Friday just as soon as it's dark. You won't forget to let me know when you're alone, will you? You won't forget to send me a message?

I wont forget promise. Id beter go now i can here my
mum coming up the stairs
Okay, bye for now. Our secret! I can't wait to meet
you. And think of a name for that pony.

She closed her laptop, lay back on the bed and
began giggling as the tension melted away like an ice
cube in the hot summer sun. Oh, you'll meet me,
you'll definitely meet me. But, you may not enjoy the
experience quite as much as you think.

5

Gravel relaxed back in his comfortable seat, glanced around the spacious premium economy cabin and decided that the extra money he'd finally decided to spend was well worth the sacrifice. Gatwick to Bridgetown was a long flight by his usual Benidorm or Palma Nova standards, and a bit of well-earned comfort wouldn't do him any harm at all. Why not live it up a bit? Why not treat himself for a change? He'd earned it. Nobody could deny that after nearly twenty-five years of West Wales policing. But, what a shame Heather couldn't be with him. She'd have absolutely loved it. What a shame they hadn't acted on their travel plans before she became ill. What a shame he hadn't taken her to visit their son before it was too late. Fucking cancer! What was the point in thinking it? It didn't change anything. Life wasn't fair and no-one said it was. You had to make the most of it while you could. A hard lesson learned far too late. That summed it up. Hadn't somebody once said that youth was wasted on the young? He was sure he'd heard it somewhere along the way. Oscar Wilde maybe? Or George Bernard Shaw? It was the sort of thing Heather would have known for sure... oh well, whoever said it had never said a truer word.

He ordered a third double whisky from the attentive slim stewardess in her tight-fitting uniform and savoured the high quality malty spirit on his tongue before looking up and grinning, revealing nicotine-stained teeth that were at least his own. 'Thanks, love, it's appreciated.'

'Is there anything else I can get you, sir?'

He lifted the drink to his lips and drained it, head back, Adam's apple protruding only slightly in his fleshy throat. 'Another one of those would go down well.'

'Another double?'

He nodded. 'What's the island like? Does it live up to the hype?'

'It's friendly and bustling with life, but you still won't have any problems finding a bit of peace and quiet, if that's what you're looking for.'

'I'm paying my son a visit. He's a golf pro at some posh five-star hotel in Holetown on the west coast.'

She looked back, smiled and winked as she walked away. 'Oh, Holetown, lovely. That's where all the famous celebs go. You'll fit in perfectly.'

'Oh, yeah, they don't come any more glamorous than me. I just hope the paparazzi leave me alone. All those flashing cameras can be bloody irritating.'

* * *

Grav was surprised to find that the eight-hour-fifty-minute flight from London Gatwick to Bridgetown, the atmospheric Bajan seaside capital, passed surprisingly quickly despite his original concerns to the contrary. By the time he'd watched two recently released and mildly entertaining films, ate the various meals on offer, completed the paperwork required by the Bajan Government, downed several double whiskies and had napped fitfully for an hour or so with his head vibrating against the window, the pilot was announcing that they were about to land and the same stewardess was checking that her passengers had their seat belts appropriately fastened. What use they would be in the case of a crash was a complete mystery to the detective, but he followed instructions anyway. It seemed best.

Grav gave her a thumbs up, raised his seat to the upright position, stretched, massaged his forehead and looked out between the white marble clouds as the island materialised below him. It was very different to anywhere he'd been before. That was clear. But the first impressions were good: vibrant green fields, pale-yellow beaches, green-blue seas, and a diamond-bright sun. Beautiful. And didn't they say travel broadened the mind? What a shame... what the hell was the point in thinking it? Always reminders of his greatest sadness. She was gone and she wasn't coming back. Not in this life. Not in this world. Everything passed for good or bad. Everything ended, however much you valued it. What was the point of regrets? They were happy for a time, which was more than many could claim. He had to count his blessings and be grateful for that.

He cursed under his breath as he raised his not inconsiderable bulk from his seat with the aid of the armrests, and his overburdened knees creaked and complained. He needed to lose some weight. He had to acknowledge that. Heather had told him much the same thing time and time again in that oh-so-familiar way of hers. She'd stand there with her hands on her hips and shake her head slowly and deliberately. 'You need to cut down on the beer, Grav. You look as if you're about to give birth to twins, my boy. And six heaped spoonfuls of sugar in one mug of tea seems a bit over the top even for you, wouldn't you agree? You'll have trouble getting through the front door if you're not careful.'

He wiped a single tear from his cheek as the past closed in and surrounded him mercilessly. She didn't smoke; she drank modestly; she watched what she ate – low fat this, low sugar that; she swam and did yoga on a regular basis; and yet she was the one who died. Fucking terrible. Where was the justice? What he wouldn't give for a bit of well-intentioned female nagging now. If only he could step back in time and stay there forever.

Grav took a deep breath, planted his feet and steadied himself. He could still see her face as clear as day. He could still hear her voice whispering in his ear. Whispering sweet nothings of love and affection. Perhaps in some unquantifiable way, she was still with him. Or was he kidding himself? She'd promised to keep a watching eye on him when she'd passed on to wherever she'd gone. She promised to look down and say hello from time to time if she could. Maybe she was doing just that right now. Was there a spirit world? Was there an afterlife? Or was it just a story we told ourselves? A story we needed to hear? Well, he'd find out one day, like it or not. There was no escaping death and taxes.

He reached up stiffly, retrieved his leather briefcase from the overhead baggage hold, slipped the long strap over one shoulder, stretched expansively and joined the other passengers waiting to disembark in the aisle. He said his goodbyes to the stewardess on exiting the plane and was struck by two things as he slowly descended the metal steps towards the ground: firstly, the pleasantly moist heat didn't hit you in the face like an almost impenetrable inferno rising from melting tarmacadam, as it often did in the Mediterranean summer months; and secondly, the degree of bird noise, both whistles and unfamiliar tweets, was much louder than in other capital cities he'd visited over the years.

As he walked the short distance from the plane to the busy terminal, he decided that they were good omens. Perhaps his time on the island would prove less stressful than he'd anticipated. Perhaps seeing Dewi again after such a long time would be pleasurable as opposed to fraught. What the hell, he may even enjoy himself.

It only took Grav a short time to retrieve his battered suitcase from all the others of a similar description circling the carousel, and within half an hour or so he'd located his passport in the inside pocket of his jacket, successfully negotiated customs, and was standing among the throng of other holidaymakers and locals on the wide pavement outside the airport's entrance. He walked towards the kerb with his heavy case in hand and glanced to his right and left between the various local taxis and tourist buses, hoping to see his son waiting to transport him to

whatever accommodation he'd finally chosen to secure on his behalf.

Grav squinted at his digital watch and swore
loudly as the strain of a long day began to take its
toll. The boy was late. He could do without that.
Here was hoping he hadn't forgotten to collect his
old dad altogether.

He rested his bulk on his upright suitcase, which
threatened to collapse under the weight, and he was
in the process of lighting a much-needed cigar when
he spotted a tall, slim and well-tanned man walking
towards him with an engaging smile playing on his
lips. He didn't recognise his son at first, expecting the
smartly dressed man to walk straight past him to
greet someone else entirely, and he was genuinely
taken aback when he stopped immediately next to
him and said, 'Hello, Dad, long time no see. Welcome to paradise,' in that familiar soft West Wales
tone that resonated from the past like nothing else
could.

'You haven't lost your accent then.'

Dewi laughed. 'No danger of that... good flight?'

'Yeah, not bad, all considered. It's a bloody long
way though.'

Dewi nodded. 'You won't hear me arguing. That's part of the attraction.'

'I guess so. An adventure. A new start.'

'Well, are you ready to make a move then?'

Grav struggled to his feet and momentarily considered reaching out to hug his son, but thought better of it at the last second and shook his hand firmly instead. Why did he find it so difficult to show affection? His mum and dad were much the same. Maybe that had something to do with it. 'You're looking really well, son. I didn't recognise you at first. I thought you were one of the natives. The lifestyle obviously suits you.'

Dewi smiled. 'Yeah, I love it here. There are some things I miss of course, the rugby in particular, when the Five Nations come around every year. But, that's inevitable I guess. Nowhere's perfect. Not even here.'

'But it was a good move everything considered, yeah?'

'Yes, definitely.'

Grav took a long drag on his cigar and coughed repeatedly as Dewi picked up the suitcase and approached a small automatic car, the make and model of which didn't interest Grav in the slightest.

'The door's open. I'll just stick this in the back and we'll be on our way.'

'Sounds like a plan. Do you mind if I smoke in the car?'

Dewi didn't reply at first, but then shook his head. 'I'd prefer if you didn't, if you don't mind, Dad. Those things make me want to puke. I don't know why you don't give them up.'

Oh shit, maybe he shouldn't have bothered asking. 'No problem. I'll finish it later.'

Grav stubbed out the glowing tip, returned the cigar to its packet, squeezed into the front seat and made a mental note to rent a bigger car more suitable for a man of his ample proportions at the first opportunity.

'Ready to make a move?'

'As ready as I'll ever be.'

As they left the bustling, densely populated Bridgetown area and made their way in the direction of Holetown, Grav was struck by how built-up the west coast appeared, with its unexpected mix of smart hotels, luxury private properties owned by the rich and famous, and dramatically contrasting wood-and-concrete shacks perched on the edge of the sea in close proximity. 'It's not quite as I expected it. I thought I'd be walking into a Bounty advert.'

Dewi checked the road, pressed his right foot down hard on the accelerator and overtook a stationary yellow bus with loud reggae music blaring from its open windows. 'Yeah, I remember thinking much the same thing myself when I first arrived. But there's some really cracking beaches all along this coast. You just need to know where they are. They're all public, unlike on some of the other islands. I've got a couple of days off later in the week. I can show you around, if you like? Maybe take a boat trip. When you see the island from the sea, you'll get a much better idea of what it has to offer.'

Grav grimaced as a front wheel collided with a large pothole and jarred his aching lower back. 'Yeah, I'd like that if I survive the journey... so, tell me, where am I staying?'

Dewi had originally planned to arrange subsidised accommodation at the luxury hotel where he worked, but after a day or two's quiet contemplation, he'd ultimately decided that the extended period of close proximity that would inevitably entail was likely to prove too much for both of them. 'The hotel was fully booked by the time you rang me. It tends to be packed at this time of year, but I've sorted out an apartment overlooking a small town beach in a place called Speightstown, in St Peter Parish, a few miles up the coast. A good mate of mine owns the place. A local lad I play golf with sometimes. He's given you a good deal as a personal favour to me.'

Okay, so it looked as if Dewi didn't want him around too much of the time. Not surprising really, when he thought about it. He'd been absent for much of the time during the boy's childhood. Pressure of work and all that. Maybe he should have made more effort like Heather told him to.

'So what do you think?'

'You'll have to thank him for me. Buy him a nice drink.'

'I will.'

'So, how far's the apartment from your place?'

'Oh, we're only talking about four miles maximum, but Speightstown's more laid back than Holetown. A little more authentic, if you believe some of the regulars. I think you're going to like it. It's your sort of place.'

'What the hell's that name about?'

'Holetown?'

'Well, yeah. It sounds like some run-down shit-hole in the valleys.'

Dewi laughed. 'It's named after a stream.'

Grav didn't respond this time despite the explanation, his mind wandering.

'Are you okay, Dad?'

'Yeah, yeah, of course I am. Never better.'

'So why now? Why visit after all this time?'

Grav swallowed hard and shifted in his seat, searching for an adequate answer and failing miserably. 'I just wanted to see you, son.'

'Oh, come on, Dad, you taking a day off is a rare event and now here you are for three weeks. There's got to be more to it. They haven't finally pensioned you off, have they?'

Grav glanced to his left and focused with keen eyes as a particularly shapely middle-aged Bajan woman in a figure-hugging white dress tottered past on her high heels, all too quickly for his liking. 'Yeah, okay, you've got me. I've been through a lot of shit at work. I had to see a psychologist. It was this or retirement. Happy now?'

Dewi nodded, taking time to compute the reality

as he manoeuvred the small car through the moderate Speightstown market-day traffic and pulled up outside the conveniently located three-storey White Haven Apartments on his immediate right. 'So that's what it's all about. You've been forced to take some leave for once in your life. Now it's all starting to make sense.'

'Is this it then?'

'Door to door, what a service. Perhaps we can have a chat over a few drinks tomorrow night. You know, a bit of a catch-up. God knows it's well overdue.'

Grav opened the passenger door and struggled onto the uneven pavement as Dewi retrieved the suitcase from the boot. 'Maybe a few pints would help oil the conversational wheels a bit. This place is growing on me already. It's going to be a good holiday.'

6

Rebecca made her excuses and left work early for a non-existent dental appointment just before lunchtime on the Friday, contending that a potentially lengthy and inevitably painful root canal treatment rendered it highly unlikely she'd be able to return to the office that day. It was an excuse she'd used once before, but she got away with it.

As she strode in the direction of her Corsa, parked in a quiet side street about ten minutes' walk away, she was noticeably shaking, nerves taut, her hands clammy and her mouth dry. But those were good things. That's what she told herself. The adrenalin surging through her system would keep her on her toes. Keep her focused on the task at hand. Razor sharp. Just as she needed to be. Just as she had to be. Today was the day. An important day. And there was no room for mistakes. She had to get everything right.

Rebecca glanced to her right and left with narrowed eyes as she opened the car's rear hatch and took a carrier bag containing a long blonde wig made of real human hair and a pair of large-lensed non-prescription glasses from the otherwise empty boot. The street was deserted. No onlookers. No nosy housebound curtain-twitchers. No unwelcome passers-by. All undoubted positives. The universe was conspiring to assist her in her quest. That seemed the obvious conclusion. It was up to her to end the predatory beast's activities once and for all. Not the police with their ludicrous limiting rules and reliance on lawyers; not the courts with their legal technicalities and inadequate sentences for the guilty, but her, just her. She could pass on the evidence she'd collated. Of course she could, if she chose to. But why take the risk? What good would it do? She could do anything the authorities could do and more. He had to be stopped. That's all that mattered. She just had to get on and do it. She was judge and jury. The sword of justice. And there was a roaring tempest coming his way.

Rebecca started the hatchback's ill-kept engine on the second turn of the key, manoeuvred out of her tight parking place and made her way through Carmarthen's quiet afternoon traffic towards the M4 on the other side of the West Wales market town. Why on earth hadn't she taken the day off? Time was getting on. Tick-tock, tick-tock. She could hear it taunting her. It was speeding away. Rushing. Why put unnecessary pressure on herself? She did it every single time. What the hell are you playing at, Becca? Would she ever learn?

She tightened her white-knuckle grip on the steering wheel as she negotiated junction two and joined the motorway, adhering slavishly to the speed limits despite her almost overwhelming desire to drive faster, faster and faster, and carefully avoiding any ill-considered manoeuvre that could potentially draw any attention to the car. Maybe the self-imposed time restrictions weren't such a bad thing after all. Maybe it stopped her mind wandering and helped her retain focus. There was no room for doubts. Not now. Not at this late stage of the proceedings. Get a grip, girl. Concentrate! She'd spent weeks planning for today and the bastard had it coming.

It began raining with ever-increasing force as she continued her journey through a Welsh countryside dulled by the attentions of winter. She increased the wiper speed as large droplets of water bounced off the road, seemingly coming from every direction at once just to spite her. She checked her watch for the umpteenth time that afternoon and howled louder, louder and louder, as the fast-moving blades battled with the volume of water hammering the windscreen. Why now? Why today of all days? Concentrate, Becca. Concentrate! Put the lights on. Yes, that was best. That made sense. No need to panic. Not just yet. Surely the rain would ease off sometime soon. And there was still time.

It took her longer than usual to reach her destination of choice on the outskirts of Swansea, Wales's second sprawling coastal concrete city, and her levels of anxiety were threatening to overwhelm her completely as she drove into the vast DIY store's shared car park and stopped in a quiet corner as far away from the entrance as possible. Come on Becca, you can do it, girl. Take a deep breath. Time pressures or not, she had to follow her tried and tested modus operandi. Wasn't that what they called it in those ridiculous TV detective shows? Keep a low profile, buy what she needed, avoid recognition, and get out of there just as quickly as she could. That's all she had to do. It really was that simple. It had worked before and it would again.

She pushed up her sleeve and checked her watch again for what she told herself was one final time, reached up, pulled down both sun visors and crouched down in her seat, making herself as small as possible before pulling on the wig, sitting up, adjusting it in the rear-view mirror and adding the glasses. Not bad. Not bad at all. Even her long-suffering mother would struggle to recognise her if challenged. It was a triumph of ingenuity over adversity.

* * *

Rebecca stood just inside the large automatic glass doors, cold, shivering, wet down to her cotton underwear and clutching her cash tightly in one hand while confirming a mental list of the various items she'd need later that day: three rolls of large black bin bags, two rolls of strong carpet tape, a good-quality heavy-duty hacksaw with a spare twelve-inch blade, bleach and a scrubbing brush. She mustn't forget the scrubbing brush. Was that everything? Was there anything she'd forgotten? Anything she'd missed? It was now or never. There'd be no coming back if she forgot something. She had to get it right first time.

She collected the smaller of two trolley styles available and rushed around the store, up one aisle and down the next, increasing her pace and searching with darting eyes as the seconds ticked by. Tick-tock, tick-tock. Can you hear it, Becca? Come on, girl. Pick up the pace. You've got to keep moving. Delays weren't an option.

Rebecca beamed as she discovered the bin bags on a bottom shelf in aisle three, and then the bleach in its large bulbous blue plastic bottle only moments later. About time. About frigging time. Why the hell did shops insist on moving their stock around on an infuriatingly regular basis? Were they trying to annoy her? Is that what it was all about? Were they involved in some kind of conspiracy against her and only her? The bastards. The absolute bastards! Come on, Becca. Focus, girl. Now wasn't the time for philosophical musings. She was making progress. That's what mattered. Two down and three to go. Everything required had to be there somewhere.

She rushed into the next aisle, dodging cans of white paint piled high in the centre of the floor as she increased her pace again, pushing the trolley faster, faster and faster. Ah, there it was. Thank God. A suitable hacksaw.

She read the product description, squinting due to the tiny print, and smiled on realising it met her requirements. A blade capable of cutting through metal and stone. And a second blade was included in the offer. That would do very nicely, thank you. Three down and just two to go. She was back in control. Back on track. A girl at the very peak of her powers. A strong and majestic alpha female. Chiomara. Boudica. Honour restored. The vengeance of justice.

Rebecca was calmer now, moving more slowly, more gracefully, her breathing easier, her heart rate falling, and within a minute or two she'd located the remaining items with relative ease and was heading for the nearest checkout with a smile on her face. She stood and waited, watching the seconds tick by on her watch, as the elderly man in front of her handed the cashier a credit card with bent arthritic fingers. She felt her facial muscles tighten as he struggled to recall his pin number, but within a minute or two he'd triumphed and left. She paid quickly, thrusting the cash into the cashier's outstretched hand and telling her to drop any change into the charity box on the counter next to the open till.

'Thanks, that's very generous of you. Have you got far to go? You look absolutely frozen.'

The nosy cow. The nosy interfering cow. What the hell did it have to do with her? Rebecca stood there, staring at the checkout girl like a rabbit caught in the headlights. Think, Becca, think. Say something. You've got to say something. 'Oh, I've been visiting an old friend in Swansea from my university days, but I'll be off back home to Cardiff just as soon as I'm out of here.' That was good. That was very good. Just walk away, Becca. Say no more. Just head to the car. She hadn't panicked. Not for a moment. One more thing to be proud of.

To Rebecca's relief, the cashier suddenly turned her attention to a good-looking young man, seemingly covered in self-inflicted tattoos, who'd appeared carrying a step ladder over one excessively muscular shoulder.

She rushed towards the exit without looking back, never looking back, and broke into a trot as she crossed the car park. Time was moving on at an alarming rate. Tick-tock, tick-tock. She could hear the seconds running away from her. Taunting her like a cat playing with a mouse. But there was still time. Things were still on track. As long as she avoided further delays. No need to panic. Not just yet. She just had to get on with it.

Rebecca returned her disguise to the bag on entering the car, flung it into the rear seat, and drove faster than was sensible on the return journey, being careful to slow to an appropriate speed in advance of any speed cameras and keeping a keen eye out for non-existent police cars. By the time she reached her 1950s council house, about forty-five minutes later, the heavy rain had changed first to drizzle and then to light flurries of intermittent snowflakes that melted almost immediately on hitting the warmer ground. Rebecca opened her front door with a smile on her face, interpreting the changes as positive signs among many. Things were on the up again. Everything was going to turn out just fine. He was going to pay. Just as he should. Just as he deserved to. Today was the day. The scales of justice were weighed in her favour. And he had it coming. He had it coming big time. That's what she told herself. That's what she screamed inside her head.

She left her various purchases on the bare floorboards of what had once been her lounge and retreated to the kitchen for a quick cup of herbal tea before stripping off, throwing her sodden clothes in the washing machine and rushing up the stairs to don a polyester onesie bought cheaply in the local market the previous week. Rebecca stood in front of her wardrobe mirror and admired her reflection as shards of winter sunshine broke through the grey clouds and illuminated the room. Okay, Becca, this was it. He'd be on his way before she knew it. It was time to get the room ready. Time to prepare.

The lounge, as she still called it, more from habit

than anything else, was totally bare – free of carpet, rugs, furniture, or anything else for that matter. It was a slight inconvenience when not used for its primary purpose, but well worth the sacrifice. That's what she thought. It was an essential part of her established protocol. A practical measure that had far more advantages than disadvantages. Time for the final arrangements. Time to get it ready. The scissors. Where the hell were the scissors?

Rebecca was well-practised in preparing the room for what she euphemistically called her 'guest's' eventual arrival. She began on virtual autopilot, unrolling the bin bags with eager fingers and pulling fifteen free from the roll before cutting them open and placing them in an ordered pile to one side against a wall. That number wouldn't be sufficient to complete the job, of course. She knew that full well from hard-won experience, but it was more than enough to be getting on with. Come on, Becca, no time to rest. Get on with it, girl. Get on with it.

She worked quickly and efficiently and was sweating profusely by the time she'd used a further thirty-one bags, making forty-six in total, to cover every inch of the space in black shiny plastic, secured in place by generous lengths of carpet tape. She knew not to leave even the slightest gap, and she paid close attention to detail, adding additional strips of tape where necessary and overlapping the bags in areas of likely heavy use. It avoided mess. That's what she told herself as her body began to ache. Undertaking the task to the very best of her ability avoided unnecessary additional work when cleaning up. Preparation was everything.

Rebecca switched on the light and walked slowly to the approximate centre of the room, being careful not to ruffle the plastic even slightly. She turned slowly in a tight circle, surveying the walls and floor space with rapidly blinking eyes. It was almost perfect. A credit to her vigilance. Just one or two tiny gaps to cover with tape and she was finished. She lowered herself onto all fours with tape in hand and shuffled around the floor, applying remedial additions as necessary... there. That was it. Done. Perfect! A thing of beauty. But, what a shame she couldn't cover the ceiling. It just wasn't practical. She'd tried it more than once and failed dismally. If she had to repaint the ceiling afterwards, so be it. She had the paint and she had the roller. She'd just have to accept reality and get it done. It wouldn't be the first time.

Rebecca approached a window overlooking the back garden and noted that the light was fading fast. Day was slowly passing into night. He'd be acutely aware of that fact, much the same as she was. She was certain of that. He'd be keenly anticipating the climax of weeks of effort on his part. He'd have fantasised and would be utterly desperate to finally make those fantasies reality. He lived for days like this. Days when he could live out his desires and satisfy his urges. They all did.

Rebecca strolled casually towards the kitchen. The beast was on the hook. It was time to reel him in for one final time. Now, where was that computer? The counter, yes, charging on the counter. Reel away, Becca, reel away.

She sat at the kitchen table with her open laptop in front of her and checked her messages. Ha! No surprises there. He'd sent multiple new messages. One, two, three, four... twelve in all. Twelve messages that became increasingly more desperate as they continued. This was going to be easy. Easy-peasy. Easier than ever before. How had she put it last time?

He was champing at the bit. Yes, that was it. Lurching forwards like a dog straining on the leash at the sight and scent of a bitch on heat. Strain away, beast. Strain away. She was ready and waiting.

She reread his final message for a third time, began tip tapping the keyboard in a sudden whirl of activity, and smiled broadly as she watched the words appearing on the screen:

sorry I couldnt mesage you before. My mum and dad have gone now. Are you still coming to see me???? Have you bought my presants????

His response was virtually instant, and she knew without doubt that she'd already won. "Will you walk into my parlour? Said the spider to the fly." Tap away, tap away, beast. Tap away.

Are you sure they've gone? You're on your own?
yer I wached them driving away. Dad beeped the horn. Their going to ring my frends mum at nine to make sure I arived safely
Is the snow sticking where you are?
Ill go and look

Be quick.

no just on the lawn but nowere else. The roads cleer.

Did you buy my pony????

Yes, yes I did. I always keep my promises. I told you that. Have you thought of a name yet?

princess

Oh, that's lovely. I'm sure she'll love it. It suits her perfectly.

wen can I see her please can I see her????

Of course you can, my dear. We'll talk about it when I get there. But there are things I want to do first. You haven't told anyone, have you?

no you told me not to

You're sure? Really sure?

yes its a secret

That's good. That's very good. I'll bring a nice treat for you. A big treat. A tasty treat.

thats brillllll

I should be with you in about half an hour at the latest. Make sure you're still alone, and delete our conversation before I get there. The quicker the better. I'll be checking your computer to make sure you've done it. And the photos, delete all the photos. You won't be able to have the pony unless you do everything I say. You do understand that, don't you?

yer

Right, that's good. That's very good. I'll see you very soon, my dear. Bye for now, D x.

7

Grav slept somewhat fitfully despite enjoying a bellyful of the local Banks beer on his first night in Barbados. Not due to the unfamiliar surroundings or time difference, but because of the constant high-pitched whistling that seemed to get louder and more insistent with every hour that passed before dawn. He was well used to the chirping of crickets that often accompanied sleepy holidaymakers in the Mediterranean. But this was different, very different, and he had absolutely no idea what it was. Perhaps a decent guidebook wasn't such a bad idea after all. Not that a book would make the little sods shut the fuck up, whatever they were.

The night could seem like an eternity for those who watched the clock until dawn. Or so thought Grav as he checked his watch, dragged himself out of bed, belched, scratched his backside with a broken fingernail, and swore loudly as one of several local cockerels welcomed the new day with a loud cock-a-doodle-doo for the third or fourth time that morning. He considered opening the bedroom's green-painted wooden shutters and hurling something at it, but he thought better of it at the last second. Ignore the damned thing. That was probably best. Why not make a quick bathroom visit to splash the porcelain, get dressed in something suitable for the tropical climes and head into town for a bit of much-needed breakfast? A plate of hot stodge to soak up the alcohol would go down very well indeed, and there must be a cash machine somewhere in the vicinity. He just had to find the damned thing... maybe in future he should close the windows and put the ceiling fan on after dark. Yeah, that made sense. Less noise and fewer insect bites. He was covered in the fucking things and they itched like hell. The decision was made. It was a win-win.

He stretched and yawned at full volume, casting

off the residual remnants of sleep. Come on, Grav my boy, things to do, people to see. What would Heather say? Something along the lines of, 'Come on now, old man. We can't go lazing around in here all day, however much you'd like to. We've got to make the most of the place now we're here. Get a bloody move on.'

He smiled warmly as he hobbled in the direction of the bathroom and whispered, 'All right, love, I hear you,' before pushing open the door with the sole of his bare foot and answering nature's call with a steady stream which seemed to go on and on. As he washed his hands with cold water and then returned to the bedroom, he silently acknowledged that he was feeling like a fish out of water. Stripped of an identity that rested heavily on his professional role. If he wasn't a police officer, what on earth was he? He thought about it for a minute or two but couldn't come up with an adequate answer. Oh well, it was only three weeks. Surely he could manage that much. He'd be back in the job before he knew it and thank fuck for that.

Grav delved into his suitcase and pulled on a pair of knee-length shorts that hadn't seen the light of day in years, followed by a brightly coloured Hawaiian-style shirt bought in a Carmarthen seconds' store, the bottom two buttons of which he left unfastened to accommodate his protruding beer gut. He finished off the ensemble with a pair of white sports socks and open-toe sandals. It was time to get out into the big wide world, or Speightstown to be more accurate, and see what it had to offer. It was time to find out what the day would bring.

As he wandered along the slowly stirring main street, the town reacted to Grav as he suspected it did to all new arrivals – with warmth and courtesy. Speightstown, while unlike anywhere he'd visited in Europe, had an unquantifiable feel of 1950s Britain about it, and that, he decided, suited him just fine. He was pleased to find a cash machine in a glass privacy booth about ten minutes' walk away from the apartment, but as eager as he was to address his hunger, he had to wait for almost an hour before the various shops and restaurants began to open their doors to customers. Grav wandered past several eateries, glancing at and rejecting menus with increasing frustration, before finally spotting a small café with an external raised seating area at the back of the quiet car park in Town Square, directly opposite the supermarket. It was, he concluded, his sort of place, unpretentious, relaxed and comfortable, and he decided immediately to make a breakfast visit a daily ritual.

A slim and attractive Bajan woman approached him almost as soon as he sat himself down and smiled warmly. 'Good morning, are you ready to order?'

Grav perused the menu and quickly focused on the bacon and sausage rolls, as if they were printed in large bold highlighted capitals. Now, that's what you called food. It was definitely one or the other. 'I'll have three bacon rolls and a cup of strong black coffee please, love.'

She nodded and made a note of his order on a small notepad with a red pencil. 'It'll be with you before you know it. Are you having a good holiday?'

He met her eyes, glad of the chance for a chat. Anything was better than lonely silence. If he could travel back in time, he'd accept their worst days without hesitation. 'It's my first day.'

'So where are you from?'

'I'm from Wales. It's a small country that borders

England. It's where Tom Jones is from. Have you heard of him?'

She laughed. 'I know where Wales is. My sister studied for an MBA at Swansea University.'

'Small world. Who'd have thought it? I actually did a bit of child protection lecturing at Swansea as part of my job with the police. When was she there?'

'She returned to the island a couple of years ago when we opened the café.'

'Did you ever visit?'

'Yes, I did. I was particularly fond of Pembrokeshire. We spent a nice sunny day in Tenby.'

'Lovely place. Sounds like you were lucky with the weather.'

She glanced to her left and nodded. 'Hang on, I need to serve other customers. I'll ask my sister to come out to say hello.'

Grav sat in silence, watching a ginger kitten as it wandered between the tables searching for any morsel of food, until a larger-than-life young woman with a beaming smile, who exuded warmth and affability, suddenly appeared in a whirl of activity with his plate of rolls in one hand and his aromatic coffee in the other. He reciprocated, but failed to match her radiant smile, and liked her immediately. First impressions weren't always accurate. But, they sometimes were, and he strongly suspected this was one of those occasions. The two talked of Swansea and South West Wales with fondness for a time, and the detective began to feel at home in a strange land. Some people could have that effect on you. Perhaps a bit of a break from police work wasn't such a bad idea after all.

8

Forty-three-year-old Derek Griffiths was twitching uncontrollably as he parked his estate car in a town centre car park, ten to fifteen minutes' rapid walk away from his destination. He knew full well that his intentions were criminal. He knew that his all-consuming sexual tastes were considered utterly abhorrent by the vast majority of the population. And most of all, he knew the likely consequences of getting caught. Getting caught would blow his life apart – bang! It could mean the end of his freedom. Just like that. In one fell swoop. And men of his type weren't treated well in prison. He'd heard stories. Bad stories. Stories from men who'd been there. Men who knew.

They were victimised. Labelled. A prison underclass. People gobbing in your food. Kicking the shit out of you at every conceivable opportunity. It just didn't bear thinking about.

He blinked repeatedly and shuddered as tiny beads of sweat formed on his body despite the December frost. What if the little bitch said something? What if somebody actually listened and acted on her allegations? It was risky, that was true, but risk could be managed. Denial would be his best defence. His only defence. And so, he had to be cautious. He had to be careful. Just as he'd been every other time. Just as he'd been over the years since his first hurried offence all those years ago. An indecent assault or gross indecency or rape. That's what the interfering authorities would call it with their frowns, judgements and virtuous moral indignation. They'd come down on him like a ton of the proverbial bricks. Unless he could convince them of his innocence. Unless he could discredit his latest victim. Unless he could shut the little bitch up and keep her silenced forever. If he was careful, he'd avoid detection. He'd outwit them. He'd get his own way. He'd win.

He was breathing more heavily now, sucking the

cold night air deep into his lungs as he hurried along the pavement in the orange sodium glow of the street lamps, head bowed, coat collar up, and hat pulled down low to cover as much of his face as possible. Be careful, Derek. Don't look up. Avoid prying eyes. Stick to the back streets as far as possible. He couldn't let his desire to make fantasy reality blind his thinking. He had to limit himself to what he could get away with, make sure she'd deleted any damning material on her computer, ensure she kept her mouth well and truly shut, and get out of there as quickly as feasibly possible. Restrictions, always fucking restrictions. It was so damned frustrating. So infuriating! One day he'd live out his ultimate fantasies. One day he wouldn't hold back. But, like it or not, today was not that day.

* * *

Griffiths hid in the shadows and stared at the house, asking himself why the hell it was in total darkness. Now, that was something he hadn't expected. Was he in the right place? Was it the right house? Yes, yes, of course it was. Of course it was. He'd checked the street name and house number three times already. Something was wrong. Fuck it! Something must be wrong.

He gagged and swallowed as he leaned heavily on a convenient wall. It was too terrible to contemplate. Too awful to even consider. Things couldn't go wrong. Not now. Not at this late stage. Not after all his determined efforts. Not after all his planning. Not when he was so very close to his prize.

Griffiths checked the watch received as a birthday gift from his wife the previous summer. It was only a quarter past six. He wasn't late. Surely the little bitch should be in. Surely there should be lights on. What the hell?

He felt light-headed as his negative thoughts rushed and tumbled in his mind like a washing machine on a spin cycle. Oh no, what if she'd left for her friend's house already? What if the little bitch had changed her mind about meeting him at all? What if she was lying all along?

He wanted to scream. He wanted to stamp and shout like a petulant child, but instead he calmed his breathing and focused. It was far too soon to give up.

Too soon to throw in the towel. What on earth was he thinking?

Griffiths pushed open the creaking metal gate with one gloved hand while clutching a packet of unopened condoms tightly in the other. It wasn't looking hopeful. Far from it, in fact. But he had to be sure. He had to be certain. He'd never forgive himself if he didn't do everything in his power before giving up and walking away. Maybe she *was* in. Maybe she'd put the lights off for some inexplicable reason. Or maybe there'd been a power cut. That would explain it, wouldn't it? No, that made no sense. There were lights on in adjacent houses. Knock the door. He just had to knock the door and see what happened. If she answered, she answered. And if she didn't, he'd just have to accept defeat and reluctantly move on.

He knocked gently at first, being careful not to attract the attention of neighbours. But, as he began knocking harder, he was surprised to see the door opening an inch or two. She was in. The little bitch was in. But why the darkness? What the hell was that all about?

Griffiths pushed the door open, inch by tentative

inch, and peered into the gloom, as Rebecca watched and waited with a partial view of the hall.

He took one step forward, then another, then another, as his eyes slowly adjusted to the semi-darkness. 'Are you there, little one? I'm sure I heard you moving. I've got presents for you. Just like I said. Just as I promised. And I want to tell you all about the pony. You want to hear about Princess, don't you? She's almost as beautiful as you are.'

Rebecca moved slowly to her right with her naked body hidden behind the room's open door. She stood there pressed against the wall, peering through the crack, frozen in anticipation but ready to strike at the first opportunity. "Will you walk into my parlour? Said the spider to the fly." She repeated it in her mind. Reel him in, Becca. You've almost got him. Reel the bastard in.

She watched as he slowly approached the room and stopped for a moment, seemingly weighing up his options. And then she called out in a hushed, well-practised childlike whisper she'd perfected over time and come to love infinitely more than any living person. 'I'm in here. Come on. I'm in here. Come and play with me. I've been waiting for you.'

He rushed towards the voice and then suddenly stopped in the doorway. 'Why are you in the dark, my dear?'

'I'm shy. Please don't put the light on. I'll cry if you put the light on.'

He took a single step forwards. 'Okay, no problem. Anything you want. We can do things your way. You are on your own, aren't you?'

'Oh, yes, I'm definitely on my own.'

'Your parents have gone, haven't they?'

'Yes, I told you. There's just you and me.'

He entered the room, acutely aware of his penis swelling in his pants. 'You can come out now, my dear. I'm not going to hurt you. We'll have some fun together. You can trust me.'

Rebecca clutched the knife tightly in her right hand and started counting. This was it. This was the moment. It was finally here. The bastard. The filthy depraved bastard. One... two... three.

She kicked the door aside and leapt forwards, grabbing his hair tightly with one hand, tearing it from his scalp, and in the same instant sinking the razor-sharp blade deep into his fleshy stomach with the other. She held him there for a moment or two, relishing the close-up and personal fear and shock in his eyes, and then used all the strength she could muster to drive the blade in an inch or two further as he sank to his knees like a slowly deflating blow-up toy. Down you go said the spider to the fly. Down you go.

The knife made a strangely disconcerting sucking sound as she pulled it from his body, before walking away and feeling for the plastic-covered light switch on the wall to her right. She screwed up her face as the bare one-hundred-watt bulb burst into seemingly enthusiastic life, lifting a hand to protect her eyes against the sudden glare. And then she looked down as he writhed and wailed louder, louder and louder, until she feared someone may hear him and intervene at the worst possible time.

'Help me. P-please. I'm b-bleeding.'

She skipped around him on bare, quick-dancing feet and closed the door. 'Shut the fuck up, you depraved bastard. Do you think I don't know you are bleeding? That's the idea. Shut up right now.'

He turned his head and looked up at her with pleading eyes that were slowly fading. 'But you're n-not a child at all. You're a—'

'Oh, so you do know the difference. Top marks. Sorry to disappoint you.'

'Help m-me, please. Call m-me an ambulance. I've got a wife, children. I don't w-want to die. Not here. Not now.'

Rebecca sat down at his side within touching distance and shook her head as he clutched his midriff in a hopeless attempt to stem the blood flow. 'Oh, I don't think so. Think about it. If you've got a wife and kids, they'll be better off without you. What good are you to anyone? Perhaps you could ask the pony to help you. What do you think? How about we ask Princess?'

He tried to reach out to grab at her throat, but he fell back heavily with a resounding thud that pleased her immensely. 'Look, I've n-never done anything like this before. Please. I've learned my l-lesson. I'm sorry. I'm really s-sorry. Help me. Please h-help me.'

She laughed, head back, multiple amalgam fillings in full view. 'Why would I believe a single word that comes out of your filthy lying mouth?'

'I w-wouldn't lie to you.'

She mimicked him typing at a computer keyboard with both hands. 'Tip tap, tip tap. Hello, my dear. I'll give you anything you want. Anything your little heart desires. Just say the word. Do you re-member all the manipulative crap you told me? Our special secrets? You've been lying to me for weeks on end. You were talking shit then and you're talking shit now. If lying were a competitive event, you'd be the champion of the world.'

'I'm sorry. I'm r-really sorry. What e-else can I say?'

'And then there were the photos you sent me. Do you remember them? Or do you need a reminder? Shall I show them to you? Your naked body. Your big fat dick in close-up. Why would *any* child want to see those images? Have you got any idea of the sort of damage men like you do to your victims? Do you un-derstand that you ruin lives? Perhaps you do. Is that it? Perhaps it excites you. Or perhaps you just don't give a toss.'

'I knew you w-were an adult all along. From the v-very start. It w-was all a game. Role-play. I would n-never have sent them otherwise. If I'd thought for one s-second—'

She snorted and spat in his face. 'More lies. Al-ways more dirty lies. Just shut the fuck up. You thought I was ten. Just ten! That's what you like. That's why you're here. That's why you brought the rubbers with you. I know exactly what you are. And I know exactly what you do to children. You bring nothing but destruction and misery to this world. I want you to understand that. I met a man like you when I was just six years old. A man who shared your inclinations and acted on his impulses. Those experiences taught me all I need to know. You destroy innocence and you destroy people. Some of them never recover.'

'I'm sorry you h-had to g-go through that. I'm sorry. I'm truly sorry. What m-more can I say? I just l-love children too much.'

'Surely not even you're that deluded? Surely you understand that your lame attempt at justification is total and utter shit? I've never heard anything more pathetic in my life.'

He was weeping now. Lost in a sea of despair. 'I'm s-sorry. How many times h-have I got to say it? Help me, please. I'm b-begging you.'

She hissed her words through gritted teeth, hating him more than she'd ever thought possible. 'You're the worst kind of criminal. The lowest of the low. I need you to understand that. What the fuck goes on in your sick mind? How does a slug like you sleep at night?'

He clutched his abdomen tightly, contemplating his mortality and what death may bring. 'Call t-the police. I'll plead guilty. I p-promise you. Just call the police. I haven't got long left.'

She ran the point of the blade along his leg from ankle to groin and then back again. 'What good would that do? You'd do a few months inside some cushy prison cell at best. And then you'd be back out in the world to sow your poison. You'd stop for a time by necessity, and then you'd do it all again just as soon as you got the slightest opportunity. Fantasy – offending – remorse, fantasy – offending – remorse. Isn't that how your mind works? Or are you one of those vicious psychos who tear lives apart and feel no remorse at all?'

'I've felt remorse. Genuine remorse. I'm s-sorry. I'm truly sorry. I can change. Just c-call the p-police. I'll confess. I'll tell them e-everything.'

She shook her head three times and placed her face only inches from his, with their noses almost touching. 'I'm afraid I can't do that. You'd be bailed and back on your computer, tip tapping, lying, manipulating, corrupting, or hanging around outside some local primary school or playgroup, or targeting some poor unsuspecting single mother. People like *you* always do. You're broken. You're lacking a moral compass. You're a machine missing a crucial cog that can't be replaced. A machine that needs crushing. Does that make any sense to you? Or are you utterly beyond redemption?'

He felt the warm blood seeping from his wound and pooling around his bottom, soaking into his clothing. 'Look, I'm losing a l-lot of blood here. I'm b-begging you. Have mercy. I've learned my lesson. I'll be a better person from h-here on in. I promise. I'll be a b-better person. I'll do a-anything. Anything at all. Just t-tell me what to do and I'll do it.'

Rebecca shook her head again, more vigorously this time, and held the knife in plain sight, waving it back and forth close to his face. 'You're a slug, a rodent, a lesser form of life. Some people don't deserve to live. Some people are better off dead. And *you're* one of those people. Perhaps now would be a good time to make peace with your maker. You never know, you may be lucky. Perhaps your God is more forgiving than I am.'

He tried to shout out. He tried to call for help. But it was hopeless. Absolutely hopeless. Rebecca perched above him on her bare knees and moved quickly, forcing his stubbled chin backwards, using all her weight and strength to maximise the impact before thrusting the tip of the blade deep into his exposed neck and cutting a four-inch gash in his throat just below his Adam's apple.

She sat back down, quietly humming a tune made popular by a recent TV washing powder advertising campaign, and smiled as red bubbles of blood and saliva erupted from the gaping wound like a grotesque parody of the childhood game. 'Now all I have to do is relax as best I can, watch you die for however long that takes, undress you, cut you up for convenient disposal and clean up the mess afterwards. That's the worst part of the process by far. Cleaning up the mess. It's a regrettable necessity that can't be avoided. That's the best way of looking at it. The lesser of two evils. You people are as dirty on the inside as you are on the out. Not surprising really, when you think about it.'

Rebecca knelt alongside him, held two blood-stained fingers to the side of his neck and felt for a non-existent heartbeat. 'Are you dead? Surely you're dead. Your staring eyes have glazed over, dulled and paled.'

She nodded twice, confirming the conclusion of her one-sided conversation. 'Yes, you're dead all right. Dead and gone. Perhaps I should take a break for a quick cuppa before continuing. Maybe even a biscuit or two.'

She looked down at the bloody corpse for a second or two longer and shook her head. 'No, no, best get it all done and dusted. Best get the whole unpleasant process over with as fast as possible. Get you undressed, cut you up, burn your clothes, a quick shower and then a bite to eat before catching a couple of hours of shuteye. What do you think? That's my usual protocol. Tried and tested. Nothing to say for yourself? Okay, fair enough. It's difficult to respond when you've breathed your last.' Come on, Becca. Just get on with it, girl. If a process worked, why change it?

She stripped his feet first, hurriedly throwing the sweaty black cotton socks aside with a distasteful expression on her face, before taking each of the shoes in hand and examining them carefully for any signs of wear. They were nearly new. Hardly worn at all. And not some cheap tat. Why not give them a clean and hand them in at that charity shop in the high street? At least then they'd be put to good use.

She jumped to her feet and placed the shoes on the windowsill before returning to the corpse, picking up the modelling knife and cutting off the remainder of the clothing, one item at a time. Experience had taught her it was easier that way. Much easier than her original efforts to undress her victims conventionally. There, done. A cold glass of water from the kitchen, a quick toilet break, and she could start the dissection.

* * *

Rebecca sighed loudly as her right arm began to ache and stiffen. Why oh why did she always underestimate the time and effort required to dismember a human body? Bones were tough. There was a surprising amount of liquid. And the stink! This was her fourth dismemberment and the stench still managed to astonish her. But at least she'd had the good sense to abandon her clothes and keep a sick bowl handy this time. Fewer things to wash and less contamination. Both worthwhile advantages. Hard lessons learned. Preparation was everything.

She took a deep breath and sat back in the pool of slowly congealing body fluids still seeping from the gradually stiffening cadaver. Maybe it wouldn't be such a bad idea to use something to mask the smell next time. A scented candle or two perhaps. Or maybe some kind of commercial air freshener. Yes, that made sense. Why on earth hadn't she thought of it before? Oh, well, put it down as another lesson learned. Come on, Becca, time was getting on. Enough was enough. It was time to focus on the now.

Rebecca admired the newly acquired hacksaw in her right hand. She began drawing the jagged blade across his upper left thigh in a slow rhythmic motion, cutting through the flesh, and then increased the pace, faster, faster and faster, when she encountered the femur. That required effort. A great deal of effort. And she addressed the task with well-practised and frenzied enthusiasm, before eventually pulling the heavy leg free from the torso and pushing it aside with a yelp of girlish delight.

She kept working. Sawing and cutting. Cutting and sawing. Willing herself on with words of criticism or encouragement when she tired or slowed. 'Come on, Becca. Get a shift on, girl. You're doing well. Really well. Nearly done. Don't slow down now. For Pete's sake, Becca. Get a move on. Get a frigging move on. Those bones aren't going to saw themselves.'

It was exhausting work certainly. Totally exhausting, but necessary. That's what she told herself time and time again when her spirits began to flag. Every minute that passed increased the risks. What if someone saw the dirty bastard entering the house? What if someone recognised him walking down her street? She had to finish what she'd started as quickly as possible and get the slimeball out of there. Saw away, Becca. Saw away.

It took her almost three hours to remove all four limbs and finally the head, which seemed to resist her determined efforts to remove it from the neck, and stared up at her accusingly until she gouged the eyes with a bloody thumb. She went to roll the head aside when it finally came free, but she thought better of it and held it up by the hair. She struggled upright with head in hand, slid and almost fell in the surrounding gore before retrieving the knife from the floor and carving the word PAEDO in large bloody capitals on the exposed forehead. Perhaps if he'd been labelled in life, she could have let him live. Perhaps that would have negated the danger he posed to an adequate degree. Or maybe not. It wasn't something that was likely to happen anyway. Society tended to frown on such things for some inexplicable reason she couldn't begin to understand. Why waste her energy thinking about such imponderables? Just focus on the task at hand. One thing at a time. Focus on the now. That was best.

* * *

Rebecca stood in her back garden and stuffed Griffiths' clothes into a metal refuse bin bought for the purpose. She poured in almost half a bottle of turpentine before striking a match and lighting one corner of his shirt. She stood back and watched as the flames leapt and danced, feeding acrid black smoke into the cold night-time air. Come on, Becca. Enough of standing around. The fire had done its work. It was time to finish cleaning up. She couldn't leave the black bags lying there on the killing room floor for a single second longer than was absolutely necessary. Get the body in the freezer for later disposal one manageable section at a time, and then her hard work was finally done. Almost time for a hot soapy shower. Almost time for a nice thick piece of wholemeal toast and strawberry jam. Yum. She could almost taste it.

She smiled broadly as she walked back towards the house.

Everything had gone swimmingly. The universe had conspired to help her in her quest. Just as it always did. It was a case of good and evil. Black and white. Yin and yang. Contradictory opposites. And she was a force for good. That's what she told herself time and time again. She was on the side of the angels. That's what mattered. God was on her side.

9

The opulent five-star hotel bar was unlike any other that Grav had known over the years, with comfortable furnishings, a highly polished marble floor, and best of all in his opinion, an uninterrupted view of a Caribbean sea lit by a sunset that made him stand and stare, as if seeing the world for the very first time. What a wonderful sight to behold. All that beauty in one place. Surely such a wonderfully crafted reality couldn't have come about by random chance. Maybe Heather was a part of it. Perhaps there was a creator after all.

He raised a hand and waved on spotting his son engaged in animated conversation with a curvy young Bajan barmaid dressed in immaculate livery, who was half hidden behind the polished wooden counter of a well-stocked bar. 'Dewi! I'm over here, mate. Sorry I'm a bit late. I had a bit of a kip before coming out.'

Grav noticed his son reach out to caress the barmaid's hand before turning towards him and nodding. 'All right, Dad. I was beginning to think you'd done a runner back to Welsh Wales, or something.'

It was only ten minutes or so. What the hell was he on about? 'You've fallen on your feet here, son. It looks like a cracking place to work.'

Dewi smiled, amused by his father's talent for stating the blindingly obvious. 'Do you fancy a glass of cold beer to be getting on with?'

Grav stepped forwards, leaned both of his bare elbows heavily on the bar and nodded enthusiastically. 'Is the Pope Catholic?'

'Two glasses of lager please, Sade.'

'Two glasses of chilled lager coming up, gentlemen.'

Grav accepted his drink gratefully, tipped back his head and drained half the contents in one swallow, before returning the glass to the bar and saying, 'Thanks, love, it's appreciated.'

Dewi picked up his glass and sipped at it, slurping the frothy foam from the top with pursed lips. 'So you can still knock them back a bit. No change there then. Shall we take a seat?'

Grav winked once and grinned. 'So, is the girl more than a workmate?'

'How the hell did you work that one out so very quickly? Always the detective.'

'I'm guessing she's your girlfriend.'

'Yeah, sorry, I should have introduced you.'

Dewi raised a hand, waved the young woman over and smiled. 'Right, let's get this over with. Sade, this is my dad, Dad this is Sade.'

'Nice to meet you, sir.'

The big man reached out and took her hand in his, before raising it slowly to his lips and gently kissing it. 'Nice to meet you too, love. And please call me Grav. No need for formalities. From what I'm told, we're almost family.'

She smiled, revealing flawless white teeth that contrasted dramatically against her smooth dark skin. 'Grav it is. I've heard a lot about you.'

'The boy's punching well above his weight on this happy occasion. Lucky sod. I hope he's treating you well, love. He's not a bad lad, all considered.'

'Oh, he's a credit to you. I'm very fond of him.'

'Glad to hear it, love. You tell me if he steps out of line, and I'll smack his arse for you.'

She looked on, tossed her hair and laughed, as Dewi took his father's arm and pulled him towards a nearby table. 'Always the bloody comedian. And the two of you are getting on. That's all I need.'

'I get on with most people, all considered.'

'So what do you think of her?'

Grav sat himself down and drained his glass with a look of contentment on his face. 'She seems like a lovely girl. I'm pleased for you, mate. Ten out of ten.'

'You don't mind that she's black?'

He stared at his son with narrowed eyes and frowned. 'Why the hell do you feel the need to ask? Why would I? People are people. She's a nice girl. That's the only thing that matters.'

'Another beer?'

Grav handed him a folded fifty BBD note. 'Yeah, and a whisky chaser. Tell Sade to have one herself. She could probably do with it.'

* * *

Dewi put down the tray and handed Grav his change. 'There you go.'

The big man drained the whisky glass with the flick of his wrist, relishing the twelve-year-old matured spirit trickling down his throat and warming his gut, before picking up his beer glass and holding it out in front of him in seeming adoration. 'Thanks, mate, that should take the edge off a bit.'

'So what have you been doing with yourself? Have you seen much of the island?'

Grav shifted his weight in his seat in a hopeless attempt to relieve his chronically aching lower back, and grinned despite the nagging pain. 'I walked as far as the bus station after breakfast and took one of those yellow buses as far as Bridgetown. That was an experience, I can tell you.'

Dewi laughed as he pictured his overweight and ageing father clinging to his seat among the locals, with loud reggae music blaring in his unappreciative ears. 'Yeah, they don't hang about, do they?'

'What the hell's that about?'

'They're totally independent with no timetable

and cheap fares. Basically, it's about forty pence to anywhere you want to go on the island. The more passengers they pick up, the more they earn. One of Sade's cousins drives one. They've got to put their foot down to make a basic living. That's the reality.'

'Ah, okay, so that explains it. Mine had a driver with long dreadlocks who seemed to think he was Mika Häkkinen on crack. It was a bit like being on a fucking rollercoaster, only faster and a lot scarier. I didn't actually shit myself, but it came pretty close once or twice. I was wishing I'd worn my brown corduroy trousers.'

* * *

The two men continued drinking to excess and making small talk for another hour or so, until a combination of the alcohol in their systems and the convivial atmosphere began to break down the long-standing emotional barriers and lift their usual British reserve. Dewi returned to their table with the tenth round of the night and fell heavily into his seat. 'So, what's going on, Dad? What the hell happened to DS Rankin?'

'Clive. Do you remember him?'

'Well, yeah, of course I do. I can remember him and his missus coming around to the house more than once when I was a kid. Didn't we all go camping in France when I was nine or ten?'

'Yeah, of course we did. Brittany. Your mother loved it.'

'So, what happened?'

'You really want to know?'

He leaned forwards in his seat. 'I asked, didn't I?'

Yes, it seemed he did. Maybe he wasn't just making conversation for once in his life. They were actually connecting on a meaningful level. 'We were investigating a serial killer case. A right fucking maniac. I'm talking five young women's bodies in shallow graves and a missing nineteen-year-old university student who met the victim profile. I was the lead detective with Clive as my second in command. And the media were all over it. Looking for anything to criticise and piss on to sell a few more miserable papers. That's pressure, son. Real pressure. It was only a matter of time until the bastard killed again. We knew it. Everyone fucking knew it.'

Dewi swallowed a mouthful of cold beer before responding. 'So what happened to Clive?'

'He was under the cosh, just like I was. There were no obvious suspects, but we were making progress of sorts. I thought he was coping. Hell, I still think he was coping. Actually, that's understating the case. I'm fucking certain of it.'

Dewi's eyes moistened as he pondered his father's very different world. 'So, how did he die?'

'He was found alone in the front seat of his car with a hosepipe leading from the exhaust.'

'So, he killed himself?'

Grav stared into the distance, focusing on nothing in particular rather than meeting his son's eyes. 'Well, that's what the coroner decided.'

'Wasn't it crystal clear? You don't seem convinced.'

'There were things that didn't fit. Things that made no sense to me.'

'Such as?'

'How long have you got?'

'As long as it takes, Dad. As long as it takes.'

'Another drink?'

Dewi nodded his confirmation and rose to his

feet on unsteady legs. 'Yeah, why not? I'll get them in. Same again?'

'I'll have a double whisky, ta, and save a bit of time. Just bring the bottle.'

* * *

'So what happened exactly?'

'I arrived at the scene just as two paramedics were confirming that Clive was dead. He was in one hell of a state to be honest, so it's not as if it was hard to work out. Swollen, red-purple, bloated. Anyway, it looked like suicide to them, but as I said it wasn't nearly so clear to me.'

'Okay, you've got me interested.'

'The car was parked right up against a high earthen bank in a quiet lane close to a remote beach. Clive would have had to attach the pipe, get back in the car and then climb over the driver's seat and gear stick, and into the front passenger seat to wait to die. Why would he do that? Can you tell me?'

Dewi shook his head, searching for a response he couldn't find as the alcohol clouded his thinking.

'And on top of that he had a seat belt on. Does

that make any sense at all to you? Because it doesn't to me.'

'No, not really... I see what you're saying. Did he leave a note?'

'No, he didn't. And that was the clincher as far as I was concerned. People leave notes. Clive would have left a note. He had a wife, family, friends. He would have wanted to explain.'

Dewi sat there for a few seconds with a confused expression on his sun-bronzed face. 'So, how come the coroner disagreed with you?'

'They'd been trying for a kid for ages. Mary had a miscarriage.'

'Anything else?'

This was starting to get embarrassing. 'Clive had been prescribed antidepressants by his GP.'

'Oh, for fuck's sake, what the hell can I say to that? Maybe your thinking's been clouded by your affection for the man.'

'I guess it's a possibility. To some extent anyway.'

'So, he may have killed himself, yeah? It's not an impossibility. Surely you have to accept that.'

'I just don't buy it. One witness claimed to have

seen Clive's car travelling in the direction of the lane with two adults in the front.'

'And nothing came of it?'

Grav shook his head. 'He was an old bloke in his eighties and seriously pissed at the time. Not exactly the most reliable witness in the world. Any half-decent barrister would tear his evidence to shreds without breaking sweat.'

'Did you believe him?'

'Fifty-fifty to be honest. He may have been saying what he thought I wanted to hear. It happens sometimes.'

'And you didn't come up with anything else?'

'Na, fuck all. The top brass knocked any further investigation on the head after the coroner's findings. Case closed. That's what they told me.'

'And you're finding that hard to accept?'

'Yes, I fucking well am. He was a close mate. Wouldn't you be?'

'So what about you, Dad? You're still one angry man. You'll have a bloody heart attack if you're not careful. What happens next?'

'Is it all right if I light up a cigar?'

Dewi staggered to his feet, glass in hand, and

cursed loudly as a splash of lager spilled over the top and soaked his feet. 'Come on, let's go out and sit on the veranda. You can smoke there without any problems.'

'Sounds like a plan.'

* * *

'So, what are you going to do with yourself once the holiday's over?'

Grav slapped the back of his neck as an insect stung. 'What the fuck is that whistling all about?'

'Frogs.'

'You're telling me that a bunch of frogs are making that racket?'

'Are you changing the subject? Saying anything to change the course of the conversation?'

'Frogs?'

'That's what I'm telling you. Tiny frogs with big voices.'

Grav sucked at his cigar, inhaled deeply, and blew a spiral of smoke high into the warm night-time air. 'Well, I've heard it all now.'

'You were about to tell me your plans.'

The little sod wasn't going to let it go. Just tell him, Grav. Just tell him and be done with it. 'I seriously considered jacking it all in for a week or two after Clive's death, but what the hell it's got to do with you I don't know.'

'I'm worried about you, Dad. That's all. You're carrying a few too many pounds, you smoke those things, you drink heavily, and you're in a high-stress job. You've told me that yourself.

You're a heart attack waiting to happen. Grandad died when he was not a lot older than you are now. Or have you forgotten that?'

Grav suddenly raised himself up, leaned forwards, and smacked the tabletop hard with an open palm, causing Dewi to jump and retreat in his seat, pressing himself hard against the backrest. 'Who the fuck are you, my mother?'

'I'm sorry.'

'I didn't come here to listen to a speech on the benefits of healthy living. If I want a lecture, I'll go and see my doctor. Got it?'

'Loud and clear. This is going well. Maybe you should have stayed away in the first place.'

'I made the effort, didn't I?'

'I'm really sorry, Dad. How many times do I need to apologise? I didn't mean anything by it.'

Grav sat back in his chair and closed his eyes tight shut in quiet contemplation. What the fuck was wrong with him? He'd upset the boy. He'd ruined what had been a pleasant evening. Other guests seemed shocked. Sade was staring. And why wouldn't she be? PTSD? It seemed the psychologist may have had her diagnosis spot on after all.

10

The young, black, flat-coated retriever bitch bounded along the windswept estuary beach, damp nose twitching, muscles and sinew straining to maximum, as she hurtled after the tennis ball flung along the sandy shoreline with the aid of a blustering wind sweeping off the Irish Sea.

Forty-seven-year-old Dr Delyth Williams adjusted her long red scarf and fumbled to fasten the top button of her wax jacket with increasingly numb fingers as the freezing temperature began to bite. 'Come on, Polly, bring it back, girl, bring it back. Come on, girl.'

The dog sprinted back towards her with a newfound enthusiasm for the game, and came skidding to a sudden halt at her feet, before jumping up with sandy wet paws that left the doctor's blue jeans with damp and muddy patches just where she didn't need or want them. 'Down, Polly, down! Go on, off you go, you daft thing. Get down, girl!'

She flung the ball again, harder this time, using all her meagre strength to maximise the distance, before striding on. No wonder she was alone on the beach. Curled up in front of a roaring log fire with a hot drink in hand would have been a far more sensible choice. Why not head into the village to buy a newspaper before going back to the house to start making lunch? That leg of lamb wasn't going to cook itself.

The doctor turned around, put her head down to protect her face from the icy wind, and started back in the direction of her Ferryside home, half an hour's or so rapid walk away. She picked up her pace again as a sudden flurry of snow filled the air and dusted the beach in white. Where on earth was that damned dog now? And at the worst possible time. It wasn't like her to wander off.

She peered in every direction, straining her eyes

before finally spotting the animal. Oh no, she'd headed off towards the water. Right through the dark river mud. Flipping wonderful. She'd be in one hell of a state. That's all she needed.

She lifted her open palms to her face and held them cupped around her mouth as she shouted out at the very top of her voice with more than a hint of irritation. 'Polly! Come on, girl! Come, come! Come on, you stupid dog!'

But the dog didn't come. She just stood there at the water's edge, ignoring her mistress with her hackles raised, and repeatedly worried at something in the mud. Something that just couldn't be ignored even for a single second.

Williams took a clear plastic bag containing several of the dog's favourite biscuits from a trouser pocket and fumbled to take one out with trembling fingers. She looked towards the animal and swore silently under her breath. That was strange – it just wasn't like her. She was usually so obedient. So well behaved. Why today of all days?

She held a single biscuit high above her head and waved it to and fro as the snow began to fall more heavily and stick to the ground. 'Come on,

Polly, Gravy Bones. Gravy Bones. Come on, girl!' Well, that was a first. She couldn't usually resist them.

She forced the bag back into her pocket, flung the biscuit to the gradually freezing ground, and began marching through the pitch-black, pungent, still-slippery mud towards the dog, who was chewing at something with enthusiasm and gusto one hundred or so yards away. 'Come on, Polly! Come on, girl, come, come!' Bloody dog. Could anything be more flaming infuriating? The doctor's booted feet sank several inches into the gluey ground with increasing frequency as she approached the estuary river, and it didn't surprise her one jot when she finally lost her footing and fell on her backside. She was soaked through. That damned dog had a great deal to answer for.

She struggled to her feet, wiped her hands on the front of her jeans and stared at the retriever, who still hadn't moved an inch. 'Polly! Come on, you stupid dog. What is wrong with you today?'

The dog glanced back very briefly, but then returned her attention to her prize, as her mistress walked towards her. It took the doctor another five minutes to reach the animal's side, and she was about to scold her like she'd never been scolded before, when she was stopped in her tracks, and stood staring at a slowly decomposing human arm in the dog's mouth. 'Drop, Polly, drop!'

She slapped the dog hard on the back with an open hand when she didn't obey the instruction. 'Drop it, Polly, drop it! Drop the damned thing! Drop it, girl!'

This time the bitch reluctantly obeyed, and the doctor moved quickly in an adrenalin-fuelled frenzy, grabbing the dog's leather collar and pulling her away. 'Sit, Polly, sit. Do what you're told, dog. Sit!'

She patted the top of the animal's head, more relieved than pleased that she'd finally followed orders despite the arm's unusual fascination. 'There's a good girl. There's a good girl. Stay, girl, stay!' So, now she was listening. About bloody time.

Williams waded out into the freezing water, almost reaching her knees before retrieving a bright-green plastic sports bag with contrasting black branding from the brown muddy mix of fast-moving river and sea water. She reached out, gripped one of the bag's two handles and made her way back towards the shore, before eventually standing shivering on the dryish ground at the water's edge. She peered in, expecting the worst but hoping for the best, and spat a mouthful of acidic green-yellow vomit from her mouth as the pungent stink of decaying flesh filled her nostrils. Oh God, it was a man's head. A man with black hair. A man who'd recently been a living, breathing individual with a life to live. She swallowed hard and dared to look for a second time, before suddenly averting her eyes and looking away. There was a second arm, that had to be an arm, and various chunks of random fatty flesh sliced or hacked from a body in the not-too-distant past. Oh God, oh God. Who would do such a terrible thing? What an awful way to end up. And where was the rest of him? She had to get help. She had to summon help.

She dropped the sports bag at her feet, desperately wanting to abandon it but feeling morally obliged to do the right thing. She gagged repeatedly as she reached down and clutched the arm so recently gnawed by the dog, and dropped it into the bag to join the other decomposing body parts. The tide would be coming in soon. It had already turned.

The beach would be engulfed with water before she knew it. She had to get herself, the dog and the bag and its ghastly contents to safer ground, and fast.

'Come on, girl, come on. Let's go, let's go!' The dog repeatedly circled her mistress, sniffing at the bag excitedly, as they made their way up the beach towards the railway track. The doctor stopped, panting hard, her lungs screaming, when she finally reached the firmer ground. She looked around to gain her bearings, trying to think clearly as the weather deteriorated still further, and the whirling snow became a full-blown blizzard that restricted her vision to no more than a few feet in every direction.

She swore loudly, screeching one obscenity after another as the debris-strewn sand and dark mud began to gradually disappear under a blanket of white on the one side and the fast-rising water on the other.

She began trotting now with the dog still circumnavigating the area, and then broke into an awkward loping run as her blood pressure escalated exponentially. The incoming tide was moving faster now, faster than before. It was moving relentlessly forward at a brisk walking pace and just kept coming, coming and coming. Should she stay on the beach and risk being cut off as the water deepened? Or should she stop running and risk clambering over the large slippery boulders that bordered and protected the railway track from the attentions of the sea? What to do? What to do? What on earth should she do? Neither option filled her with joy, that was certainly true, but she had to choose one or the other and get on with it quickly. Which was the lesser of two evils? That's what she had to decide.

She looked down, witnessed the water creeping around her feet, and in that instant the decision was made. She had to climb over the boulders and cross the track. It was the only viable alternative left open to her. She just had to stop pondering and get on with it.

Up she went, inch by inch, using her one free hand to support her weight as she climbed onwards, slipping repeatedly on the jagged surfaces again and again and again. By the time she reached the wire fence bordering the rails and climbed over it with the dog in close attendance, her jeans were ripped and both knees were grazed and bleeding. She clutched the bag still tighter and began to cry salty tears which ran down her face as she wailed in pain. A walk on the beach had turned into an ordeal. Could life get any better? Yes, it flipping well could.

The doctor made her way across the track, down a steep snowy bank leading towards the quiet road that led through the village, and seriously considered knocking on the front door of the first house she came to before instinctively deciding against it and trudging on. She could do without the drama such a visit would inevitably entail. Just get home and use her own phone. That seemed best. It wasn't every day you turned up at someone's abode with a bag of body parts, head included, even if you were a local GP.

11

Thirty-two-year-old Detective Sergeant Laura Kesey sat in her small cluttered Carmarthen Police HQ office and stared at the seemingly endless mountain of paperwork piled high on the desk in front of her. She was new to the force after transferring from the West Midlands Police, and was starting to seriously doubt the wisdom of the move. West Wales was a comparatively small force with such limited resources despite its vast geographic area, and more importantly, she missed her close friends and family much more than she'd anticipated. Her partner seemed happy enough in their new role with the local social services department, but up to that point she'd struggled to fit in. She had to accept that. Maybe an intensive Welsh course would be a good idea. Not that many of the local officers seemed to use the language all that often. And they all spoke English anyway. Still, it was worth considering. Show willing. Why not have a chat with the detective inspector when he finally turned up? Perhaps the force would even pay for a course. It certainly wouldn't do any harm to enquire.

She rose from her seat with flagging enthusiasm, pushed her auburn fringe away from her eyes with the fingers of one hand, and approached the room's only window with its view of the car park two floors below. What a first week in the job, and now it was snowing. Just when she thought things couldn't possibly get any worse. Perhaps it was God's idea of a joke. And now it was getting heavier. Maybe He was looking down and laughing. It wouldn't surprise her. Would she even get home for the night?

Kesey was bending down to switch on the stainless steel kettle on the floor in one corner of the room when a sharp knock on the office door made her jump. Who wanted her now? It would mean more paperwork no doubt. Oh well, there was only one way to find out.

She raised herself to her full height and shouted, 'Come in,' in a strong Birmingham accent that some found hard to decipher.

PC Kieran Harris pushed the door open and smiled. 'Sorry to bother you, Sarge, but we've had a phone call from a local woman claiming she's found a bag of human body parts on the beach in Ferryside. It's about eight miles away from here, if you were wondering.'

'A bag of body parts?'

'Yeah, that's what she said. A head with something carved into the forehead, two arms and various other small lumps of flesh she couldn't identify.'

She glanced towards the window. 'Today, in that lot?'

'Just over an hour ago.'

'Are you sure it wasn't some nutter ringing in to wind us up? It wouldn't be the first time.'

He stepped forward, reached out and handed her a single A4 sheet of paper with the doctor's name, address and telephone number written on one side in black ink. 'Sorry, Sarge, it's a local GP, a Dr Delyth Williams. I think we can assume it's kosher.'

'Oh, that's bloody marvellous. Why on a Sunday of all days, with all the brass tucked up nice and warm in front of their tellies? So where's this bag now?'

'In her garage.'

'Well, at least it's cold enough. That's one positive.'

'Yeah, I guess so.'

She looked down at the details, holding the paper approximately six inches from her eyes to accommodate her gradually deteriorating eyesight. 'Okay, so where's this Ferryside place?'

He pushed some cardboard files aside and rested his eleven-stone frame on the corner of her desk. 'Maybe it wouldn't be a bad idea if you bought yourself a map of the force area. It's on the coast, halfway between here and Pembrey.'

'Like that helps. In which direction's that exactly?'

'About four miles from Kidwelly. Are you with me?'

She nodded, but in reality was less than certain.

'Ah, yes, I think I know where you're talking about. There's a view of the castle over the water.'

'Yeah, that's it.'

She approached the window for a second time, looked out and sighed. 'So what are the chances of me getting there this afternoon?'

He screwed up his face. 'I'd say somewhere between close to zero and zero.'

'Oh, terrific.'

'My sergeant said I can run you there in the Land Rover, if that helps? Four-wheel drive and all that.'

She took a deep breath and steadied herself. 'Give me ten minutes, Kieran. I need to make a call. I'll meet you in reception at five to, yeah?'

'Okay, Sarge, I'll go and find my wellies.'

DI Trevor Simpson answered his phone on the third ring and immediately recognised Kesey's Brummie twang on the other end of the line. 'So why the hell are you ringing me at home? Do you think I haven't got better things to do with my time?'

Her brow furrowed. 'I need some advice, sir.'

'Why aren't you talking to Grav? He's your divisional DI, not me.'

'I'm very sorry to bother you, sir, but DI Gravel's still away on holiday.'

'All right for some. The vicious bastard shouldn't even be in the fucking job.'

'I can't comment on that, sir.'

'What about DCI McGregor? His number should be on the on-call list. Why not get hold of him instead of bothering me? You do realise I'm on sick leave, don't you?'

She shook her head, beginning to regret ringing at all. 'I'm sorry, sir, I've tried. I can't get hold of him. From what I'm told, some of the phone lines are down because of the snow.'

'Have you tried his mobile?'

'I have, sir, but no joy. There's no signal.'

'Okay, so it seems there's only one way of getting you off the damned phone. I'm all ears. What can I do for you?'

Kesey spent the next five minutes or so succinctly explaining the reason for her call, as the DI listened in hushed silence.

'Is that it?'

'That's it, sir.'

'Have you got a pen and paper handy?'

She delved into her handbag and took out her police-issue pocketbook and a plastic biro. 'Go ahead, sir. I'm ready.'

'About bloody time. I want you to get yourself down to this doctor's house, confirm what we're dealing with, take a statement, and contact the on-call pathologist. With a bit of luck, it will be Dr Sheila Carter. She's got a lot of experience and knows what she's talking about.'

She took a deep breath and noted his orders in barely decipherable scribbled handwriting. 'Is there anything else, sir?'

'The River Tywi's tidal. Anything thrown in anywhere downstream of Carmarthen is going to end up somewhere in the estuary at some point or other. We're going to have to search the river, but that's going to take some arranging. You're talking several miles of fast-flowing water. Do what you can today and speak to the detective chief super first thing tomorrow morning. She's usually in by about half eight at the latest. She can take it from there.'

'Thank you, sir, that's very helpful.'

'And check the missing persons records. See if anyone who's been reported missing meets the victim's description, once the pathologist's given you an idea of his approximate age and height.'

'So we're assuming he's a victim?'

'I don't think he carved up his forehead before putting his own head in a bag, do you? That would be some trick if he managed it.'

She winced. 'No, sir, I wasn't thinking.'

'Just do your best, Laura, that's all anybody can ask of you. And give me a ring before you clock off tonight if you need to talk again. I'm not going anywhere.'

'Thanks again, sir, I really appreciate your help. I hope you're on the mend very soon.'

* * *

It took the two officers about forty-five minutes to make what was usually a twenty-minute journey, and there was a good four to five inches of fresh snow on the ground by the time PC Harris pulled up outside the Williams family's three-hundred-year-old detached stone cottage. The doctor had been keeping a keen eye out for their arrival and she'd already pulled on her coat and hurried halfway down the path to greet them by the time they exited the vehicle.

Kesey met her with a wave of her hand as she opened the wooden gate and stepped onto the pavement. 'Dr Williams? Dr Delyth Williams?'

'Guilty as charged. You managed to get here then.'

'Yeah, eventually, thanks to PC Harris here. He's my chauffeur for the day.'

The doctor smiled in response, acknowledged the young constable with a subtle nod of her head and began trudging along the path towards a concrete garage topped by a snow-covered asbestos roof, located to the far right of the main house. 'I'd prefer if we didn't talk in the house if at all possible. My partner's looking after our two young children. They're old enough to know what's happening, but not old enough to understand it. I'd prefer to keep today's events from them if at all possible. I don't want their Christmas ruined.'

'Good luck with that. If you find a head, it's likely

to make the news sooner rather than later. The villagers will talk of little else soon enough.'

The doctor didn't respond, choosing to ignore the observation.

'So, let's take a look at the offending items.'

Williams opened the garage's side door and switched on the overhanging fluorescent light before ushering the two officers in behind her. 'Okay, there it is. The quicker you get the damned thing out of here, the happier I'll be.'

Kesey walked slowly to where the bag was located on top of a chest freezer surrounded by various items of gardening equipment, which she silently observed gave the scene a misleading normality. She hesitated momentarily, took a deep breath through her open mouth, and then pulled apart the two sides of the bag with gloved hands and peered in. It was a head all right. There was no mistaking that. And it was real. Not some convincing stage prop as a part of her had hoped. What a world we lived in. She'd seen enough. It was time to get hold of the pathologist as instructed and proceed from there.

She gripped the bag and struggled to close the degraded zip for a few seconds before giving up on the idea and carrying it out into the daylight as it was. 'Do you want to take a look inside, Kieran?'

He shook his head repeatedly and took a single step backwards towards the garage wall as unwelcome mental images filled his mind. 'No, you're all right, thanks, Sarge. I'll pass on that one, if that's all right with you?'

She nodded and gagged, ready to throw up at any second. 'I couldn't have a glass of water, could I, Doctor?'

'Of course you can. I'll just fetch one from the kitchen. I can only apologise for not inviting you into the house. As I explained...'

'We completely understand. That's not a problem. Now would be a good time to get that water I asked for.'

The doctor returned a minute or two later with glass in hand, to find the DS bent over and vomiting in a corner of the garden next to a large thorny bush. She spat the remaining puke from her mouth, and accepted the drink with an outstretched hand.

'I'm sorry about that. I don't know what came over me.'

The doctor smiled humourlessly. 'It had much the same effect on me. It's not every day one sees a head in a bag.'

'We don't seem able to get a phone signal. Any ideas?'

'Oh, you've got no chance at this end of the village. It's the high bank at the back of the houses that's the problem. We never can. But if you drive as far as the small humpback bridge you crossed on your way here, you should be okay.'

'I really need to take a statement from you before we head off. We can do it in the Land Rover, if that helps? It shouldn't take more than twenty minutes maximum.'

'I'll just tell my partner what's happening and be back with you before you know it.'

'Okay, that's great, I'll get the forms ready.'

* * *

Sheila Carter was seated in the lab at Carmarthen Morgue and enjoying a chicken and mayo sandwich when the two officers trudged in later that afternoon. She introduced herself on opening the door and led them into a white-painted room that Kesey silently acknowledged looked not unlike a hospital operating theatre. 'Do you fancy a hot drink before I take a look? The two of you look as if you could do with it.'

Both officers refused with thanks, thinking that their queasy stomachs were unlikely to welcome refreshments, however warm and well intentioned.

'If you're sure. That's the bag in question, I presume?'

The DS answered in the affirmative and handed the bag over just as quickly as she could.

'Right, let's take a look at what we're dealing with.'

PC Harris quickly retreated towards the exit as the consultant forensic pathologist began emptying the bag, one item at a time, onto a stainless steel dissection table. 'Is it all right if I wait in the vehicle, Sarge? My stomach's doing somersaults here.'

She smiled. 'Yeah, why not? I'd join you if I could. And keep the heater on. I'll see you when we're done.'

'Thanks, Sarge. I owe you one.'

She turned back towards the doctor who was in the process of carefully examining the head. 'What are your first impressions?'

Carter focused on the forehead with a puzzled expression on her heavily lined face, and talked as she worked. 'So what's happened to Grav? I'd have thought he'd have been here for this one. I can't keep him away usually.'

'He's on holiday in the sun for the next couple of weeks, lucky man.'

She revolved the head slowly in both hands. 'Oh, yes, he mentioned something the last time I saw him. Barbados, wasn't it?'

'Yes, I think so.'

'They'll have to drag him out of the police station kicking and screaming when he finally retires.'

'Yeah, I'm told he's a character.'

'You haven't met?'

'No, I'm new to the area.'

She glanced back and laughed. 'Oh, he's a character all right. But he's a good detective. Remember that. You'll learn a lot from him if you look past the thunder.'

Kesey dabbed a spot of perfume below her nostrils and approached the table. 'So, what can you tell me about this lot?'

'It seems you're just as impatient as the rest of them. He didn't commit suicide, if that's what you were wondering.'

'Yeah, I'd worked that one out for myself.'

'So what do you want to know?'

'Anything you can tell me.'

'I wouldn't like to guess at his age beyond that he's an adult male at this stage, but someone appears to have carved the word PAEDO into his forehead with a sharp instrument and there's an ear missing, if that helps.' She held the head up so that the face faced the light. 'Here, see?'

Kesey nodded. 'Do you think an animal could have chewed it off?'

Carter revolved the head in her hands. 'No, it's a clean cut. Almost surgical. I'd say a scalpel or a very sharp knife.'

'A trophy?'

She nodded. 'Yes, that's a possibility. Or it could be an indication of torture. I think that's a logical conclusion on first impressions.'

The DS held a hand to her mouth. 'Oh, for God's sake.'

'Do you need some fresh air, detective? You're looking a little green around the gills, if you don't mind me saying so.'

She swallowed twice. 'No, I'm good thanks… how long's he been dead?'

'Well, now you're asking. It seems much of him's missing from what I can see, and what little we do have has been in the water, as you're very well aware. It's been exposed to changes of temperature, not to mention PH and salt content. That complicates matters somewhat. And bacteria and various waterborne creatures seem to have had a good go at the various bits and pieces too. That certainly doesn't help us a great deal. I'll let you have my report sometime tomorrow, but don't hold your breath. Determining a time of death is going to be something of a challenge, if not impossible.'

'Can we identify him?'

She looked up and met the officer's eyes with a sneer. 'You're the detective.'

'Talk about walking on eggshells. I'm just trying

to do my job here. Can you help, please? I'd really appreciate your insight.'

Carter forcibly prised what was left of the man's lips apart and peered into the gaping mouth. 'His teeth are still in situ, so there's nothing stopping us comparing dental records to confirm his identity. Not that that helps you identify him in the first place, of course. Have you thought of missing persons? I can see that fingerprints are a lost cause.'

Sarky cow. 'Yeah, I'm already looking into that, thanks. What about DNA? If he's got convictions, he may be on the National Database.'

Carter turned away, walked towards a nearby sink, turned on the hot water and thoroughly washed her hands right up to the elbows. 'You appear to have a talent for stating the blatantly obvious, young lady.'

'So, what's the answer?'

'Now, that's where things become rather more complicated, I'm afraid. DNA, for the most part, is obfuscated and negated by the decomposition of the soft tissues. That's going to be a real issue in our friend's case.'

'Obfuscated?'

'Obscured. That's probably the best way of explaining it in lay terms you can understand.'

'Oh, shit! Just my luck. Any ideas?'

'We could use a piece of the long bone, of course. They're always useful due to their long preservation. The process is a little more complex if no bone marrow is present, but the results are much the same in the end.'

'That's something you could arrange for me, yes?'

Carter rested her hands on her bony hips and nodded. 'I'd say so, as long as your lot are going to pay the additional lab costs.'

'Why does red tape always seem to get in the way of basic policing? I'm sure the answer's going to be a resounding yes, but I'll consult the detective chief super and give you a ring in the morning with an unequivocal answer.'

'Okay, Sergeant, I believe we're done for today, unless there's anything else you want to ask me before you leave me in peace.'

She shook her head. 'No, I think that's it.'

'Glad to hear it.'

'Thanks for your help, Doctor. You came recommended. It was good to meet you, circumstances apart... I'll take the sports bag with me for evidential purposes, if that's all right with you?'

'Of course, no problem. It's of no further use to me. And give my best wishes to DI Simpson. I assume that's who you were referring to when you mentioned the recommendation?'

'That's right, and I will.'

'Oh, there is one more thing I should probably mention before you head off into the sunset with that sensitive young constable of yours.'

The DS turned and looked the pathologist firmly in the eye on approaching the door with the bag in hand, half expecting another sarcastic or patronising comment to be tossed her way. 'What's that exactly?'

'The two arms belong to different men.'

12

Rebecca lay face down on her single bed with her upper body resting on her elbows, and focused on the computer screen just a few inches in front of her eyes. Tip tap, tip tap. Tap away. There were so many out there. So many to choose from. So many to target. But she had to choose well. Who posed the highest risks? That was the important question. It was a matter of weighing up what she knew of each of them. Probing them for information until she was satisfied with her assessment. She couldn't kill them all in one lifetime, however much she'd like to.

Ah, it was him again, alias Teddy Bear. That wasn't a name she'd forget in a hurry. This was the fifth time he'd contacted her in just two short days. He seemed keen. More than keen. *Desperate* would probably be a better way of putting it. It would be as easy as shelling peas if she chose him. Given some of the depraved filth he'd sent, he was definitely on the shortlist. The current out-and-out favourite. Perhaps find out a little bit more about him before reaching any final conclusions. It was best to be sure.

She reached out with one of the red-painted nails she was so very proud of and typed one single word:

Hi

His reply was almost instantaneous:

Hello again, I missed you.

"Will you walk into my parlour? Said the spider to the fly." Give him time, Becca. Make the bastard work for it. A few seconds more.

Are you still there, Rebecca?

Why had she given him her own name? Why do

that? It was stupid. Really stupid. What was the point of adopting carefully considered security measures to protect her identity and location, if she then handed out potentially traceable information before she was ready, like some ignorant amateur?

She tugged at her hair, pulling a bloody tuft from her scalp and hurling it to the floor with a loud yelp. There, that felt a little better. It was amazing how a little pain clarified her thinking at times of stress. It wasn't so bad. She knew what she was doing. It was nothing really. She'd invested far too much time and effort to give up now. She couldn't just let the slime-ball off the hook. He had to be punished. It was just a matter of how and to what degree.

Yes Im still here

Are you alone?

She could sense his relief. It was almost palpable. And always the same predictable questions. The depraved bastard only had one thing on his mind. Just like the rest. Just like they all did.

Yes Im on my own in my bed room

Where are your mother and father?

Why do you want to know

I just do.

Mums down stairs making super and dads gone
to work

At this time?

He works for the counsil. He drives one of those big
griting lory things. Its yelow

Ah, now I understand. Remind me how old you are?

She reached down, picked up a small notepad
from the floor next to the bed and checked her handwritten records. R – S – T, yes, there he was: Teddy
Bear, Teddy Bear. Nine. She'd told him she was nine.

I was nine in June. I had a pool party with my frends at the leisere centre

That's a nice age. My favourite. Have you got any photos of the party? I'd really like to see them.

Will you send me sum more fotos first. I liked the ones you sent last time

Which ones did you like the best?

What the hell could she say to that? They were all as revolting as each other. Think, Becca, think. Leave the bastard hanging. That's all she had to do. Leave him dangling and see if he signed his death warrant.

I liked all of them

Shall I send some now, then?

yer

What of?

you choos

I'll send you some of my best ones. But you must never show them to anyone else. Especially adults. They wouldn't understand. You'll get into terrible trouble if you break our secret. The police and social workers would take you away from your parents and put you in a children's home. A horrible children's home where people would hurt you.

She clenched her hands into tight fists and pictured herself pummelling his face to a bloody, unrecognisable pulp. Oh, this one was a right manipulative bastard. Evil to the core. One of the very worst she'd ever encountered. He'd pay all right. He'd really pay.

I wont tell any body

Promise me. Give me your word and hope to die.

I promise

Okay, I trust you. I'm sending some now. Are you ready?

OK

There, sent. Have they arrived?

yer

Tell me if you like them.

She stared at the screen with narrowing eyes as three colour photographs appeared before her. Oh, for God's sake. They were pictures of children. No, no, no! One, two, three, four, five. Five children. Five young children. Five children ranging from toddlers of two or three, to boys and girls of eight or nine years. And that must be him. Teddy Bear. The naked monster in the black face mask. The devil in human form. The bastard. The absolute bastard! He was evil to the very core. Just as she'd thought.

She sat up and began punching her mattress hard with alternate fists: one, two, three, four, five, while screaming expletives at the screen. 'You dirty fucking bastard! Oh, you're guilty. You're guilty all right. I will hurt you bad.'

She looked away from the computer, closed her eyes, and took repeated deep breaths, in through her nose and out through her mouth, to calm her pounding heart. That's it, Becca, that's it. Focus on the endgame. Focus on the prize. This one wasn't going to get away. Not a chance. Not if she had anything to do with it. And he'd suffer. Yes, he'd suffer all right. She'd tear his fucking face off one small piece at a time.

She focused back on the screen and began typing:

I realy like the new fotos you sent me

That's good. That's very good. Which one do you like best?

Is it you in the funy mask????

Yes, it is. I bought it on holiday in Amsterdam.

why are you wering it????

It's a game.

what sort of game

A funny game. My favourite. I play it all the time. It's great fun.

Can we play it some time

Yes, of course we can. Will you send me the photos? The photos of your birthday party? I'd really like to see them.

Now what? She had to come up with something. Something convincing. Something he wanted to believe. Something he was desperate to believe.

I havent got them on my new computer but mum had some printed from the place in the super market. she put one in a frame and hung it on the wall in our lounge above the tely

Do you know where they are now?

yes you can see them if you want to

When? How?

you could come and play

I'd really like that.

Do you live in Carmarthen

Where's that?

its in wales

Near Swansea or Cardiff?

Not to far away. I think swansea is nearer

That's quite a long way from where I live, but I'd still come. We can be best friends.

Okay, so when was best? She'd need time to buy everything. Time to prepare. There was no point in rushing things. Not if it could lead to potential mistakes.

My mum and dad go out every friday nite. They wont be back until late

How do you know?

They never are. Its always after ten. I usualy watch a dvd or play computer games until they get home. some times one of my frends from school come over

She sat and waited for an instant response that didn't materialise. He'd paused before responding. That was a first. He was suspicious. The bastard was definitely suspicious.

Are you still there teddy????

That was a very long sentence. Are you sure you're only nine?

Thank you. my mums a teacher at the big school. She

gives me extra lesons and makes me practise my
words at week ends. Im the best in my class

She shifted an inch or two on the bed. The dirty
bastard had paused again. What the hell was that
about? Was he still having doubts? Damn, damn,
damn! No, hold on, he was typing again. He was still
chewing on the bait.

Where do they go?

who????

Your parents.

To the cinema first and then for a piza or some thing
like that

And they go every single week?

Yes allways

Don't they arrange a babysitter?

No they all ways leave me on my own unless a frend comes to play. Im a big girl now

You're certain? Always?

Yes always. they say Im old enough. I can ring my gran if I need help. she lives down the road

How do they get to the cinema?

In my dads car

What make is it?

I dont know

What colour is it?

blue

Where does he park it?

on the drive

Always?

yesssss

That's good, that's very good. I'll come and play on Friday. It's best if you don't ask one of your friends to join us this time. Is that okay?

yer ok

That's good. Our secret. Now I just need your address.

ill send it now

Rebecca jumped off her bed with easy athleticism, reached back to close her laptop, and giggled helplessly. It had been a close thing. He'd almost got away more than once. But it seemed his criminal lust had overcome his caution. Here was hoping he wouldn't have second thoughts and slink off into the night. This one really did deserve to die a horrible death. "Will you walk into my parlour? Said the spider to the fly." Come in and see what you get.

She retreated to her kitchen after a quick bathroom visit, sat at the table drinking chamomile tea from a porcelain cup, and planned Teddy Bear's torture and eventual murder with what she considered military precision. She was going to need everything she'd required on every other occasion: the bags, the tape, the saw. That was true. But this time was different. Special. This time there'd be additional requirements to make him wince: a hammer, pliers and maybe a car battery. She could give it more thought and come up with a definitive list later in the day. If the snow didn't clear in time, she'd have to don a suitable disguise and walk into Carmarthen town centre to buy them there. Oh, well, needs must. Such was life.

13

Kesey had set her radio alarm clock for six thirty a.m. sharp that morning, half an hour earlier than usual, and she was showered, dressed in a smart navy-blue two-piece suit usually reserved for court appearances, and leaving the house with a mug of warming coffee in hand about forty-five minutes later. It was time to impress. Time to make her mark.

The previous day's snow had turned to unrelenting driving rain overnight that had swept in off the sea at the behest of the wind, and returned the fields to their original winter green. She silently observed that it didn't look anything as atmospheric or scenic as the erstwhile stereotypical white chocolate-box vista, but it was a great deal more practical. And that, she decided, suited her just fine.

The roads were still relatively quiet at that time of the morning, and the journey passed quickly as she negotiated the country roads while listening to Radio 1. Hopefully it was a good omen. Hopefully things were looking up. Maybe, just maybe, the move to Wales wasn't such a bad idea after all. At least she didn't spend half her life stuck in lines of traffic. A herd of dairy cows or a few wandering sheep were a more likely problem these days.

She briefly considered heading straight to the Police HQ canteen for another coffee as she drove into the car park with a Culture Club hit blaring in her ears, but she abandoned the idea almost immediately on exiting the vehicle. What was the point of making an effort to arrive early if she didn't take full advantage of the fact? She was there to see the chief super, and that's what she had to do.

Kesey hurried across the car park as the rain began to fall, avoiding the many puddles with quick-dancing feet despite her two-inch heels. She said a cheery good morning to the receptionist seated behind a glass security screen at the entrance to the building and smiled. 'Is the detective chief super in yet, Sandra?'

'Not as yet, Laura, but she shouldn't be long. She mentioned she'd be in first thing.'

'Her office is on the top floor, yeah?'

'Yes, you've got it, right at the end of the corridor. Her name's emblazoned on the door.'

'It bleeding well would be, wouldn't it? And in big bold capitals, no doubt. As if anyone needs reminding.'

* * *

The DS was already standing outside the head of the Criminal Investigation Department's office door when the chief superintendent drove her sleek and much-admired four-door sports saloon into the car park a few short minutes later.

Kesey stood, waited, adjusted her hair, brushed non-existent fluff off both shoulders, and silently acknowledged that she was feeling a bit like a naughty child standing outside the headteacher's office. She badly wanted to impress. Perhaps more than she should. But the chief super was an influential woman despite her comparative youth. A successful woman who'd crashed through the metaphorical glass ceiling like a charging raging bull, in what was largely still a men's world. One day she wanted to be just like her, and she wasn't ashamed to admit it to herself. Maybe playing her part in investigating this case, an inevitably high-profile case, for however long and in whatever capacity the boss deemed appropriate, would aid her journey along that same rocky path. The greasy pole was greasy for a reason, but she fully intended to climb it as fast as feasibly possible. One day she'd be an officer with the authority and the increased salary that went with it. She felt driven. Impatient. And it couldn't come quickly enough.

Kesey was leaning against the wall and picturing herself sitting behind a big light-oak kick-ass desk in an excessively big office that yelled status and power when DCS Hannah Davies suddenly stepped out of the lift and appeared in the long corridor, resplendent in a knee-length military-style coat, which the

DS silently noted made her look even taller than her natural five-foot-ten-inch frame. Or was it the boots? Maybe it was the boots. Anyway, whatever it was, she looked just like a woman at the top of her profession should look: efficient, stylish, elegant, and dare she think it, sexy, in a hot, professional, secretarial sort of way.

'Are you waiting for me, Laura?'

'Yes, ma'am. I was hoping for five minutes to update you on some events that happened yesterday. A body or rather the body parts of two adult males were found on the tideline in Ferryside by a local doctor walking her dog.'

The DCS opened her office door with a gloved hand and walked into the room with a confident swagger Kesey thought typical of those who know they're in charge. 'Come in, Sergeant, I'm aware of the case. Sheila Carter gave me a quick call at my home late last night. She feels you're rather too young and inexperienced to be dealing with a murder case. Nothing personal, you understand. It's just an honest opinion. But I have to say I've known her for some time and I trust her judgement.'

The DS opened her mouth momentarily, but

then closed it again, suddenly lost for words.

'Nothing to say for yourself?'

Kesey just stood there, shifting her weight from one foot to the other, still searching for a response that didn't materialise, and watching as the DCS took off her gloves, one finger at a time.

'Coffee?'

She tugged at her sleeve. 'Yes, please, ma'am.'

Davies reached out and pointed towards a large picture window with an uninterrupted view of the town. 'The kettle's on the windowsill; it should be full. Now remind me, how long have you been in the job?'

The DS switched on the kettle and turned to face her boss as it slowly came to the boil. 'I joined the West Midlands force shortly after leaving Sunderland University a few years back.'

'Ah, yes, I remember reading that in your file. You didn't actually complete your Criminology degree, as I recall.'

'No, ma'am. I decided student life wasn't for me.'

The DCS glanced briefly at the various framed

academic certificates festooning the office walls, before returning her attention to her junior colleague. 'There's a jar of coffee on the silver tray over there. There's only powdered milk, I'm afraid. My secretary isn't in this morning. She's expecting another child any day now.'

'Milk and sugar, ma'am?'

She shook her head. 'Neither for me, thanks. I'm in training for a half-marathon in Paris next month, but help yourself.'

The DS poured the boiling water into two overly fussy porcelain cups and added a single spoonful of powdered milk and a sprinkle of brown sugar for herself. 'There you go, ma'am.'

'Thank you, Sergeant, take a seat. You were telling me about your career path.'

She sat as instructed and immediately noticed that her chair was smaller and lower than the chief super's, who appeared perched on a pedestal by comparison. 'I was a community PC initially, and then joined CID soon after finishing my probationary period. It's what I've always wanted to do.'

Davies sipped her coffee and paused for a second

or two before speaking again. 'And how did that work out for you?'

'I worked as a detective constable for almost three years, mainly in the Handsworth area of Birmingham. It went pretty well overall. My evaluations were positive and so I sat my sergeant's exam. I was promoted to detective sergeant about nine months after that.'

'So you've only been a police officer for about six years in total, correct?'

Kesey took a gulp of gradually cooling coffee, oblivious to leaving a powdery milky moustache above her top lip. 'Look, I know I've only got six years' experience, but I'm a hard worker and a fast learner. I worked in a high-population, high-crime, multicultural division and dealt with a wide variety of cases. Some fairly high profile. I gained a lot of valuable experience in a relatively short time, and put some serious villains away in the process.'

The DCS stared at her without speaking for a second or two, and then said, 'I'm pleased to hear it, Laura. I'm sure we can put that hard-won experience to good use. Now tell me, what happened yesterday?'

Kesey spent the following fifteen minutes or so

succinctly summarising the salient events of the previous day, and decided she felt significantly better for it. At least the boss was taking her seriously. At least she was treating her like the police officer she was. Maybe she'd been too quick to judge. Maybe the chief super wasn't so bad after all.

The DCS tapped her desktop repeatedly with the first two fingers of her right hand. 'That's very helpful, Sergeant. I'd be glad if you'd prepare a full report before the end of the day. Leave it on my desk if I'm not in my office. I'll check it first thing in the morning. And chase up Dr Carter's report. Collect it yourself if you have to. She assured me that it would be ready by eleven o'clock this morning at the latest, and she won't let us down. I like to have all the facts at my fingertips. No unwelcome surprises. Capisce?'

Kesey stood to leave. She had absolutely no idea what capisce meant, but she got the gist. 'Will do, ma'am.'

'Sit down, Laura, sit down. I haven't finished with you quite yet.'

'Ma'am?'

'Look, Sergeant, I'm going to be honest with you. You're only sitting here because of the limited resources currently at my disposal. I've never had a time when so many of my senior detectives are either on sick leave, out of the country on leave or attachment, or fully committed to other cases. Detective Inspector Gravel is our longest-serving and most experienced murder detective. I've made a reluctant decision to ask him to return early from his holiday to head up this investigation, but in the interim, I want you to manage it for me. It shouldn't be for more than a day or two, assuming he can get a flight. I'll keep a watching brief until he arrives, and, of course, you won't be left without support. We'll meet to discuss progress on a regular basis if you accept. I can assure you of that. So, tell me, what do you think? Are you up to it?'

The DS looked down and removed a spot of dust from her sleeve in silent contemplation.

'Well, are you going to give me an answer, Laura? Or are you going to sit there twiddling your thumbs?'

'I'd be happy to do it, ma'am. Thanks for putting your faith in me.'

Davies linked her fingers together and nodded. 'That's what I hoped you'd say. This is an opportunity, Sergeant. It's an opportunity to make your mark in your new force. Don't cock it up.'

'I won't, ma'am.'

'Let's hope not. It could come back to haunt both of us. We have to be better than the men, Laura. Remember that. Carve it in stone. We have to beat them at their own game. It's the only way females can progress.'

'I understand, ma'am.'

The DCS smiled warmly for the first time that morning. 'Right then, now that that's out of the way, let's decide where we go from here. Have you got a pen and paper?'

Kesey delved into her overburdened handbag and nodded twice. 'Yes, ma'am.'

'Then I suggest you take some notes.'

She placed her pocketbook on her lap and poised her biro above the first blank page.

'We've used the training room on the second floor as a serious incident room in the past. It's fitted out with phone lines, computers, whiteboards, maps and the like. I suggest we do likewise this time. I'll let the Training Department know what's happening, and you can base yourself there for the foreseeable future. Give them an hour or so to free it up.'

'Okay, ma'am.'

'Are you familiar with the H.O.L.M.E.S. crime intelligence software?'

The DS paused before responding. 'I'm aware of it, but I haven't got a great deal of experience using it.'

'The Home Office have got this one spot on for a change. It's proved extremely useful in managing complex cases for some time now. The system ensures everything's processed in the one place and helps us make links that might otherwise be missed. Invaluable really. I like to think its use makes the chance of vital clues being overlooked far less likely. Have a word with DI Gravel when he returns to the fold. He was part of a working party that helped shape the system's development. Ask him to give you a brief tutorial. It's well designed in the main. I feel sure you'll master it in no time.'

'Okay, will do, ma'am.'

'We've got two dead adult males, yes?'

'Yes, ma'am.'

'Let's try to get them identified as quickly as possible. That'll give us a sound starting point when it comes to catching our killer. I'm assuming you've made a start with the missing persons records?'

'I've asked DC Rees to get on with it, ma'am. Looking at our force area initially, but then moving on to other forces both within Wales and beyond the border.'

The DCS shook her head slowly with her glasses perched on the very tip of her nose. 'That's going to be a very long list. We'll need to narrow it down if it's going to be even remotely manageable. We do at least already know that both victims are male, white and that one had short cropped dark hair. It's not a great deal, but it's a lot better than nothing. We also know that one of the two men had "paedo" carved on his forehead, either before or after death. Someone obviously believed he was a sex offender, and he, or she, felt strongly enough about that to take a knife and let the world know. Check to see if the location of any known or suspected paedophiles is currently unknown. The sex offender register should go some way in helping you in that regard, but don't rely on it exclusively. It has its limits.'

She scribbled frantically, and spoke without looking up. 'Yes, ma'am.'

'Make sure you talk to the child protection unit sergeants in each division, and to the West Wales Social Services Department's child protection team managers. They all have a great deal of local knowledge, some of which may well be relevant to this investigation.'

'Will do.'

'Let's see what conclusions Sheila reaches in her report, and we should be able to build further on our profiles. She should at least be able to provide us with an age range, and she mentioned signs of what could be a tattoo on the degraded skin of one of the two arms. That may help us somewhat. I've given her the go-ahead on the DNA tests. We should get them back within a few days. She'll get the samples sent off sometime this morning.'

'Thank you, ma'am.'

'Don't worry yourself too much about Sheila's opinion of you, Laura. She was young herself once. Hopefully you can prove her wrong.'

She nodded. 'I will, ma'am.'

'Right, where were we? We're going to need to

search the river, of course. Starting in the estuary and progressing back towards Carmarthen. That's quite a task, as I'm sure you've already realised. The Tywi's in flood at the moment, due to a combination of high tides, heavy rain and the melting snow. Sod's law I guess. But we're going to have to do what we can. There's got to be other body parts to find, assuming they haven't already reached the open sea. We've just got to locate them.'

Kesey drained her cup as the true enormity of the task ahead of her began to sink in. 'I've got to be honest, ma'am. This isn't like anything I've dealt with before. I'm a city girl. How do I arrange all that?'

'We need to get started early this afternoon and make as much progress as we can before the light begins to fade. We're only talking of a small window. I'll bring the chief constable up to speed immediately after our meeting and ensure there are sufficient uniform officers available to make the search viable. I'll cancel all leave for the foreseeable future, and bring in officers from other divisions as required. That will include dive teams where necessary, and dog handlers as a prerequisite. If there are further body parts to find, which as I've said seems inevitable, let's get them found. I don't want another member of the public having the sort of experience suffered by our GP friend. It doesn't look good for the force.'

'Do you think it's worth me checking CCTV, ma'am?'

'I don't know what purpose it would serve, to be frank. There's no cameras in the area of the Tywi anywhere between here and the estuary on either side of the river. I guess it makes sense to dedicate a junior officer's time to the task of examining the tapes from the surrounding area once we've got some sort of timescale, but it seems highly unlikely that whoever dumped the bodies wouldn't have sought out a more remote location. It's not like we're short of them in this part of the world, as you'll see for yourself soon enough. You've got a young probationary constable attached to CID at the moment. A PC Benjamin Reid. Not a bad lad, if a bit full of himself. I know the family. If we're going to do it at all, he seems the obvious choice. Don't waste the time of a more experienced officer.'

'Okay, ma'am, that makes sense. I'll have a quick word with him once I've read the pathologist's findings. At least then I can give him an estimated start and end date.'

The DCS rose from her seat, circumnavigated her desk and approached a large framed map of the force area on the back wall directly opposite the window. 'I'm aiming to have the search officers in the relevant areas by one p.m. today at the latest, starting here in Ferryside and here in Llansteffan on the opposite side of the estuary. They'll then gradually work their way upriver on both banks, and in the river itself, for however long it takes. It's approximately eight miles by road from Carmarthen to both villages, and so I'm expecting a thorough search to take several days given the early sunsets. It's dark by four thirty at the latest.'

'In the river, ma'am?'

'Take a seat, Sergeant, take a seat. We've got an inflatable powerboat for the purpose, and trained divers with experience of this sort of thing. When it comes to searching waterways, they know what they're doing a lot better than you, or me for that matter. All you'll need to do is point them in the right direction and let them get on with their jobs.'

'Will do, ma'am.'

JOHN NICHOLL

'I suggest you arrange a briefing for twelve p.m. today sharp. You can use the conference room on the ground floor for the purpose. Every officer involved needs to know what they're looking for and why. I'll make a brief appearance at the start to spell out that you're standing in for DI Gravel, and then leave to let you get on with it. That should keep them on their toes.'

'You want me to bring them fully up to date, yes?'

She nodded. 'That's exactly what I want you to do... and get yourself down to Ferryside sometime today to familiarise yourself with the ground. You can get back to Carmarthen once you've done that, to get on with the other tasks we've discussed. Overtime isn't going to be a problem given the nature of the investigation.'

'Does that apply to all the officers under my supervision, ma'am?'

She checked her watch before looking up again. 'Yes, it does.

Any final questions before we bring the meeting to a close?' Kesey closed her eyes and thought for a few seconds, before opening them again and asking,

'Shouldn't we let the public know?' less than convincingly.

A transient smile played on the chief super's lips before disappearing as quickly as it appeared. 'Yes, I haven't forgotten, Sergeant. I'll be putting out a brief written press release just as soon as I've apprised the chief constable of the situation.' She laughed. 'I think he'd like to hear it from me before he reads it in the papers, don't you?'

Her face reddened. 'Yes, ma'am. Of course.'

'We'll delay a full-blown press conference until DI Gravel's back from the tropics. You needn't concern yourself in that regard. Hopefully by then we'll have something positive to tell the journalists. These things require careful management. You've got more than enough to be getting on with in the interim.'

'Thank you, ma'am.'

Davies rose from her seat, reached across the desk and shook the sergeant's hand with a surprisingly firm grip. 'Glad to have you on board, Laura. Us girls have got to stick together.'

'Thank you, ma'am. I won't let you down.'

'Let's hope not... there is one last thing I wanted to mention, before you head off. I don't think I'm speaking out of turn when I say that DI Gravel is somewhat old-school. I think that's probably the best way of putting it. But, with that said, he gets results, even if he does sometimes bend the rules a little more than I would wish in a perfect world. Do your best to get on with him. If you focus on his good points and try to ignore his more obvious flaws, you'll learn a lot and be a much better detective for it.'

14

Kesey sat in the driver's seat with the engine ambling and wolfed down one chocolate truffle after another while waiting for the Carmarthen-to-Swansea train to thunder past with a loud toot of its horn a minute or two later. All that was left of the snow of the previous day were various intermittent piles of dirty grey slush at the sides of the road, and she said a silent prayer of thanks to a God whose existence she sometimes doubted as the safety barrier slowly rose into the air with an electric buzz, enabling her to drive over the railway crossing and into the stone-strewn parking area that bordered the exposed beach.

She parked to the side of the Yacht Club, next to a walled compound housing variously sized boats, and donned a bright-orange waterproof coat before locking the car with a single click of a button. She walked to the edge of the uneven track to look out on the wide estuary, and found herself gratified to see that the search was already in progress. But surveying the scene with her own eyes in real time, rather than perusing a map and picturing the geography as she had earlier in the day, left her in no doubt as to the enormity of the task at hand. If the killer had chosen to dump the body parts either here where the river met the sea, or in an even more remote location, probably in the unlit darkness of the night, the chances of him being seen were virtually zero. Good detective work and a lucky break or two were her best hopes of success. If she worked fast, really fast, and things somehow went her way, she may even make some real progress before the infamous DI Gravel arrived back from his holiday in the winter sun.

She pictured herself making a dramatic single-handed arrest and receiving the enthusiastic plaudits of her previously dismissive colleagues. Wouldn't it be marvellous if she broke the case before he even turned up? That would win her some favour like nothing else could. She'd be a heroine, admired for her achievements. Flavour of the month.

The DS looked out and watched as small groups of uniformed officers made their way along the beach in an organised formation on both sides of the rising water. Maybe the dog handlers had the best chance of success. PC Rob Lawler had mentioned that his German Shepherd bitch had specialist training in finding bodies at the briefing. You couldn't ask for better than that. He reckoned she'd never failed. But then how would he know?

She took another chocolate from a coat pocket, unwrapped it, and had just popped it into her open mouth when a warmly dressed blonde woman in her early thirties walked along the track towards her with a plump black-and-tan Rottweiler bitch in tow. The woman smiled warmly, stopped, and stood at the officer's side. 'I wonder if they'll find anything else. It's horrendous, isn't it? Imagine finding a human head. Ghastly! I was on the beach with the dog yesterday before it started snowing. I'm just glad it wasn't me who found the horrible thing.'

The DS took her warrant card from a coat pocket and held it up at eye level. 'DS Kesey, local police. And you are?'

The woman was beginning to wish she'd walked right on by without saying anything at all. 'Dianne Davies. I'm a practice nurse at the local health centre.'

'Nice to meet you, Dianne. Do you live locally?'

She nodded and patted the top of the large dog's head as it snuggled up to her thigh and licked her gloved hand. 'Yeah, about five minutes' walk away.'

'Is the reason for the search common knowledge?'

'Oh, yes, it's the talk of the village.'

'You haven't seen a search boat here today, by any chance?'

She nodded. 'Yeah, three officers with diving equipment took an inflatable down the slipway about an hour ago. You'd have seen them out on the water yourself if you'd been here a bit earlier. They haven't long gone.'

The DS took her few remaining chocolates from her coat pocket and offered one to the local, who accepted it gratefully and began sucking, as the dog slobbered and dribbled next to her. 'I'm assuming they were making their way in the direction of Carmarthen, correct?'

She reached out a damp hand and pointed to their right. 'Yeah, they disappeared around that bend in the river. Just where it's flooded over the marshy area.'

Kesey nodded. 'Okay, thanks. Is there any talk locally that may be of interest to the police?'

'What sort of thing have you got in mind?'

The DS looked on as the dog gave up on the chance of a chocolate, wandered onto the beach, and began sniffing at nothing in particular. 'Is the dog okay?'

'Yeah, she won't go far. Come on, Marge! Here she comes.'

'Any missing local men, or anyone seen dumping something in the river. That's the sort of thing I'm thinking of.'

Dianne looked into the far-off distance as the coastal wind began to blow harder and the temperature dropped very close to zero. 'One of the health visitors mentioned that one of her new mums complained that she hadn't heard from her husband for a few days. He'd missed an important meeting they were supposed to attend together. Something to do with the children... the health visitor joked that she wouldn't mind her own husband disappearing once in a while.'

'Okay, that's helpful. Do you know if he's been reported missing?'

The nursing sister shook her head. 'No, I can't say for certain, but I very much doubt it. It's something he does on a fairly regular basis, apparently. He wanders off the radar and then comes back into her life when it suits him. Some men are like that. Unreliable. It's what he does.'

'Can you tell me anything else about the family?'

'Not a great deal. I haven't met him myself, but the mother brought one of their three kids into the surgery for her immunisations a week or two back. She seemed nice enough on first impressions. A little nervous, perhaps. They've only been in the area for a few months at most. Helen told me that the kids' names have been included on the child protection register.'

'Helen?'

'The health visitor I mentioned.'

'Any idea why the children are on the register?'

'No, I probably should do, but I haven't been involved with that side of things. I know Mel Nicholson, the social services manager, knows the case, because Helen mentioned him chairing a child protection case conference she attended.' She grinned. 'She told me she thinks he's quite dishy, but she'd hate me for telling you that.'

The DS smiled. 'I don't suppose you know what this errant husband looks like?'

'Sorry, no. Not a clue. More cesspit than Brad Pitt's my bet.' She laughed.

'What about a name?'

'The mum called herself Lucy and the baby Kylie. There's a few Kylies on their estate to complement the Britneys and one Madonna.'

She shook her head and grinned. 'Maybe they'll form a band.'

'Yeah, you never know. The family name is Griffiths, but I seem to remember Helen mentioning that the parents were known under a different surname in London. She had some problems tracking down the health visiting records.'

'Okay, so it looks as if they may have something

to hide. What's their current address?'

'I know it's one of the new housing association places on the estate near the English language primary school in Kidwelly, but that's about it. Number six or sixteen maybe. That seems to ring a bell.'

Kesey took her police-issue pocketbook from the top pocket of her coat and opened it at a page marked with an oversized paperclip. 'What's your home number please, Dianne?'

She gave the number as requested and volunteered her address without being asked.

'Have you got a mobile number?'

'Get down, you daft dog. We'll be going in a minute... sorry about that. She's probably hungry.'

'The mobile?'

'We can't get a signal at our end of the village. It's probably best to ring me either at home or at the clinic if you need to get hold of me.'

'Okay, I doubt I'll need to, but thanks anyway. It was good to meet you, and thanks for the information.'

'You're welcome.'

'Another sweet before you go?'

'Oh, go on then, thanks... bye for now.'

'See you again.'

'Our paths'll cross again at some point, no doubt... come on dog, the sky's about to open. It's time to head for home.'

* * *

As the detective sergeant drove back through the small coastal village, across the humpback bridge and along the narrow lanes in the direction of the main road, she was thinking that she might just have won the investigative lottery. What were the chances? The information could be totally irrelevant, of course, and it very probably was knowing her luck, but stranger things had happened. A lucky break broke the Yorkshire Ripper case wide open. Maybe, just maybe, this Griffiths character was one of the victims. That would be one way to impress the DI on first meeting. All she had to do was make some phone calls, track this Mel Nicholson down as soon as practically possible and keep her fingers well and truly crossed.

* * *

Sheila Carter had already left for a meeting by the time Kesey arrived at Carmarthen Morgue later that afternoon. She had a quick look around the lab and its adjacent rooms without success, and was about to give up on any chance of obtaining the post-mortem report that day, when a young female secretarial worker with long legs and a very short skirt called after her and waved a large brown envelope in the air above her head. 'Are you the police officer? The new one? Dr Carter told me to keep a look out for you.'

The DS smiled and accepted the envelope with an outstretched hand. 'Many thanks.'

'You're welcome.'

Kesey sat back in the driver's seat, ripped open the A4 envelope and began reading the contents line by line. She hadn't been expecting a great deal of worth given the extremely limited material at the pathologist's disposal, but she was surprised to find that Carter had, at least, reached some tentative conclusions which were likely to make a positive contribution to the investigation. The two arms belonged to two different men, which she already knew, but it seemed that the longer of the two and the head belonged to the same individual in life. The pending

DNA test results would, of course, confirm that as fact or otherwise. But Carter's conclusions stated it was likely given the skin tone, bone density, hair colour and the estimated length of time the particular body parts had spent in the water. She'd also concluded that this particular individual was likely to have been approximately five foot nine or ten inches in height, while the second man was significantly shorter at about five foot six or seven. The taller of the two men was thought to be in his late thirties or early forties, and the second man younger, but of indeterminate age, due to the more advanced state of decomposition. The older of the two men's body parts had been in the water no more than two or three days, while the younger man's arm was likely to have been in the water for a week or longer. She considered that this one arm may have been frozen for an unspecified period prior to disposal, but she stressed that this was an informed hypothesis rather than an established fact. What was known with certainty was that both the arms and the head had been removed from their respective bodies with a serrated blade such as a saw, and that the ear had been removed with a sharp blade prior to death.

Kesey refolded the report and placed it on the passenger seat together with the envelope. It wasn't all bad. There were positives. While nothing the pathologist said went any way to identifying the killer, it did at least bring the identification of the victims that much nearer. That was a reasonable starting point. She'd had worse days. The chief super had said that Carter was reliable. It looked as if she was right.

* * *

The DS made four phone calls before finally tracking down Mel Nicholson, senior social services department child protection manager, at a local three-star hotel where he was presenting a lecture on the assessment of risk to a small gathering of police officers and social workers. It was Nicholson's policy always to put operational matters ahead of his many other responsibilities, and he was more than happy to make his apologies to the attending group and take the call just as soon as he was summoned. 'Hello, Mel Nicholson speaking.'

'Hello, Mr Nicholson, we haven't met. My name's

Laura Kesey. I'm a detective sergeant based at West Wales Police Headquarters.'

'I don't recognise the name; you must be new. What can I do for you, Laura?'

'I'm hoping you can tell me something about the Griffiths family from Kidwelly.'

'Which one exactly? It's a common surname in this part of the world.'

'Yes, of course it is. There's the mother, Lucy, the father, three kids, the youngest of whom is called Kylie. I don't know if that helps? I'm told you chaired a recent child protection case conference attended by DI Simpson.'

'Yeah, I know who you're talking about. It was the last conference Trevor came to before going off on sick leave. How's he doing by the way, any news?'

'I spoke to him only yesterday, as it happens. He's doing okay, thanks. Hopefully it won't be too long before he's back in work.'

'Glad to hear it. Give him my best the next time you speak to him.'

'I will.'

'So, what do you want to know?'

'Anything you can tell me.'

Nicholson found a chair and sat himself down. 'Okay, I can manage that much. The mother's a stay-at-home parent, they've got three kids as you said, two boys aged six years and four years, and a baby girl of about five months. All three children's names were added to the register under the sexual abuse category and a multiagency protection plan agreed.'

'What about the father?'

'Yeah, I was just coming to him. This is where it gets interesting.'

'Interesting how?'

'He calls himself Derek Griffiths these days, but his surname was Rodgers before they left London. He was employed as a residential worker in the Blackheath area until a few months back. An indecent assault allegation against a seven-year-old resident put an end to his less-than-glittering career, but it came to nothing in court when the alleged victim fell apart under cross-questioning. Not surprising really, when you think about it. The shit kids sometimes have to go through at the hands of the defence barrister is unbelievable. How they can do it and still sleep at night is a mystery to me.'

'So, do you reckon he did it?'

'Oh, yeah, there'd been previous allegations of a similar nature that came to nothing due to a lack of corroborative evidence. I read the transcript of the most recent joint investigation video interview. He's guilty all right. I've got absolutely no doubt in my mind. Either the seven-year-old had read a sexual abuse textbook or she was telling the truth. I know which one I'd put my money on.'

'So if he was found not guilty, how come the kids are on the register? It doesn't make a lot of sense.'

'Child protection is a civil process governed by the Children's Act. We assess risk on the basis of the balance of probabilities, rather than reasonable doubt as in the criminal courts. Griffiths has reluctantly agreed to move out of the family home for a twelve-week period while the NSPCC team in Swansea carry out a comprehensive risk assessment. He moved in with his mother in Llanelli from what I heard, in case you're interested. That's where he grew up before heading to London.'

'Ah, okay, I didn't realise that. The bit about the legal framework.'

'Why would you? It's a specialist field.'

'I'm assuming they came back to this area to

make a new start. You know, to try to escape his past, that sort of thing.'

Nicholson stifled a laugh. 'Yeah, that was a part of it, but it turns out he targeted the wrong victim this time. Not that I'm suggesting there's ever a right one.'

'What are you talking about?'

'Unknown to him, the victim's father's a south-east London heavy with high-end criminal connections in the illicit world of drugs, people trafficking and prostitution. A hard case named Shane Taylor. Word is Taylor put a contract on him. Ten grand in unmarked notes for whoever killed the bastard. Griffiths was running for his life. He shits himself whenever anyone knocks on his door.'

'Now things are beginning to make sense. He isn't white and about five foot ten inches tall with short dark hair by any chance?'

'Yeah, he is as it happens, but why do you ask?'

'We'll need to complete the scientific checks before coming to any firm conclusions, but I think that someone may have claimed that ten thousand quid you were talking about.'

15

Grav was suffering from yet another skull-splitting hangover as he completed the reams of paperwork required before taking charge of his rental car, and he decided to leave the vehicle parked exactly where it was for another half an hour or so while he walked as far as his regular Speightstown café of choice for a belated mid-morning breakfast.

He received his usual warm welcome on seating himself below a bright-blue sun umbrella, and was feeling a little better about life in general right up to the point his mind began wandering back to the events of the previous evening. Oh, shit, he'd behaved like a complete prat again. That summed it all up very nicely. What the fuck was wrong with him? Why so quick to anger? Why so fucking obnoxious for no apparent reason whatsoever? Dewi was making an effort, and he'd gone and ruined it in two minutes flat. What a bloody temper on a man. A grovelling apology might be a good idea when he next saw the boy. Put it down to the booze, say he was sorry, shake him by the hand, buy him a drink or two, and the boy would have to be satisfied with that. You couldn't press rewind in this life, more's the pity. What more could he do? What more could he say?

He decided to forgo his usual meaty rolls, ordered an extra-large banana omelette with several rounds of brown buttered toast and strong sweet coffee, and watched, open-mouthed, for ten minutes or more, as a black-and-yellow Antillean Crested Hummingbird, no more than three inches in length, hovered with its long beak probing a white flower in the bush to his immediate left. He raised a trembling hand to his face and gently massaged his bloodshot eyes. He spent so much of his time looking in the gutter and under stones, so much time focused on humanity's seemingly unlimited capacity for evil that witnessing such exquisite beauty could prove to be strangely hard to bear. He thought about it for a minute or two longer while continuing to focus on the bird as it manoeuvred from flower to flower with seemingly effortless ease, but he couldn't come up with an adequate resolution. How the hell would he explain it in the unlikely event that anyone was ever interested enough to ask? Maybe any explanation he could come up with would be inadequate anyway. Yeah, that was probably the case. Maybe it was something you had to experience yourself. Something you had to have lived.

Grav's ruminations were brought to a sudden halt when the same smiling waitress arrived at his side carrying a tray laden with his freshly prepared refreshments only moments later. 'Thanks, love. That looks delicious as always. Say thanks to that nice sister of yours for me. You two have made an old man very welcome, and it's appreciated.'

'Glad to be of service, Grav. Any plans for today?'

He took a slurp of hot coffee without waiting for it to cool and winced as the boiling water blistered his top lip. 'I thought of driving over to the other side of the island. My son mentioned that it's very different to the west coast. Any recommendations?'

'Bathsheba's beautiful. There's a lovely relaxed restaurant overlooking the sea, if you're still hungry after that lot.'

He patted his large overhanging gut and grinned. 'Thanks, love, I may well check it out.'

* * *

It took him a little under forty minutes to reach the east coast, despite getting lost more than once. He stared at the vista appearing before him as he manoeuvred down the long twisting road leading to Bathsheba, with its wide pale-yellow sandy beach, coral rock formations and large white-topped Atlantic rollers that roared and crashed onto the beach time and time again. He was surprised to see several surfers waiting to catch the big waves far out in the water, and struck by how very different this side of the small island truly was. It was as if someone had drugged him and dropped him onto a completely different island in another part of the world. A bit like parts of Cornwall's Atlantic coast, but with sun. That was a fair comparison. And Heather would have loved it. It was her sort of place. Wild, unspoilt and unpretentious. He heard her still-familiar voice whispering in his ear again, and silently acknowledged that he had never felt more alone in his life. What was the point of new experiences when he didn't have his lovely girl to share it all with? Would he ever come to terms with his loss? Did he even want to? Maybe he did, but probably not. That was the bitter reality. Why move on when you were still in love with the lost?

He glanced in the rear-view mirror as he parked the vehicle, and thought for a fleeting moment that he saw her sitting in the back seat with a disapproving look on her girlish face. 'Come on now, Grav. Stop wallowing in the past, old man. I'm fine where I am, and life has to go on. Now get out of this bloody car and stretch those legs of yours before you get rooted to the spot.'

He nodded and smiled. 'All right, love. I hear you.'

Grav made his way past several stalls staffed by friendly locals selling brightly coloured towels, hand-crafted jewellery and other potential souvenirs, and strolled along the seaweed-strewn foreshore for half an hour or more, before finally turning around and heading back towards a wooden ramshackle bar he'd spotted a few minutes' walk from where he'd parked earlier in the day. He pondered that he probably shouldn't drink and drive. Heather would certainly frown on it. But what harm could a bottle or two of beer do? And maybe buy a couple of packets of those fried plantain he liked so much. Yeah, what the hell, go for it.

* * *

The big middle-aged Bajan bar owner placed his hand on Grav's shoulder and shook him gently, causing his ever-expanding beer belly to wobble like a birthday jelly. 'It's time to wake up, sir. You've been sleeping for almost an hour.'

Grav blinked repeatedly and yawned, emitting a loud bellow. 'Can I have another beer?'

'It's time to be on your way, sir. I'm about to lock up. I've got a home to go to.'

He struggled to his feet and stumbled against the balcony's wooden safety barrier as his left knee gave way under his weight. 'Well, isn't that just dandy? You take my money and then you kick me out when it suits you. Fucking charming! And your beer's shit. You want to try switching your bloody fridge on. It's hot, in case you hadn't noticed.'

The big Bajan visibly stiffened as Grav leered at him with bleary eyes. 'I'm not going to tell you again, sir. You're drunk. It's time to be on your way.'

Grav briefly considered throwing a punch, but thought better of it and stumbled down the three wooden steps leading to the road. 'All right, I'm going. If you don't want my custom, I'll take it somewhere else.'

'You do that, sir. And please don't come back.'

* * *

The light was fading fast as Grav drove away from the east coast with a string of expletives ringing in his ears. He took three wrong turns and almost two hours to make what should have been no more than a thirty- to forty-minute journey, and he had the look of a condemned man on his face by the time he reached his apartment. Who the fuck was that looking his way? That had to be a police car. And with a rather tasty female officer sitting in the driver's seat. Oh for fuck's sake. Surely the bastard barman hadn't contacted the plod. Or was it the drink-driving? Maybe it was the drink-driving. He'd certainly had a few. Should he do a runner? Na, that wouldn't do him any favours. He'd run and she'd catch him. And that wouldn't help anybody, least of all him. Face up to whatever was coming. Take it on the chin, grovel and play the fellow copper card. It had worked before. Why not this time?

Grav parked behind the building and threw up against a wall in a corner, before staggering around to the front with tears welling in his eyes and an acidic taste in his mouth. He spat a mouthful of green bile to the pavement and glanced in the direction of the police car as he struggled to slot the key into the lock. Come on, Grav. You can do it, boy. Come on, come on. That's it, open.

'Is that you, Inspector Gravel? I need a word with you.'

Oh shit, she was getting out of the car. She was crossing the road towards him. 'If that fucking barman is trying to stitch me up, he's got to be kidding. He had a go at me, not the other way around. I was the innocent party.'

She stopped on the spot and stared at him open-mouthed as he fumbled in the pockets of his over-sized shorts for his warrant card. 'That's not why I'm here, Inspector.'

He tripped over on attempting to negotiate the doorstep and crashed to the tiled floor, grazing both knees and cracking the top of his head against a wall. 'So I've had a few drinks. What harm did it do? I'm on holiday, aren't I?'

She hurried towards him and took his arm in hers. 'A few! Who are you trying to kid? Come on, Inspector, let's get you upstairs. Isn't alcohol a wonderful anaesthetic?'

'Oh, you're a lovely girl. And beautiful too. Have you come to look after your Uncle Grav?'

She lifted him to his feet, guided him to the bottom of the stairs and began pushing him up one step at a time. 'Where do you keep your coffee, Inspector?'

'I hope you're not one of those kissy, kissy types. But, if you are, no tongues.'

'Just what I need, a badly behaved wannabe funny man. I think you need to cool out a bit while I make that coffee.'

'Whatever you say, love. Whatever you say.'

She shoved him onto the small landing, supported him there with one hand, and tried one door, then another, before guiding him into the white-tiled bathroom, lowering him into the shower cubicle and turning on the cold water. 'Now, you stay there till I tell you to come out. Are you going to behave yourself?'

He lifted a hand to the side of his head and saluted. 'Yes, ma'am.'

She shook her head and headed for the kitchen.

* * *

'Come on, out you come. Your coffee's made and waiting for you.'

'Give me a hand, love.'

She bent at the waist, reached out a hand, helped him to his feet and handed him a bath towel taken from the heated rail next to the sink. 'Right, can you stand up by yourself?'

He began towelling what was left of his hair. 'Yeah, the room stopped spinning a minute or two back. It was like being on a fucking merry-go-round.'

She looked across at him and frowned. 'Didn't your mother ever wash your mouth out with soap and water?'

'Sorry, love.'

'Strip off, get yourself dry, wrap that towel around yourself, and meet me in the kitchen just as soon as you're ready. I haven't got all day, so get a move on.'

So, if she wasn't there to question or arrest him, what the hell else did she want? Oh God, was it bad news? Had something happened to the boy? He secured the towel tightly around his waist, hurried across the landing in three strides and opened the kitchen door. 'This isn't about Dewi, is it?'

'I don't know who Dewi is, Inspector, but no, it's not about him. Now sit yourself down before you fall down, and make damned sure that towel doesn't fall off. They don't pay me enough to be looking at that sort of thing.'

He laughed, sat as instructed, and said, 'Thanks, love,' as she handed him his cup.

'Right, do you think you're actually capable of a sensible conversation, or do I need to put you back in that shower?'

He took a gulp of coffee and grinned. 'I'm sorry,

love. I've been a right prat. One drink too many. What can I do for you?'

'So, you're sobering up at last. And not before time. We've had a Detective Chief Superintendent Hannah Davies on the phone. She wants you to phone her urgently.'

What the hell did she want? One minute she was trying to get rid of him, and the next asking him to ring. Women, they were all as mad as fucking hatters.

'Did you hear me, Inspector? Am I not speaking English?'

'Sorry, love, I was deep in thought. Did she say what she wanted?'

She handed him a piece of paper with the DCS's contact number written on it in blue ink. 'No, she just stressed the urgency. That's her home number if you miss her at the station.'

He nodded and made a mental note of the number. 'Can I borrow your mobile, love?'

'What's wrong with yours?'

'I didn't bring one with me.'

She reached across the table and snatched the

paper from his hand. 'Give me that, I'll ring the damned number myself... right, it's ringing. Be polite now. Don't go upsetting the woman or you'll have me to answer to.'

He saluted for a second time, hoping to make her laugh, and accepted the phone when she didn't. 'Hello, it's Gareth Gravel. I was given a message to contact you.'

'Good of you to get back to me so promptly, Inspector. How are you?'

'You didn't ring halfway across the world to enquire about my health. Just get to the point, woman, and let me get on with my holiday.'

'Charming as always... okay, I'll put my cards on the table. I'm hoping you'll agree to help me with a small problem this end.'

'Is it another complaint?'

'For once the answer's no.'

'Just say it like it is, woman. I've got a holiday to get on with.'

'I do not appreciate your attitude, Inspector. I would strongly advise you to remember to whom you are speaking.'

'I was in uniform when you were still in school,

love. If you've got something to say, now would be a good time. I'm not in work now.'

'You're really trying my patience, PTSD or not.'

'Just get to the point.'

'We've got a double murder case, two as yet unidentified victims. I want you back here and heading up the investigation.'

'I'm only here because that fucking psychologist insisted I make the trip. You were behind that. She told me that herself. You couldn't get me on a plane quickly enough.'

'I'm trying to be patient, Inspector. Now's your chance to get back to work.'

'Perhaps I don't want to come back to work. Perhaps I like it here.'

She resisted the impulse to end the call prematurely. 'Now look, Grav, I've asked you nicely. You can cooperate, or I can recommend early retirement. If you're not up to the job any more, all you have to do is say so.'

'Did I say that?'

'So, you're in agreement then. You're choosing to cut your holiday short of your own volition.'

'Yes, I fucking well am.'

'Well, thank you, Inspector. That's good to know. You're booked on a plane at ten past five tomorrow evening. You'll be back in Gatwick by six twenty a.m. The ticket's paid for. You can collect it at the airport.'

'Business class?'

'Economy I'm afraid. It's all the force could stretch to.'

He chortled to himself as he handed back the phone. She'd played him like a pro. 'Thanks for the use of the phone, love, it's appreciated.'

The Bajan officer drained her coffee, stood to leave and slotted the phone into a pocket as she approached the staircase. 'I'm very glad you're not my inspector.'

'Sorry I've been such a pain in the arse, love. And thanks for the help.'

She shouted out without looking back on opening the front door. 'Do men ever grow up? Sleep it off. And don't miss that plane. I'll put you on the damned thing myself if I have to.'

16

When forty-one-year-old Gary West, alias Teddy Bear, first regained consciousness on the cold, black plastic-covered floor of Rebecca Smith's killing room, he thought for one moment that he was waking from a frightening and unpleasant dream that felt all too real. But the pain seemingly emanating from every inch of his bloody face brought reality into sharp focus as he remembered approaching the house, knocking on the open door and wandering, one cautious step at a time, into the darkness to find that oh-so-elusive little girl he'd been grooming for weeks, with all the anticipation that entailed. He looked up at the hazy pink light somewhere above his head and wondered why everything appeared to be shrouded in a red mist he couldn't begin to compute or comprehend. He tried to blink repeatedly to clear his sight, but the results were limited to a further eruption of pain, which left him trembling uncontrollably. Rebecca had used a razor-sharp modelling knife to cut away his eyelids, and there was nothing left to blink with, just ragged edges of skin and red-raw sinew that leaked blood onto his exposed eyeballs.

Rebecca approached him slowly from an unseen corner of the room, looked down, studied his injuries with interest, and threw a glass of cold water in his face. 'Good to have you back in the land of the living, Teddy Bear. I thought I may have clubbed you one too many times with that new hammer of mine. I get rather carried away sometimes when an invited guest first arrives. I was beginning to wonder if you'd come around at all.'

He stared at her as his eyes cleared of blood and witnessed a reptile-like coldness. He went to scream, but the resulting sounds were limited to muffled noises that would be impossible to decipher or even hear beyond the immediate vicinity. Rebecca had taken her time to sew his lips together with a darning needle and a length of fishing gut.

'Don't bother trying to speak. I wouldn't want to hear anything that comes out of your filthy mouth anyway. You said more than enough online for one lifetime. That told me all I needed to know.'

Teddy Bear tried to struggle upright with the intention of hitting out and overpowering her, but he immediately realised that both his arms and legs were bound tightly with reams of plastic tape that wouldn't budge an inch. He attempted to force them free, using all his remaining strength to move them even slightly, but it was hopeless, absolutely hopeless. If she didn't cut him free, he wasn't going anywhere.

Rebecca stood at his side and laughed as he lost control of his bladder and a large dark patch appeared on the front of his trousers and pooled under him where he lay.

'"You walk into my parlour, said the spider to the fly. 'Tis the prettiest little parlour that ever you did spy." It's my favourite poem of all. Do you know it? If you do, you'll know what happens next. It didn't go well for the poor fly. I can tell you that much. The spider tore that unfortunate little fly apart one tiny morsel at a time. Tore him apart with forethought and brutal intention. He never had a chance. I think much the same thing is going to happen to you. What do you think of that? How does that make you feel? Are you scared, Teddy Bear? You've tried to free yourself. You've tried to shout out. You've pissed yourself. You seem scared enough to me.'

His eyes were burning now, shining like cat's eyes in the light of the naked bulb. She sat at his side and studied them as he attempted to pull away. 'Hold still, Teddy, that's not going to do you any good.'

He tried to shout out again, but to no effect.

Rebecca clutched his hair tightly with one hand and began slicing off his right ear with the same knife used to remove his eyelids earlier that evening. It was tough, really tough. It must be the cartilage. And there was a surprising lack of blood where ears were concerned. Interesting. Perhaps she'd have been better off using the saw. She'd gone to the trouble of buying another one. So, why not use the thing? Oh, well, another lesson learned. Put it down to experience. She could do that with the left one anyway. Nothing lost. She'd have the second ear off before she knew it. 'How are you doing there, Teddy? Are you finding the process as fascinating as I am? Some say the anticipation of pain is far worse than the torture itself, but I'm far from convinced.'

He stared at her and then at the saw in her hand, and began writhing on the floor in an attempt to snake himself, inch by inch, towards the door and the safer world beyond the walls.

'Now, now, Teddy Bear, you're not going any-where, however much you'd like to. Don't you re-member the poem? The fly doesn't get away. He never gets away. If you recall the verse, he never came out again.' She kicked him hard in the ribs just above his left hip and smiled. 'Oh dear, what's that terrible stench filling the air? Have you gone and soiled yourself like a helpless little baby? You like ba-bies, don't you, Teddy. You told me that yourself. You sent me photos which proved it. Do you remember them? The baby, you and the mask. That mask that hid your identity so very effectively. And now you're just like one of those little babies yourself. A help-less, crying, bleeding baby, and nobody gives a flying fuck about you. Not me, no one! Oh, the irony. I hope you can see where I'm going with this. I'm not over-complicating matters, am I?'

He moaned quietly to himself and began to shake even more violently.

'Can you still hear me, Teddy? Can you hear your life force draining away towards oblivion? You'll be begging to die before I finally finish with you, if you're not already doing so. You may be, of course. Not that I'll hear you. Not with your mouth sewn shut. But I'll get the gist anyway. I think they call it non-verbal communication. I read it in a textbook once upon a time. Your body talks. Expressions. Gestures. And what's left of your face is still somewhat expressive, in a pathetic subhuman sort of way.'

He tried to scream out again, but no words materialised.

'No comment? Nothing to say for yourself? No? Well, back to work then. A busy girl's jobs are never done. It's surprising how many body parts it's possible to remove before the donor breathes their last anxious breath. You'll find that out for yourself soon enough. My record's only five up to now, but I'm sure I can do much better than that with your able assistance. What do you think, shall we go for six or even seven?'

He was silent now, imagining what was to come, resigned to his seemingly inevitable fate and anticipating the relief death would eventually bring.

Rebecca stood, stretched slowly and deliberately, conscious of her movements, and gripped the saw tightly before holding it in plain sight and watching his expressions closely. She lowered herself to the floor and removed the second ear quickly and efficiently with three rapid movements of the blade. 'There you go, Teddy. Done. Now, wasn't that so much easier than all that hacking away with the knife? No comment? Still nothing to contribute? No? Oh well, it's up to you. You can't say I didn't give you the opportunity. Lie there and groan incoherently if you must. I'll just have to put up with it as best I can.'

She giggled as she held the severed ear up a few inches in front of his popping eyes, and allowed the blood to drip, drip and drip onto his face for a few seconds before speaking again. 'Two eyelids and two ears. That's four down and three to go. Or shall we really push the boat out and aim to blow the record right out of the water? Perhaps we're not being nearly ambitious enough. Tell me now if you disagree. No? Then I'll assume you're in full agreement. I was thinking nose, penis and testicles initially. But you've still got ten fingers and ten toes. Why didn't I think of them before? Silly me. What about those, Teddy? What about those?'

She suddenly threw the ear aside and reached out to touch his right foot, tap, tap, tapping it in time with her singsong rhyme: 'Eeny, meeny, miny, moe, catch a Teddy by his toe, if he screams *don't* let him go... yes, what the hell, let's go for it. Toes first and then your fingers. What do you think? One to twenty. And then we can finish with that ever so active tiny little prick of yours, if I can manage to find it without a magnifying glass. Tell me now if you've got any objections. It'll be far too late once I've started.'

She shrieked with laughter as he shook his head violently, causing small droplets of blood to spray in the air and onto the floor.

'Come on, Teddy, now's the time. Speak up or forever hold your peace. No? Still nothing to say for yourself? This is becoming something of a pattern. But I can't say I'm surprised. I think you're enjoying yourself almost as much as I am. I'll just pop out and fetch the loppers from the shed, if that's all right with you? Be patient. I won't keep you waiting for long. It goes through thick branches without any resistance or difficulty.

We'll have to take off those shiny black leather shoes of yours, but I don't think your little piggies will prove too much of a problem, do you?'

He held his breath in an attempt to breathe his last, but his basic instinct to suck in oxygen overcame his desire to die, just as Rebecca returned to the room and closed the door behind her.

'You're a little blue in the face, Teddy Bear. I hope you haven't been holding your breath again. That wouldn't do. It wouldn't do at all.' She knelt down at his feet and began removing his shoes as he kicked and bucked in ineffective resistance. 'Is there a hell? That's what you've got to ask yourself. Is this a flavour of what's to come for eternity? Or maybe you're in hell already. Have you considered that possibility? Maybe I'm a shape-shifting devil in human form.' She stood, turned her back to him and wiggled her bare bottom. 'Maybe there's a tail coming out of my arse. Or maybe I'm just an ordinary human being out for revenge.'

Rebecca threw his shoes and socks aside for later disposal, took the loppers' handles in both hands and removed the big toe from his right foot. 'Well, that one came off without any problems. Easy-peasy. Do you think I should stop now, Teddy Bear? Do you think you've suffered enough? Am I a monster? Is that what you're wondering? Why don't I bring the process to a rapid conclusion, as I would for an injured animal? Because you're worse than an animal, that's why. You're below an animal. You're the lowest of the low, and I'm going to make you suffer for every second of however long you've got left in this life. Why? Is that what you're asking yourself? Because I want to, Teddy. Because I can.'

She removed the second toe with an audible crunching sound and frowned. 'Did you show mercy to the children whose lives you destroyed? Did you empathise with your victims' suffering and choose a different path? Ever? Even once? I doubt it. I really doubt it. Because you're here, aren't you, Teddy? That's why you came. You planned to ruin yet another young life for your own deviant reasons.'

In less than a minute, the toes were lying together on the black plastic in a neat and bloody pile.

'There, we've broken the record already. Three cheers for us, eh. It's amazing what can be achieved when you work together.'

She jumped to her feet rather than move onto the second foot as she'd originally planned, and casually threw the loppers aside with a thud as they hit the floor. 'Time for a break, Teddy. All that cutting and sawing was surprisingly hard work, even for a strong and experienced girl like me. I'm going to make myself a nice cup of herbal tea, have a quick bite to eat, and I'll be back with you just as soon as I can. Don't concern yourself. I won't let you down. But I think we'll leave your pretty little nose until last, if that's okay with you? A previous guest spluttered and choked on his own blood very soon after I cut it off. It was all over far too quickly for my liking. What a tragic shame. So leave the nose until last. That's what I concluded. I won't be making that unfortunate mistake again, I can tell you.'

* * *

Teddy had lost a good deal of blood and had drifted into semi-consciousness by the time Rebecca completed her refreshments, made a quick toilet visit, and returned to the room about twenty minutes later. She kicked him hard in the upper thigh three times in an attempt to stir him, and thought for one moment that he'd died prematurely, before rushing upstairs, two or three steps at a time, and returning with a small mirror, which she held right up close to his face. It was misting up ever so slightly before fading away again. There were signs of breath. He was alive. But she had to make a start and work quickly. Such a terrible shame. Why, oh why, had she taken a break? It seemed he didn't have long to live. There was no time to lose.

Rebecca sprinted to the kitchen and back, hurled a second glass of cold water in his face and began. 'One toe... two toes... three toes... four. There you go, Teddy. Only one to go. We're making marvellous progress, wouldn't you agree? Snippety snap. There. Done. That's much better. And now for your fingers. Count down from ten to zero for me and you'll get the picture. Just count in your head if you like. I appreciate you can't vocalise your thoughts. I wouldn't ask you to do the impossible.'

She shuffled along the floor on her bare bottom

from his feet to his upper body, rather than stand. 'I've been on the radio, Teddy. My fifteen minutes of fame. Or at least my work has. They didn't mention me by name... there you go. That's your thumb done. And with a nice satisfying snap too... someone found two of my previous guests in the Tywi Estuary and notified the police. Such an unfortunate inconvenience. I don't know which bits were found. It could have been anything, now that I think about it. But it hardly matters. I'll have to be a lot more careful from here on in. But they've got absolutely no idea who I am. That seems obvious, wouldn't you agree? They'd be knock, knock, knocking on my door if they did. That's their job after all... right, it's time for me to stop prattling on and get on with what we're here to do. Just that second hand of yours and our work is almost done.'

He was moaning constantly now, drifting in and out of consciousness, praying for death, silently pleading for death and whatever it may bring, as she unfastened his trousers with bloody fingers, pulled down his soiled underpants and removed his genitals. 'There, that's much better. Someone should have done that long ago.'

She tore loose his lips and stuffed the testicles into his open mouth, with the flaccid penis hanging out in place of a panting tongue. 'There, now you know exactly how some of those poor unfortunate children felt at your hands and those of the other scum you offended with. I'm guessing you're not actually enjoying the experience a great deal more than they did... now, that only leaves that pretty little nose of yours before I cut your throat... snippety snap! There, that's your nose gone.'

She threw the loppers behind her, picked up the mirror, held it in front of his face, and moved it repeatedly, tracking his movements as he tried to turn his head and look away. 'Take one last look at yourself before I put you out of your misery, Teddy. You're a slug, a rodent, a lesser form of life. This is your final opportunity to repent and seek forgiveness before you're on your way to the nether world. Would you like to say anything in your defence? Any last words? No? Then, head back, hold yourself still, the knife's here somewhere. Ah, yes, here it is. It's time to meet your maker.'

17

Kesey parked the Mondeo directly opposite the Griffiths family's three-bedroom semi and watched as a demure young woman in her mid-twenties made her way along the pavement, pushing an aged pushchair that looked almost as bedraggled as she did. If it was Lucy Griffiths, as she strongly suspected, it seemed likely that she'd just delivered her two older children to the nearby primary school. Not bad timing all in all. The interview would be a lot easier without two busy kiddies running around all over the place and looking for attention.

The detective sergeant wound down the window with an electric hum as the woman walked up the weed-strewn pathway towards the front door of number sixty-six Kings Road. 'Mrs Griffiths? Mrs Lucy Griffiths?'

The young woman paused in mid step and looked up. 'Who the fuck are you? The police, some stuck-up overeducated social services do-gooder, or the fucking social after my benefits again? It's always one of the three. If you're looking for Derek, you can piss off. I haven't seen him for days. And neither's his mother, by the way. I know cos I've asked her.'

Kesey wound up the window, exited the vehicle and walked towards the woman, who was unlocking the front door. 'It's you I need to speak to, Mrs Griffiths. It won't take too long.'

The woman manoeuvred the pushchair over the doorstep, pushed it inside the hall, and turned to stand in the doorway like an obstructive bouncer at a late-night nightclub. 'So, who the hell are you then? I haven't seen you sniffing around here before.'

The DS looked into her face and thought that she looked tired, defeated, older than her years. 'DS Kesey, local police. We need to talk.'

She stared at the officer with a blank expression

on her face. 'What's that fucking idiot done this time?'

'Why do you stay with a man like that? Why would anyone stay with a man like that?'

'What the fuck's that got to do with you?'

'Okay, sorry, let's start again... can we speak in the house, please, Mrs Griffiths? It'll be easier to talk inside. This won't take too long, as I said before.'

'What harm can it possibly do? The quicker I answer your questions, the quicker you'll sod off and annoy somebody else. Come on in then, in you come, you're not going to piss off otherwise. Your sort never do.'

'You know it makes sense.'

She steered the pushchair into an unkempt, sparsely furnished lounge that smelt of the unspecified and unmistakable ingrained filth common to chronically dirty houses. 'Okay, let's get this shit over with. And don't wake the fucking baby. I've only just got her off.'

'When did you last see or speak to your husband?'

'Why do you want to know?'

'Just answer the question, Mrs Griffiths.'

'Are you going to plant your fat arse then? You're making the place look untidy.'

The DS examined the available seating and sat herself down on what appeared to be the cleanest of three seats. 'So, what's the answer?'

Lucy stood there on slender white legs that looked ready to give way at any moment, and picked up the baby as she began to stir and whimper. 'Now look what you've fucking well done. She'll be as miserable as fuck if she doesn't get her sleep. That's down to you, that is.'

'Sorry, I didn't mean to wake her.'

She held the child over one shoulder and patted her back gently with an open palm. 'There you go, little one, back to sleep, mummy's here... I haven't heard from the ugly git for over a week. What's he accused of this time? If it's something involving kids again, he can fuck right off. It nearly got him killed the last time. I don't need that sort of hassle. That's why we're in this shithole in the first place.'

Kesey looked at her and frowned. 'We've found a body that meets your husband's description. We're still to confirm the identity with any certainty, but I think you need to prepare yourself for the worst.'

She sat herself down and broke into a smile as the possibility of a new reality dawned. 'So, they finally got him then? I can't say I'm surprised. It was only a matter of time.'

'As I said, we need to confirm it's him. I'm hoping you can help in that regard.'

Lucy adjusted the baby's position, and gave her a dummy to suck on while continuing to comfort her. 'Can I see him? You could take me in the car. That would be the easiest and quickest way, yeah?'

The DS paused before responding. 'You haven't heard any stories locally or in the media? Nothing relating to the body?'

'Fuck all. What are you talking about?'

'Seeing the body's not going to be a good idea. The man in question was found in the estuary in a small village called Ferryside, about five miles from here. He was in the water for quite some time before being found, if you know what I'm saying.'

She flinched as unwelcome images invaded her mind. 'Did he drown?'

'We don't think so.'

She pointed towards a teak wall unit with her free hand. 'There should be a photo of the ugly git in one of the drawers somewhere, if that's any good to you?'

'We've got photos on file, thanks, but like I said, he'd been in the water. Do you know if he's visited a dentist since being in Wales?'

'Not that I know of, but he wouldn't tell me anyway.'

'What about in London?'

'Look, I can't help you. He tells me fuck all. Are we done?'

'Has he got a hairbrush, anything like that?'

'Nope.'

'Are you trying to be obstructive? It won't do you any favours if you are. What about a comb, or some-thing along those lines?'

'There's a pair of his bloodstained underpants at the bottom of the wardrobe, if that's any good to you?'

'Which bedroom?'

'The larger of the two at the front of the house.'

'So, how did he get blood on his pants?'

She smiled without parting her lips. 'Piles. He always was a pain in the arse.'

The DS ascended the stairs one slow step at a

time with the hint of a smile on her face, and came back down a few minutes later with a pair of blood-soaked Y-fronts in a clear plastic evidence bag.

'Did you find what you wanted?'

'Yes, ta, I'll get back to you as soon as we've compared the DNA. It's likely to take a few days.'

'Is that it then?'

'Do you have the internet in the house?'

She shook her head. 'You know we fucking well don't. It's a condition of the child protection plan. No internet and no computers.'

'What about at his mother's place?'

'So, you definitely think it's likely he's dead?'

'Yeah.'

'Okay, Derek's a fucking liability, but he's not a complete idiot. He uses the library, or cafés or his mate's place. He likes the sort of filth Derek likes. Dirty bastard.'

Her eyes widened. 'Can you tell me this man's name and address?'

'I'd tell you if I could. Straight up I would. But he never told me.'

'And the man never came here?'

'No fucking way. I wouldn't have the bastard in

the house. Derek knows that. He pushes me. He's a bully. But he knows where to draw the line. What's wrong with screwing adults? That's what I used to ask him. Isn't my pussy good enough for you? Why not leave the kids alone?'

'So, what did he say in response?'

'Fuck all. He'd just shrug and walk away if he was in a good mood, or give me a slap or three if he wasn't. I gave up asking in the end.'

The DS scowled, oblivious to her expression. 'Has he ever touched any of your children inappropriately?'

'I'd cut his fucking dick off if he tried it, and he knows that, shitting myself or not.'

'So if it's someone else's kids it's okay with you? That's a strange version of morality.'

'Did I say that? No, I fucking well didn't.'

She nodded her acknowledgement. 'Has Derek got a computer hidden away anywhere? Anywhere at all?'

She paused, attending to the baby, and then said, 'Yeah, he has.'

Kesey met the woman's eyes, which were flickering like a faulty bulb. 'Are you going to tell me where it is?'

'You don't think he's coming back?'

'No.'

'There's a clear plastic box with a lid buried in the garden to the right side of the path, about halfway down. It's covered with loose turf. He thought it was fucking hilarious that you lot hadn't found it. He said you were a right bunch of numpties.'

The DS rose to her feet and approached the back door. 'I appreciate your cooperation, Lucy. You're doing the right thing.'

'It feels good to help for a change. Good to come clean. And if you're wrong, and I stitch the bastard up in the process, so be it. Maybe the time's right.'

* * *

'Did you find it?'

She nodded while walking down the hall towards the front door. 'Yeah, I did, ta. I'm going to stick it straight in the boot of the car. I'll be back with you in two minutes.'

'Okay, leave the door open. The baby's wide awake now anyway.'

* * *

'Is there anything else I need to know before I make a move?'

Lucy unbuttoned her blouse, took the dummy from the baby's mouth and encouraged her to suckle on the exposed nipple. 'Fuck all I can think of.'

'Is there anyone you want me to call for you? A relative or a friend maybe?'

She shook her head, screwing up her face. 'There isn't anybody. It's just me and the kids now. He made sure of that.'

'Can I get you a cup of something before I head off? I'm in no rush. It's no bother.'

'Sharing a cup of tea with a fucking pig, who'd have thought it? Yeah, why not? Tea, a splash of milk and one sugar for me. And there's half a packet of choccy biccies on top of the fridge, if you fancy one.'

* * *

'There you go, Lucy. Do you want me to hold her for you? You look as if you could do with a bit of a break.'

The young mother clutched the baby tightly to her chest and turned away in her seat. 'Is this a trick? It has to be a trick. He'd told me not to trust you people even for a single second. He said you'd pretend to be nice. Worm your way in. He'd warned me time and time again. You can fuck right off! You're not taking my baby.'

Kesey backed off quickly, sat herself down and smiled thinly, thinking that Lucy looked ready to bolt for the door. 'That's not going to happen. That's never going to happen. I'm just going to sit here and drink my tea, okay? I'm investigating two murders, nothing more. I'm not here to take her from you. The thought never crossed my mind.'

She was breathing more heavily now, clinging to her young child more and more tightly. 'Are you lying? You seem friendly enough. But, maybe you're lying. Do you promise?'

'I'm not going to take your baby. That's a promise. One hundred per cent guaranteed.'

She relaxed almost immediately, her face softening. 'Nice biscuits.'

'Yeah, lovely. Where did you buy them?'

'In the Co-op down the road.'

'Ah, yeah, I know the one.'

'Do you want another one? You can have one if you want.'

She smiled. 'Oh, go on then. They're seriously moreish.'

'He used to be a residential worker.'

'Are we talking about Derek?'

'Yeah, that's how we met. He was one of the staff.'

'At a children's home?'

Lucy dunked her second biscuit into her tea and began licking off the chocolate. 'Yeah, Lee Hill. That's what the home was called, Lee Hill. I think it's closed now, thank fuck. It wasn't a particularly nice place to be for any child. A right fucking dump.'

'Were you working there as well?'

She shook her head and laughed. 'What a question. My mum was on the game to fund her heroin addiction, and Dad, whoever the fuck he was, pissed off just as soon as he knew she was pregnant. Or, at least, that's what she told me. She may not have had the slightest clue who he was, now that I think about it. You know, he may have been some miserable punter who screwed her and paid for her time. I grew up in care. Foster homes from the age of seven and then residential care when I was twelve, and none of them wanted me any more. I was one of the kids.'

'Ah, now it's all starting to make sense. You were one of Griffiths' victims. Just like the rest of them.'

'I guess so. If that's how you want to put it.'

'So how on earth did you end up living with him?'

She looked up and stared at a spot on the ceiling as she recalled times past. 'I left the home when I was sixteen and moved into a one-roomed bedsit in Hackney. The social paid for it. He started calling around whenever he felt like a shag, and he got me pregnant a few months after that. It made no difference whether I said no or not. He just fucked me anyway. I went to the police once and tried to tell them, but they didn't want to know.'

'It seems you've been let down all your life. No silver spoon in your mouth... are you scared of him?'

She nodded twice as tears welled up in her eyes. 'Yeah, he can be one vicious bastard when he wants to be. Always ready with a slap or a punch, or worse. But never where it shows. He makes certain of that. I see the bruises, but nobody else does. I left him more than once in the early days after he moved himself in. I slept on the streets for a while. In doorways, under bridges. Anywhere out of the rain was better than living with that tosser. But he came after me. He always came after me. I belonged to him. That's what he told me. I was his property to do whatever the fuck he wanted with. How dare I try to leave him? How dare I try to escape? Who the hell did I think I was? He was my owner, my master and my god. He kicked the crap out of me that last time, after dragging me back. I pissed blood for a week... I really hope it's him. I hope the bastard's dead and rotting.'

The DS nodded as Lucy's facial muscles relaxed. She looked suddenly younger. As if the years had melted away. 'As soon as I've got a definitive answer, you'll be the first to know.'

'He's never left the laptop hidden in the ground for as long as this. There's no way he'd do that. It's going to be him. I can feel it. I fucking well know it. How about a glass of wine? Let's celebrate. It's nearly Christmas. Life's looking better already.'

18

It only took Rebecca just over an hour to access Derek Griffiths' laptop on Kesey's request, despite the security features. She'd had a lucky break. That's what she told herself. And she planned to take full advantage. Deleting any links to herself was a given. A no-brainer. But maybe, just maybe, there was a way of pointing the police investigation in the wrong direction. Smoke and mirrors. That's what she needed. It was just a matter of how.

Why not make a cup of coffee for a change? She'd need it. Her brief initial review of the computer's content had not been a pleasant experience. She knew what he was. She knew what he did. But that stuff was never easy to see on the screen, right there in front of you. There appeared to be thousands, literally thousands of indecent images of children. Some featuring Griffiths himself, engaged in various sexual acts that almost defied belief. The man was a monster. A predator at the peak of his powers. That's what she repeated in her head time and time again. She'd been right to kill him. Right to make him suffer. The world was a better place.

Rebecca pushed the computer aside and spooned what she considered just the right amount of instant coffee granules into a pottery mug. She poured in the boiling water, followed by a splash of soya milk and finally, unusually for her, a single sugar lump from a box normally reserved for visitors to her office. She stirred the resulting concoction vigorously and sat back in her black leather swivel chair, trying her best to relax. The very existence of the investigation was starting to get to her. She had to accept that. It was starting to eat away at her fragile confidence. The police were getting nearer, closing in on her as their target, even if they didn't yet know it themselves. Maybe, just maybe, if she used all her cunning and deceptive skills honed by hard adversity, she could keep it that way and they'd never find out how very close they'd been.

She was sitting back with her eyes closed, breathing deeply, attempting to clear her mind, when the shrill tone of her office phone made her jump, causing her to spill a small amount of the hot beverage onto her lap in the process. Damn it! Who the hell was this now? Demands. Always demands. It really couldn't be at a worse time. 'Hello, computer section.'

'Is that you, Becca? You're sounding very formal this morning.'

She dabbed at her skirt with a paper tissue held in one hand while holding the phone with the other. 'Oh, hello, Laura. I was planning on giving you a ring sometime later today. How's the investigation going?'

'It's been a lot of dead ends so far, but I like to think we're finally making progress. I'm hoping you've got some good news for me. Any luck with the computer?'

At least she hadn't come to her office in person. At least she hadn't come snooping. 'Not as yet, sorry. I'm working on it as we speak. Give me another couple of hours and I should be into it.'

'Is it that difficult, even for you?'

Come on, Becca, hold it together girl. She'd been successfully conning people for years. Why should that change now? 'Griffiths knew what he was doing. Quite impressive really. There are various layers of security, but I'm making progress. Is it urgent?'

'Yes, it's urgent. It's always urgent. We need to know who he's been in contact with. Other sex offenders. Children. You never know, it may point us in the right direction.'

Well, that was one thing she wasn't going to be finding out anytime soon. 'Oh, that's awful. There's some terrible people out there.'

'Certainly are. It's my job to catch them.'

'I'll make this my number-one priority. No holds barred.'

'Surely it already was? What's more important than a murder enquiry?'

'I'm giving it my full attention. I can't do more than that.'

'Thanks, Becca, that's great. You're sure you'll crack it today, yeah?'

She nodded, getting into the role and beginning to enjoy herself. 'Yeah, I'm ninety per cent confident.

But tomorrow morning at the very latest. Promise. I'll make sure I get it back to you just as soon as it's done.'

'But it will be tomorrow at the latest, yeah?'

'Haven't I already said as much clearly enough? I'll get it back to you. Perhaps now would be a good time to let me get on with my work.'

19

Grav joined the long line of passengers waiting to negotiate the check-in desk, dropped his suitcase to the floor and kicked it twice. What the hell was wrong with the boy? He'd made the effort to call on him en route to Bridgetown. He'd offered his heart-felt apologies. Not quite on bended knee, but not far off. And that still wasn't good enough for the sancti-monious little prick. Maybe he shouldn't have both-ered visiting at all. Maybe he should have stayed away. The boy didn't have a fucking clue.

He nudged the suitcase forwards with the sole of his shoe as the traveller in front of him accepted her boarding card. Oh well, such was life. It was back to

Welsh Wales and all that entailed. Back to being a working copper again. Back to a world where his life made sense. Where he mattered. Where he didn't feel like the proverbial floundering fish out of water. Another hour and he'd be on the plane.

* * *

Grav silently cursed Detective Chief Superintendent Hannah Davies and his life in general as he lowered his not inconsiderable backside into the economy seat. He turned to face the elderly woman next to him and smiled as he noted the look of obvious irritation on her face. It seemed that her long return journey home had just become a little more onerous. 'Sorry, love, you've drawn the short straw. I like to spread out a bit.'

The flight passed more slowly than had the outbound journey, as the woman repeatedly attempted to engage him in conversation. Grav relied heavily on strong alcohol, pretended to be asleep more than once, and finally resorted to telling her that he had absolutely no interest in her family or her fucking pet poodles, even if she claimed that one of the little blighters had won best of breed at some prestigious dog show three years running. The remainder of the journey was spent in silence, as both of them chose to actively ignore each other to the nth degree.

When the pilot finally announced the early-morning approach to London's Gatwick, Grav swore he'd never go on holiday again, unless it involved copious amounts of beer, like-minded mates, and international rugby. If the psychologist thought his enforced Caribbean trip had been in any way cathartic, the silly cow was very sadly mistaken. He had never felt so pissed off in his entire life. Getting called back to the job sooner than expected was a lifesaver.

It was almost seven a.m. by the time he'd collected his suitcase, negotiated passport control, and was heading in the direction of Paddington Station. As he boarded the direct train to Swansea, he acknowledged that he was experiencing a degree of elation he hadn't felt for quite some time. He wouldn't describe his mood as orgasmic, but it wasn't far off. Almost as good as Wales winning a Grand Slam or defeating the old enemy England at their own ground. The implications were bloody obvious.

He needed to work. Why not go directly to the police
station on his eventual arrival in Carmarthen, however knackered he felt? He was wanted. He was
needed. He was important again. They couldn't do
without him, and that suited him just fine. He had an
investigation to get on with. A murderer to catch. A
life worth living.

* * *

Grav had a skip in his step as he sauntered into
Police HQ and said a cheery, 'Afternoon, love, good to
see you doing something useful for a change,' to a
slim female constable, who was arranging various
advisory leaflets in a wall-mounted rack next to the
main doors.

'Thank you, sir. Did you have a nice holiday?'

'No time to talk now, love. Things to do, people to
see. But thanks for asking.'

She made one final adjustment to the display
and stood back to admire the results of her efforts as
Sandra reappeared at reception. 'Sarky sod. Things
are back to normal. The place just wasn't the same
without him.'

20

Kesey looked up as Grav burst through the door, and knew immediately that the infamous Detective Inspector Gareth Gravel was back in charge. He was just as he'd been described. Larger than life and twice as ugly. No, that wasn't fair. He was worn, creased, world-weary rather than unattractive. 'Hello, sir, nice to meet you. It's good to have you back.'

He approached her desk, stood immediately in front of it with his protruding gut resting on its edge, and cocked his head at an approximate forty-five-degree angle. 'So, who the hell are you then? You look young enough to be my granddaughter.'

She stood and reached out a hand in greeting, but withdrew it quickly when he left her hanging. 'DS Kesey, Laura Kesey. I've been covering in your absence.'

He grinned. 'So you're my new sergeant, are you? Are you sure they didn't mix you up with somebody a bit longer in the tooth and promote you by mistake?'

She stiffened, not appreciating his brand of humour. 'I'm old enough, sir. You needn't worry about that.'

'That's right, love. Put a smile on your pretty face. It may never happen.'

'Did you have a good holiday?'

He stood stiffly, shifting his bulk from one foot to the other, and pointed to the kettle on the floor behind her. 'Fucking terrible, thanks. Mine's a coffee. Milk and five sugars if you want to win a few brownie points. Let's start as we mean to go on, shall we, love?'

'Did I hear you right? Are you serious? You did say five sugars?'

He sat himself down and nodded. 'Yeah, I'm on a diet. I've cut it down from six. I was thinking of starting yoga next week. Do you think I'll look good in a leotard?'

She laughed at the mental picture and then suddenly stopped. 'I was sorry to hear about DS Rankin, sir.'

'Clive? Yeah, he was a good copper and an even better friend. He's missed. And don't go thinking you're going to replace him in my affections. He served his time.'

She handed him his coffee and frowned. 'I'm just here to do my job, sir. I hope we can work effectively together. I'm not looking to take anyone's place, least of all Clive Rankin's.'

'That's my mug you're using. The Neath Rugby Club one. That's mine. Nobody else touches it without my permission.'

'I'll keep it in mind.'

'You do that... now, tell me, do you like a drink, Sergeant?' He raised his mug in the air, causing a splash of coffee to spill over the top. 'I'm talking about a real drink, not this stuff.'

'I'm partial to a glass of wine or a cold beer. Why do you ask?'

'So you like beer?'

'Well, yeah. Lager mainly. The bottled stuff.'

'And have you heard of rugby union? I'm talking about union mind, not that pale imitation they play up North.'

She nodded. 'My husband's taken me to watch England versus Wales in Cardiff a couple of times over the years.'

'And what did you think of our great capital city?'

'I loved it. The atmosphere was brilliant.'

'And the match, would you go again?'

'Yes, absolutely. What a great day out.'

Grav broke into a broad smile that she thought looked strangely out of place on his heavily lined face. 'You're not Rankin. No one ever will be, but you'll have to do.'

'I'll do my best, sir.'

'Okay, Sergeant, you'll no doubt be pleased to hear that you've passed the job interview. You can call me boss here, or Grav in private, if that suits you better. Got it?'

'Yes, boss.'

He checked the wall clock to his left and rose to his feet with the aid of the desktop. 'Come on, love, Carmarthen Rugby Club's open. We can get a bite to eat and a drink or two while you update me on the case.'

* * *

Grav grinned at the middle-aged, dyed-blonde barmaid on approaching the otherwise empty rugby club bar, and looked on appreciatively as she bent at the waist to retrieve two reasonably clean glasses, revealing a plunging cleavage that threatened to burst out of her low-cut cotton blouse at any second. 'So, how's life with you, Liz, my lovely? I hope that husband of yours is treating you well. You can always move in with me if he's not up to it any more.'

She laughed and smiled at the DS, assuming she'd be seeing a lot more of her in the future. 'Two pints of Buckleys?'

'Is that all right for you, Sergeant? You won't be sorry when you taste it. It beats that lager you like hands down.'

'Yeah, why not? I'll try anything once.'

'Thanks, Liz. And two of your gourmet pasties with brown sauce when you're ready.'

'Two pints of amber nectar coming up. Do you want the pasties heated up?'

Both officers replied in the affirmative.

'Take a seat, Grav. I'll bring them over when the microwave pings.'

'Cheers, Liz, you're a star.'

She turned to the DS and met her eyes. 'You've got a lot to put up with working with that one. Nice to meet you.'

'And you too.'

* * *

The two detectives sat at Grav's regular table behind a worn-out pool table haunted by Rankin's memory. Kesey slurped her beer, placed the glass back on a sodden beermat and looked across at her boss. 'So, do you want me to summarise the investigation up to this point? I can run you through the salient points in chronological order, if that helps?'

Grav lifted his glass to his lips and emptied over half its contents in one gulp. 'You don't fancy a game of darts then? Or we could put some music on the jukebox and have a dance.' He slipped a hand into the inside pocket of his jacket. 'I've got fifty pence here somewhere.'

'Do you know, I never know if you're joking or not.'

He drained his glass and laughed until tears ran down his sun-reddened face. 'Just kidding, love, the look on your face. I haven't got the legs for it these days. The old knees are gone. Now, get another drink in, start at the beginning and tell me exactly what we're dealing with.'

She handed him his pint, sat herself down, and leaned forwards with her elbows resting on the table. 'So, how much did the chief super tell you?'

'Two murder victims, one an alleged nonce, the other as yet unidentified. That's about it. I'm playing catch-up. I want to hear it in your own words. The more you can tell me, the happier I'll be.'

Kesey felt glad to get down to business. Glad of the opportunity to impress. And glad of the chance to share the responsibility for the case with a more experienced officer. She spent the next fifteen minutes clearly outlining the investigation's key developments as Gravel sat and listened in contemplative silence.

'Is that it then?'

'That's it, boss.'

'Another pint?'

She checked her watch. 'It's going to be another late finish.'

'So, is that a yes?'

'Just half a weak lemonade shandy for me please. I just can't handle that volume of liquid.'

'Women and their sensitive bladders. I'll get them in.'

* * *

'There you go, Laura.'

'Thanks again, boss.'

He grimaced and massaged his right leg as his arthritic knees stiffened and complained. 'So, the DNA results confirmed that our head belongs to this nonce who arrived from London, yeah?'

'That's right, boss. I received the report this morning. The lab rushed the results through, in fairness. His name was Derek Griffiths, previously Rodgers. He moved to London a few years back after growing up in the Llanelli area. From what I can gather, he's always worked with kids in one capacity or another.'

'Yeah, that makes sense. It gives his kind easy access to potential victims. Their inclinations often drive their life choices. Fucking terrible when you think about it. Have you let his missus know he's dead?'

She nodded her head in confirmation. 'I've met her the once and told her we thought it likely it was him... she was one of the kids at the home he worked at. She seems all right really. I think she'll do okay now he's gone.'

'She'll be doing cartwheels.'

Kesey smiled on picturing the scene. 'I would be. It must be better than winning the lottery.'

'So, she's aware of the DNA results?'

'No, I was planning on calling on her again first thing in the morning to confirm the good news, if that's all right with you?'

'Yeah, no problem, the quicker you see her, the

better. If she knows anything relevant, do you think she'd tell us?'

'Yeah, I do. She gave us the computer without any problems. I really think she wants to cooperate.'

* * *

Grav took the last cigar from a packet of five as the busty barmaid collected the dirty plates with a beguiling sway of her hips and a smile. 'How was the food?'

'Fucking awful as always, thank you, Liz. Good to see you're keeping up the club's usual standards.'

She laughed as she walked away. 'Kind of you to say so, Grav.

I'm here to please. Glad to be of service.'

He struck a match, lit the tip and sucked on the cigar, savouring the nicotine hit as the toxic fumes filled his lungs. 'So what do you make of the death threat made against this Griffiths character? Are we talking about serious intentions or empty words?'

Kesey coughed as the smoke swirled around her head and irritated her windpipe. 'Oh, it was a genuine threat all right. I had a long chat with a DS Connelly at the Met who'd had extensive dealings with Taylor. The guy's a heavy end criminal with a history of serious violence: GBH, kidnap, threats to kill, attempted murder on one occasion, although he got off in court due to a lack of corroborative evidence. The case against him looked solid. He'd been witnessed beating the crap out of a local dealer with a pickaxe handle: two broken legs, several fractured ribs, blinded in one eye, concussion; but the two witnesses withdrew their statements in court. They claimed the police had put pressure on them to fabricate evidence because of some sort of vendetta against the defendant.'

'Intimidation?'

'Yeah, that's what the Met thought. The risks of helping put him away were just too high. You can't blame them when you think about it. Why would you put everything on the line for some drug dealer you didn't even know personally?'

'So where's this Taylor character now?'

She took a swig of shandy to clear her throat before responding. 'He's still banged up for another two years for another unrelated conviction, but he's got numerous serious criminal contacts. Connelly reckons there'd have been any number of people ready and willing to claim the ten grand on offer. He said there's quite a few who'd have done it for a lot less. It seems two grand's the going rate on their patch.'

'Two grand. As little as that. Life's cheap in the big city. Did any obvious suspects spring to mind?'

'He said he'd give it some thought and get back to me if he came up with anything useful, but I'm not holding my breath. I got the distinct impression that a dead nonce in Wales isn't a particularly high priority.'

Grav nodded twice and took a long drag on his cigar before turning his head stiffly and blowing clouds of smoke behind him. 'Maybe the killer's done everyone a favour. Is one dead sex offender really such a bad thing?'

'Except for the other arm.'

'Yeah, exactly.' He grinned. 'That rather complicates matters. Any ideas as to the owner's identity?'

'There's nothing on the DNA database, fingerprints were a non-starter, and the tattoo on the arm was degraded to such an extent that the design couldn't be identified with any sort of certainty. Dr Carter says it could have been an anchor, but stressed that's more guesswork than anything else. We can say he had a tattoo, but that's about it. We've got nothing.'

'At least you're thinking along the right lines, love. That's a positive.'

'Thanks, boss.'

'You're sure this Connelly character didn't have any ideas?'

'No, like I said, nothing.'

'I've got a few potentially useful contacts in the Met. I might make a few phone calls myself. It couldn't do any harm.'

She put her glass on the table and looked him in the eye. 'Is it okay if I take five minutes to give my hubby a ring, boss? Just to tell him where I am. I don't want him thinking we've eloped.'

He grinned. 'Chance would be a fine thing... yeah, of course, I'll get another drink in.'

'Do they do coffee?'

He laughed hoarsely. 'Our lovely Liz might have a

heart attack when I ask her, but I'll see what I can do.'

* * *

'Sorted?'

'Yeah, no worries. He's started cooking tea, God bless him. It'll be a quick bite to eat and then off to my class at the leisure centre for seven o'clock.'

'What, is it some sort of keep-fit class or something?'

'Kick-boxing.'

His eyes widened. 'What? All that Bruce Lee stuff? That's a bit full on, isn't it? Are you sure you wouldn't prefer something a bit less physical?'

She laughed. 'I've been doing it since I was a kid. I've fought in competition a few times. Full contact. I've even won some medals. I was runner-up in the British championship a couple of years back. I love it. It keeps me sane.'

He shook his head. 'Are you winding me up?'

'No, straight up. My dad got me involved when I suffered a bit of bullying in school. He used to run a club. I got a black belt when I was sixteen.'

'No more bullying.'

'It stopped long before then, but yeah, no more bullying.'

Grav took a slurp of beer. 'So, tell me, what's your husband do?'

'He's a social worker.'

'Ah, okay, I've got a couple of mates in the job. Childcare or adult services?'

'Childcare. He came here to take up a vacant senior practitioner post in the Llandeilo team. You know, to get away from the big city and enjoy a slower pace of life.'

'Good luck with that. Shit happens everywhere, love. Not just in the concrete jungles of this world. There's a lot fewer people, but there's less of us to deal with them too.'

She picked up her cup and lifted it to her lips before returning it to its saucer with traces of red lipstick on the rim. 'Thanks for the coffee. It's surprisingly good.'

'Wonders never cease.'

She smiled.

'So, what's happening with the search?'

'It's going to take a further two days to reach Carmarthen, apparently. The river's still very high at the moment, which has made the entire process a lot more difficult than it should have been. I think they'd probably have been done by today if it wasn't in flood.'

'Yeah, I noticed from the train. You couldn't miss it. Half of the low-lying fields are still covered with a couple of feet or more. It happens on a regular basis in the winter months.'

She added a second sachet of powdered cream to her hot drink and stirred. 'So I'm told.'

'So, they haven't found anything else of interest, no?'

'Not as yet.'

'If what's left of the bodies made it out to sea, they could be washed up anywhere along the coast.'

'Yeah, I can see that.'

'What about this sports bag you mentioned? Does that help us at all? Any chance of tracking down where and when it was bought?'

She shook her head. 'Not a great deal, to be honest, boss. It's a popular brand stocked by all the major sports stores in the UK and most of Europe. The particular style and colour has been a bestseller.

Tens of thousands have been sold over an eight-year-plus period in Britain alone.'

'So it seems that's a non-starter.'

'I'd say so.'

Grav leaned forward to stub out his cigar in a black-and-gold-coloured ashtray before relaxing back in his seat. 'You mentioned a computer. What does that tell us?'

She swallowed hard and lifted a hand to her eyes as they threatened to fill with tears. 'The tech team had a look at it for me initially. Everything was password protected, but the girl in charge managed to hack it surprisingly quickly in the end. He'd used the first name of the last child he's alleged to have assaulted before leaving London. Sheena. Taylor's daughter. There are literally thousands of indecent images of children stored on the hard drive. Some in the most extreme category. Rape. Torture. Both boys and girls. There's some sick bastards out there. Why would anyone do those awful things? Why would anyone want to look at anything so utterly ghastly?'

He took a clean white cotton hankie from his pocket and handed it to her. 'Beats me, love. I think it's best not to know. We had a case a few years back involving a consultant child psychiatrist employed by the child guidance service. He headed up a local organised abuse ring for years. Dr David Galbraith. I'll never forget that name. It'll be engraved on my psyche until I breathe my last. He was one sadistic cunt, I can tell you. The worst I've had the misfortune to encounter in a very long career. Some of the things that scumbag and his like-minded nonces did were mind-blowing. And the bastards came from all walks of life. You're talking unemployed and poorly educated lowlifes to professional scumbags in positions of influence. Some of them actually moved to the area and others travelled fucking miles. And they weren't fussy. They abused their own kids, each other's kids, and any other vulnerable children they could get their dirty hands on. There was no end to the bastards' depravity. Kids of all ages and both genders manipulated into silence by psychological and physical violence. The entire case was fucking horrendous.'

'I don't envy you that one.'

'Nothing's harder to deal with if you've got an ounce of empathy or sensitivity. My advice would be to focus on putting the offenders away. That's the key.

Don't get caught up in the whys and wherefores. It'll drive you nuts if you think about it too much. And avoid getting emotionally involved if you can manage it. Easier said than done, I appreciate, but you've got to try. I saw what that shit did to a few of the investigating police officers and social workers. One of our lot was puking up after every joint investigation interview. She was in one hell of a state by the end. And an experienced social worker never worked again. She went off sick and didn't make it back. Some of us shout, some of us scream, or kick something, or get seriously pissed on a regular basis. And some of us move on to do other things: training, management. Do whatever you need to do to survive. Just gather evidence, lock the bastards up for as long as possible and walk away. Maybe that kick-boxing's not such a bad idea after all.'

Kesey was lost in her thoughts, and she sat in silence for a second or two, pondering the intensity of Grav's statement before speaking again. 'The child protection team covering the Kidwelly area are going through the various photos and videos. Jane Pritchard's been given lead responsibility by her DS. She's already made a start, but why go through them all? That's what I can't figure. We know what Griffiths was.'

'It's got to be done, love.'

'We know he was a predatory paedophile. But he's dead. Can't we leave it at that and just focus on the murders?'

Grav took a swig of beer and swirled it around his mouth, savouring the rich yeasty flavour before swallowing. 'You've got to remember that every one of those photographs and videos is of a real-life boy or girl who's experienced things no child should ever suffer. They're not just celluloid or digital images. They're depictions of real crimes. Serious crimes against the innocent. We have to do all we can to try and identify as many of those kids as possible. They need our help. They need our urgent help. And we have to look for any clues as to the locations and more importantly the abusers' identities. Jane's a good officer with a lot of relevant experience. She's skilled. Hard-working. Dedicated. If there's evidence to find, she'll find it.'

For the first time, Kesey understood what the chief super had meant. Ignore the detective inspector's many obvious flaws and learn from him. It seemed he had a great deal of practical knowledge. Wisdom of sorts. A clear and uncomplicated view of right and wrong. There was more to him than she'd thought on first meeting. A lot more. There was a deeper, more thoughtful man behind the contrived brash tough guy image he chose to present to the world.

'Are you still with me, love?'

'Sorry, boss, I was deep in thought... I get it, but sooner her than me.'

'And me too. I don't know how they do it day in, day out. Has Griffiths been in direct contact with any children on social media? Locally or otherwise?'

'Oh, shit. That's not something I've considered, to be honest.'

'Well, at least you're not a bullshit merchant. A good straight-talking Midlands lass suits me just fine. Have a chat with Jane in the morning and ask her to prioritise it. We can't assume why he was murdered. I appreciate that the Taylor contract is the most likely theory, but it's not a given. And ask her to explore his links with other nonces. Didn't you say his missus mentioned he'd been in contact with somebody locally?'

'Yeah, she did. I'll follow it up.'

'Let's find out who the bastard is and pay him a visit.'

She checked her watch and nodded. 'Okay, boss. Did the chief super mention the press conference?'

He drained his glass and raised himself stiffly to his feet, the pain in his knee joints negated to some extent by the alcohol. 'No, she fucking well didn't. Has her majesty decided on a time and date?' He raised an open hand to the side of his head in mock salute. 'Doff my cap, curtsey, and all that.'

She shook her head as he broke into a smile. 'You're going to really love this. It's arranged for two o'clock tomorrow afternoon.'

He slumped back into his seat rather than approach the bar as he'd intended. 'Oh, for fuck's sake. Is it a full-blown affair, the newspapers, TV, radio, the whole shebang?'

'I'm afraid so, boss.'

'And what the fuck are we going to tell them? We've got these bits of two bodies. A head and two arms. Both blokes. Fuck knows who one is, but the other's a nonce. No, we haven't got any suspects. No, we won't be making an arrest anytime soon. Any more questions? No, we don't know where the rest of the bodies are. And, yes, we've looked. Anything else before I go and lie down in a darkened room? Yes, we are next to fucking useless. You're spot on, madam. I can hear them laughing now.'

'I'm sorry, boss. I had no say in it. She just told me it was happening and I'm telling you. That's the way it was.'

'It would have been nice to be consulted. That's all I'm saying.'

'She's in charge, boss. You know what it's like. It was out of my hands.'

He nodded his head slowly. 'Yeah, that's the reality of top-down policing. She's in charge. And don't I know it. She never misses an opportunity to remind me. She's got all the qualifications in the world. MA this, PH fucking D that, but fuck all real frontline experience. She wouldn't know a criminal if one ran up and bit her on the arse. I was arresting offenders when she was still in nappies.'

'It's not all bad, is it, boss? We can at least appeal for information. Ask if any member of the public has seen anything that could help us. Someone dumped those body parts. Someone may have seen something. You never know your luck.'

He rose to his feet again with his empty glass in hand.

'Ignore me, Laura, I'm just sounding off. Things are changing too fast. I don't recognise the force sometimes. I'm the last of the Mohicans. The final dinosaur awaiting inevitable extinction in an evolving world.'

'Oh, come on, it's not that bad.'

'Another coffee, or are you going to have a proper drink with your old Uncle Grav?'

She checked her wristwatch again, more obviously this time, and looked up at him. 'Is it all right if I make a move, boss? It's been a long day and I've got that class to get to.'

'So, I'm going to be drinking alone again. I should be well used to it by now. Such is life.'

'Are you okay, boss?'

'Yeah, of course I am. You get yourself home to that husband of yours. I hope he realises he's a very lucky man.'

'Oh, he knows all right. I never stop reminding him.'

'Good for you, love. I'll see you in the morning.'

'I'm calling on Griffiths' missus on my way in, yeah? To confirm the good news.'

'I'll be at the station all day, love. I'll see you whenever you get there. And don't forget to dress up in your best bib and tucker. You're going to be on the telly.'

21

Rebecca Smith sat naked and cross-legged on the plastic-covered floor of her killing room with the gas central heating turned up to maximum, and repeatedly prodded the semi-frozen male torso laid out in front of her with the tip of a carving knife. Time was getting on again. It was rushing away from her. Second by second, minute by minute, hour by relentless hour. She was already physically and emotionally exhausted, and it was going to be another late night. Teddy Bear was taking a frustratingly long time to thaw, and she wouldn't be able to chisel off the flesh for at least another two hours or more, however hard she tried. Damn it! Why was life always so very complicated? So challenging? Why so many hurdles? Such things were sent to try her. That was the only feasible explanation. Her cross to bear.

She balanced the knife on his mottled chest and rose to her feet with her thoughts tumbling over and over in her mind, faster and faster, pondering the same nagging dilemmas time and time again. Her life was seriously in danger of unravelling completely if she didn't up her game. She'd been complacent. Careless even. And that simply wasn't good enough. Disposing of two of her previous guests as she had had drawn attention to her activities. It had made the Welsh TV and radio news, for goodness' sake. And the local papers too. The front pages with big bold headlines: *Human remains discovered in Ferryside.* That really couldn't happen again. Not if she was going to continue her mission. Not if she was going to put an end to their criminal activities. Not if she was going to protect as many children as feasibly possible. He took her innocence, and she'd take their lives. Not all of them, of course. That wasn't possible. They were a plague. A disease. There were far too many for that. But as many as possible. She'd make it her life's work. Her reason for living.

* * *

Rebecca switched on the kettle and leaned against the rounded edge of the kitchen table, waiting for the water to come to the boil. One section at a time. That made sense. The torso tonight, a leg tomorrow, and then the second leg the night after that. Then worry about the arms and head once that was done. Five days and she'd be finished. Bite-sized chunks. Organisation. That was the key. Don't get over-whelmed, and do everything in a logical sequential order. The river was no longer a viable option. Not with the police sniffing around as they so obviously were. Not if she wanted to continue her quest. And so flushing chunks of freshly cut flesh down the toilet and into the sewage system was her next best option. Shit joining shit. That could work. As long as she was careful not to block the pipes. As long as she didn't overdo things. As long as she cut the flesh into small enough pieces. It wouldn't take care of the skeletal remains, of course. They still posed a signifi-cant challenge. But it was far from insurmountable if she gave it further thought. All she had to do was use her intelligence and be entirely practical.

Rebecca switched on the radio and listened as the disc jockey announced the next hit record with an enthusiasm that seemed at odds with the solemnity of the night's activities. Smashing and grounding the bones would be difficult if not impossible. Maybe fire or acid would do the job? Didn't John George Haigh use concentrated sulphuric acid back in the nineteen thirties? Yes, the Acid Bath Murderer, that was it. She'd seen something on the telly a few months back. A documentary or a drama maybe. But could she get hold of the stuff in sufficient quantity without drawing suspicion? Maybe. All she had to do was do the research. Avoid rushing. Get it right. And the chest freezer would have to do in the interim. It wasn't ideal, but there was nothing intrinsically wrong with that. That's why it had a lock. That's why she'd bought the ridiculously expensive, oversized catering version in the first place.

She dropped a herbal tea bag into a favourite pottery mug, poured in the boiling water and tried to relax as the rising vapour warmed her face. Righteous vengeance was totally exhausting. All the inherent complications required adequate resolution. It had taken over her life, dominating her thoughts during every waking hour. Work had become an unwelcome necessity that provided occasional useful insider information and paid the bills, but nothing more. There was no time for relationships. Not even if she wanted one. And no time for hobbies. But it was worth it. That's what she told herself as she added a few drops of cold water from the kitchen tap and sipped her drink. Her life was dedicated exclusively to one crucial purpose. That's the way it worked out. The direction in which her life events took her like an irresistible fast-flowing current she couldn't hope to resist even if she wanted to. Maybe in another parallel universe she'd never met Sheridan with his deviant criminal perversions. Maybe there, in that very different world, her parents' lives were in one wholesome piece. Hell, maybe there she was happy. Deliriously happy with a good man, if such a thing existed, children of her own, a cat or even a friendly lapdog to spoil with treats and affection... but she did meet him. That bastard. That filthy evil bastard! And things didn't work out that way. She didn't find happiness. Not even close.

As Rebecca sipped her warming berry tea, black-and-white pictures played behind her eyes like an old cinematic film she was keen not to watch. She was back there. A child again. Just as she'd been so many times before. A small confused and unhappy six-year-old little girl who'd been unlucky enough to encounter a monster. One of many predatory brutes that lurk not in the shadows, but in plain sight, hidden behind the mask of apparent respectability, status or manipulative charm. The teachers, the youth workers, the priests, the residential workers, the sports coaches and the rest of them. Bad apples that, she silently observed, could be depressingly hard to spot.

She dropped the mug to the floor and was instantly back in the present. An adult again in an adult world she understood only too well. Maybe if Sheridan had been convicted it would have provided some form of therapeutic solace. Maybe. Just maybe. Perhaps if he hadn't disappeared to God only knew where, killing him would have been sufficient to alleviate her melancholy obsession with that short but causative period of her past. Maybe if she could finally track the vile bastard down and make him pay, that would give her some sort of lasting peace. Was he listening for a knock on the door? Was he watching his back? Was he haunted by the ghosts of his crimes as she was? As her parents were? She hoped so. She really hoped so.

Rebecca took a hand-knitted cardigan from the back of a kitchen chair and pulled it on urgently, suddenly aware that she was shivering. Why not set her radio alarm for five in the morning, have a quick breakfast and cut up some of the melting torso before heading to work? That made sense. There was no real urgency despite her many anxieties. It wasn't as if he was going anywhere. It would probably mean a bit of mopping up before the butchery could start. But she could manage that much. All she had to do was use a few towels and throw them straight in the washing machine afterwards. It wouldn't be the first time or the last.

She tilted her head back and smiled, pleased to have finally reached a resolution she found acceptable. Why not spend half an hour or so on the computer before heading upstairs for the night? Yeah, why not sit back, relax and check her messages again, tired or not? Teddy Bear would be gone soon enough. She could dispose of the soiled bags, the tools and whatever else. And metal didn't float. It was time to choose her next guest. Time to send an invite that couldn't be ignored. But to whom? That was the question. The butcher, the tailor, the candlestick maker? Ah, this one looked interesting. Lover Boy. What a ridiculous name. He appeared to have all the required qualifications. A scratch that needed itching. "Will you walk into my parlour? Said the spider to the fly." Tip tap, tip tap. Tap away, Becca. Tap away. He could be the one. He could be. But there were so many to choose from.

22

Grav glanced at his reflection in the operation room's large picture window and made one last ham-fisted adjustment to his frayed but much loved Carmarthen rugby club necktie. He was a man notorious for his fashion sense, or rather the lack of it, and that fact didn't bother him in the slightest. He'd never been a looker, as he'd often told his wife in times gone by. But he was comfortable in his own skin, creases and all. And there was nothing wrong with that. 'How am I looking, Sergeant? Will I do for the cameras?'

She pushed her paperwork aside, looked up,

smiled, and tried to sound as sincere as possible. 'Very smart, boss.'

He looked her in the eye and laughed. 'Yeah, yeah, don't go overdoing it now. I don't think I've ever looked very smart in my life. My missus used to tell me that all the time. Passable maybe, if duty calls, but that's about it. Have you got a comb I can borrow? We've only got about twenty minutes before kick-off.'

She reached into her leather handbag and handed him a plastic hairbrush without the need for words.

'Thanks, love. How did it go this morning?'

'With the Griffiths family?'

He ran the brush through his short scanty salt-and-pepper hair, and handed it back almost immediately. 'Well, yeah, that's where you've been, isn't it?'

She peeked down and spotted two grey hairs contrasting against the black plastic bristles. 'I called early before school. She asked a neighbour to come in to watch the kids while we talked in the kitchen over a cup of tea.'

'And?'

'She was well pleased with the news. Not quite

doing cartwheels, but not far off. She's thinking about going back to London if she can find anywhere she can actually afford to live. She says it's the only place she feels at home.'

'Has she got any sort of support network?'

'She's got an older sister who she thinks is probably still living in the city somewhere, but she hasn't seen her for years. Griffiths prevented her trying to contact her when he was alive, but she's planning to get back in touch if she can track her down.'

'Makes sense.'

'Yeah, I think she'll make the move just as soon as she can. Maybe some kind of house swop if the housing association can arrange it.'

'She's not planning a funeral then? She'd only need a small coffin unless we find the rest of him.'

She shook her head. 'I can't see it happening. She wants to forget him as best she can, and move on with her life with the kids.'

He checked his watch for the third time in less than half an hour and pointed towards the kettle. 'And who can blame her? Mine's a coffee, if you're making one. You know how I like it.'

The DS spooned instant coffee into two mugs,

added a splash of cold milk to both, and finally sugar, one level for herself and five heaped for her boss. 'She'd been giving the situation more thought. That nonce she mentioned her husband meeting. She thinks his name's Peter. She recalls Griffiths crashing out of the house late one night a few weeks back when he was seriously pissed, and saying he was walking over to Peter's place for some decent company.'

'How sure was she of the name?'

'She reckoned eighty per cent plus.'

'No surname?'

'Nope. I tried to push her, but she couldn't come up with anything. I'm certain she wasn't trying to be obstructive.'

'Have a chat with Jane and put her in the picture. If there's a known or suspected nonce who goes by that name living in the area, she'll know about him for sure.'

She poured the boiling water, stirred, and handed him his mug with a smile. 'There you go, boss. You can stand your spoon up in it if you try hard enough.'

'Thanks, love, it's appreciated.'

'I gave the child protection unit a call from the car as it happens. Jane was out, but the DS in charge thinks she knows who Lucy's talking about. There's a Peter Harrington with an indecent assault conviction living not twenty minutes' walk away from the Griffiths' house. The boy was eight at the time of the offence. Harrington was volunteering in a local church youth club.'

'Okay, that's useful to know. I might well pay him a surprise visit myself. Let's see what he can tell us with a bit of gentle encouragement.'

23

The detective chief superintendent was already waiting at the front of the conference room, seated directly behind two adjoined tables covered with pristine white linen tablecloths, when Grav pushed the doors open with his recently appointed DS in close attendance. They were stopped in their tracks momentarily when met by a barrage of flashing, clicking cameras and loud chatter, but they soon took their seats alongside their boss. Grav looked around him and observed that the event reminded him of another similar conference not so very long ago. And just like then, the DCS had chosen to wear her newly dry-cleaned dress uniform, rather than her usual plain clothes, silver-coloured buttons highly polished in a blatant attempt to make a good impression on the attendant mass, representatives of the media baying for the next big story. Anything that could make a positive impact. Anything that could potentially help her scramble, inch by inch, up the greasy pole to the very top. She never missed a trick.

Davies rose to her feet and faced the room as Gravel and Kesey remained seated alongside her. Why the hell hadn't he made more of an effort? Look at the state of his damned shoes.

Hadn't he heard of polish? But at least his hair was reasonably tidy for a change. That was something to be grateful for. 'Right, if you could all settle down, I'll introduce you to the panel and we'll make a start.'

She waited for the chit-chat to gradually subside and spoke again, clearly enunciating each and every word in her crisp, public-school-educated, south of England accent. 'My name is Detective Chief Superintendent Hannah Davies. I'd like to welcome you all to West Wales Police Headquarters. The gentleman seated to my immediate left is Detective Inspector

Gareth Gravel, as some of you are already aware, and seated immediately next to him is Detective Sergeant Laura Kesey, who has recently joined us from the West Midlands force. The purpose of this afternoon's meeting is to bring you all up to date with developments in the case as far as investigative restrictions allow. There may well be some questions we are unable to answer at this time due to operational reasons, but with that said, I feel sure that the inspector will clarify matters to your satisfaction.'

With her introductions done, she returned to her seat and frowned as Gravel assisted himself slowly to his feet with the aid of the tabletop and glanced around the room for the second time with an inflexible turn of his head. Oh, she was sure, was she? If she was, it was more than he was. Perhaps *she* should give the fucking talk. See how she liked that. Keep it short and sweet. That was probably best. Stick to the basic facts. Come on, Grav my boy, get it done.

He coughed, clearing his throat, and began speaking with a tobacco-ravaged smoker's rattle that could sometimes be difficult to comprehend even with excellent hearing. 'As I'm sure most, if not all, of you are already aware, the partial remains of two adult males were found in the Tywi Estuary at Ferry-side by a local doctor in recent days. We are treating both deaths as suspected murders and an investigation is currently underway.'

He pulled his tie loose at the collar, rested his weight on the table's edge and waited for the resulting chatter to die down again before continuing. 'Enquiries have identified the first victim as a Derek Griffiths, previously known as Rodgers, a dark-haired, forty-three-year-old Caucasian male of average build and height, who was resident in the Kidwelly area of the county up to the time of his death, having moved there from London in recent months. Mr Griffiths was last seen alive on the eleventh of this month. His partial remains were found in a green plastic sports bag with black branding, a photo of which DS Kesey will now show you.'

He looked on as the DS switched on a desk-mounted slide projector, displaying a large and clear image of the bag on the white-painted wall behind her.

'Thank you, Sergeant. I'll be saying a little more about the bag later in the proceedings.' He walked slowly around the table and stood in front of it, no more than three feet away from the first row of seated journalists. 'The identity of the second victim, another white-skinned adult male of more diminutive stature, possibly five foot six or seven inches in height, is as yet unknown. Enquiries are ongoing in that regard. An extensive search of the river and estuary area has been undertaken and will be completed sometime later today. Nothing further of significance has been found up to this point. Are there any questions before I continue?'

A long-in-the-tooth journalist, who was all too familiar to both the DI and the DCS, raised his arm and waited for silence. 'Why isn't the chief constable here? He's not at the golf club again, is he? I'm told he spends more time there than he does here.'

Gravel glared at him as the attendant crowd burst into laughter, and turned and focused on the DCS. 'Do you want to respond to that one, ma'am?'

The chief superintendent remained seated, waiting for the laughter to subside before standing. She didn't have any idea where the chief was, but saying that wasn't an option. Not if she were to secure her next promotion. 'The chief constable is away on urgent business. I will, of course, be keeping him fully up to date with developments just as soon as the press conference is at an end.'

This time the same gutter press journalist rose to his feet. 'It's more of the same. The usual non-committal bullshit. Almost exactly what you said last time. He wasn't here for the serial killer press conference either, was he? Am I right? Five dead girls and he didn't bother turning up. I guess he's not going to put himself out for two unimportant men. It seems to be becoming something of a habit.'

Her face was reddening now, her senses in a state of adrenalin-fuelled hyperarousal as her fight-or-flight response fully kicked in. The particular journalist was nothing if not predictable. Always looking for something to criticise. Any angle to tear down to sell a few more wretched papers. 'Mr Brown, it is Mr Brown, isn't it?'

'Yes, it is. So what's your answer? My readers will want to know. They'll demand to know.'

What an infuriating individual. 'The purpose of this afternoon is to focus on the investigation of two murders. I'm the head of the force's Criminal Investigation Department, and Detective Inspector Gravel is the lead investigating officer for the case. We are very well placed to answer any questions pertinent to this enquiry. I want to make it crystal clear that our answers will be exclusively limited to that end. I have absolutely no intention of being distracted by other unrelated matters, which at the end of the day are not going to help us catch a killer. Two men are dead. It's our job to find out who killed them. Discussing matters not directly related to the investigation isn't going to aid that process. I'm going to hand back to DI Gravel at this point, and would ask that all further questions are limited to issues that relate directly to the investigation and nothing else. I hope that's clear to all of you.'

Grav was inclined to give her a resounding round of enthusiastic applause as she returned to her seat with a dark and sullen look on her face, but he resisted the temptation as he looked slowly around the room. So, it seemed she'd grown a pair. He would perhaps have put it in blunter terms, but she'd said what needed to be said, and good on her for that. Things were looking up. 'Has anyone got any more questions that are actually worth answering before I crack on?'

A young female journalist with purple hair met

Grav's eyes and spoke out, pronouncing each word in nasal North Wales tones that resonated from his childhood holidays in Snowdonia. 'Some Ferryside locals are saying that a man's decapitated head was found, and that the head had something carved into, or written on, its forehead. Can you confirm that, please?'

'That's not something I can discuss at this stage for operational reasons.'

She held his gaze. 'So, it's true then? The locals seem to think so.'

Grav shook his head and pulled his tie a little looser. 'Didn't you understand me the first time, love? It's not something I can confirm or deny... anything else before I move on? No? Then I'll crack on.' He turned, took a single step to his right, and looked directly into the lens of a BBC Wales television camera, almost at touching distance. 'I would appeal to any member of the public to contact the police urgently if they have any information that could potentially assist us with our enquiries, however seemingly insignificant it may seem.'

He raised a hand, pointed firstly at Kesey and then at the slide projector on the table in front of her.

'My team can be contacted twenty-four hours a day, seven days a week on the telephone number displayed on the wall behind me. People can also contact their local police station if they'd prefer. It makes no odds. If anyone's seen someone throw or put anything into the river or estuary in recent weeks, I want to know about it. If anyone was seen carrying something in the same area which could have been a body part, get on the phone immediately. You've seen the photograph of the bag. Have you seen someone with a bag meeting that description? Did anyone have a bag like that which is now missing? Has anyone been acting strangely or taking an overly active interest in the case? If you've got any suspicions, whatever their nature, I want to hear about them. Don't hesitate, just ring. No one's going to tell you you're wasting our time. Let the police decide if the information's worthy of attention.'

Davies stood as Grav paused for a moment or two, catching his breath and panting slightly. 'Unless anyone has any further questions relating to the investigation, I think we can thank DI Gravel and bring the proceedings to a timely close.'

'I haven't finished.'

She turned to face him. 'You haven't?'

He shook his head. 'No, ma'am.'

She remained standing, scanned the room, weighing up the mood, and said, 'It seems that DI Gravel has something to add.' She looked at him with a steely glower, but resisted the temptation to tap her watch. 'We won't keep you too much longer.'

Grav waited for her to return to her seat before addressing the room again. 'We've already talked about the fact that both bodies were dismembered after death. That takes the right tools, time and effort. There'd have been a lot of blood. If anyone was seen with what could have been blood on their clothes, contact us urgently. Even if he's a family member. Even if you think they're the last person who could potentially be involved. If you do nothing and they kill again, you will be at least partly responsible.' He paused again as his chest began to tighten. 'And finally, if anyone has any ideas as to the identity of the second victim, we'll be glad to hear from you. Now, are there any final questions before I ask the chief super to bring the press conference to a close?'

A broadsheet journalist seated at the back rose to his feet and said, 'Yeah, it's not a question, but there is one thing. I was told that a human leg was found on the beach in Pendine shortly before the meeting.'

* * *

Gravel called after the DCS as she strode quickly in the direction of her office with notes in hand. 'Well, that went well.'

She stopped, turned, and glared at him with a look that could wither lesser men. 'I'm assuming that's your idea of humour.'

'Why the hell did we hold a full-blown conference? What numpty came up with that stroke of genius? Put out a press release, appeal for the public's help, yeah, fair enough, but that charade did us no favours at all. We had fuck all new to say. I looked like a right plonker. What were you thinking, girl?'

Her eyes narrowed as she took a step forwards and glowered at him. 'Maybe ordering you back from Barbados wasn't such a good idea after all. I'd be extremely careful what I said next if I were you, Inspector. There's only so much of your disrespectful crap I'll tolerate before putting you on a disciplinary charge. Do not go thinking that your long service and the general affection with which you're held within the force will stop me pensioning you off faster than you can blink. Are we clear?'

He looked at her, breathing heavily, his blood pressure reaching potentially dangerous levels as he bit the tip of his tongue and swallowed his words.

'Nothing more to say for yourself, Inspector? No? Okay, if we're done here, I suggest you find something constructive to do with your time. You've got a killer to catch. Get on with it!'

He turned and walked away, mumbling crude obscenities under his breath.

As she entered the lift and pressed the appropriate button, she was scowling, angrier than she'd been in quite some time. He was disrespectful, objectionable, infuriating, and worst of all, as if that wasn't bad enough, he was right.

24

Rebecca felt a sudden surge of alarm as she sat in her small, dated kitchen with a cup of freshly brewed herbal tea in hand and watched the lengthy report relating to the afternoon's press conference on BBC Wales's early evening news. It was a high-priority case. That's what the familiar dark-haired female presenter stated more than once, as if to goad her and only her. It seemed that the police would stop at nothing to catch the killer. To catch her and lock her up forever.

Her heart was pounding in her throat now. She could hear it. And for a moment, as she struggled to breathe, she thought she may actually die there and then on the spot. Just collapse to the floor and take her last breath, with Teddy Bear's bare white bones lying on the killing room floor for anyone to wander in and discover at will. Was she going crazy? Losing her mind? Is that what was happening? Or was her reaction entirely justified in the circumstances? That's what she asked herself as her head began to pound, bang, bang, bang, as if something were attempting to break out of her skull with a jackhammer.

She reached forward, increased the television's volume to maximum and screamed out at the very top of her voice, feeling a little better almost immediately. Yes, yes, of course it was justified. She shouldn't be too hard on herself. What was she thinking? Her activities had never been subjected to such an intense degree of attention before. It was the lead story. TV, radio, the lot. *And* DI Gravel was an experienced detective with an excellent reputation despite his past failures. That was pressure. Real pressure. The type of intense pressure she hadn't experienced before.

She screamed again as the potential implications of the investigation fully sank in. She had to be more careful. She'd disposed of two bodies efficiently and effectively, but then she'd got careless. She became complacent. Really complacent. She didn't weigh the body parts down. She didn't bag them and use stones to stop them floating to the surface. It was stupid. Really stupid. Almost unforgivable.

Rebecca sipped her warm tea and placed the cup back on the pine tabletop as the news programme came to an end. It wasn't so much the possibility of getting caught that fazed her so very badly. A prison sentence held no particular fears she could think of. It was her essential quest coming to a premature conclusion that worried her most. She'd killed five, which was to her credit, but five wasn't nearly enough. Not when there were so many children at risk. Not when there were so many predators out there in the big bad world to hunt down and eradicate. If they were the plague, she was the cure. What purpose would she serve if incarcerated? She'd be almost as worthless as they were.

Her breathing was easier now as she wiped the sweat from her brow with the sleeve of her cardigan, leaving a small damp patch on the cuff. Maybe she should speed things up a bit. Maybe she should contact Lover Boy again and invite him along to the house just as soon as the remains of the corpse were disposed of. Yes, that made sense. But what about the bones? The arms, the legs, the torso and the head? The drains weren't a viable option. It would entail weeks of work. Sawing and sawing and sawing again, until each and every one was small enough to flush away. It was too onerous a task to even consider. Totally out of the question. And the river, her oh-so-convenient dumping ground of choice, was always going to be a high-risk option from here on in. People would be looking out for her, watching with keen eyes and ready to interfere. Ready to pounce and snare her at the slightest opportunity. Another unwelcome obstacle in her seemingly insurmountable world of woe.

She stood and hurled her empty cup into the stainless steel sink, smashing it to pieces. She had to come up with an alternative means of disposal and soon. An alternative that was both practical and minimised the risks of being detected. There was no time for delays. No time for inaction. What about the garden? It was far from ideal, but it was at least a conveniently located graveyard. A graveyard without mourners. Without memorials. Without tears. Yes, like it or not, the garden would have to do.

* * *

Rebecca sat and waited until precisely three in the morning before switching off every light in the house, unlocking the back door with quivering fingers, pulling on a warm winter coat and striding out into the back garden with a determined expression on her face. She stood at the edge of the lawn for a few seconds, allowing her eyes to adapt to the limited light, and then surveyed the scene in the pale-yellow glow of a half-moon shrouded at least in part by dark grey-black clouds, seemingly seeking to dominate the leaden sky.

She glanced to her right and left, walked out to the approximate centre of the lawn and turned slowly in a circle, searching for any hint of electric light or early-morning snoopers in any of the over-looking houses. She repeated the process for a second time, revolving slowly, ever so slowly, until she was finally satisfied that, with the exception of a dog howling somewhere in the far-off distance, Carmarthen's residents were fast asleep with their dreams and oblivious to her very existence. Just as she wanted it. Just as she needed it. The time was precisely right. It was time to get on with it. Time to get it done.

Rebecca took a shovel from her overly cluttered shed, approached the longest of three flowerbeds located at the far side of the lawn furthest from the house, fastened the top button of her padded coat against the December nip, and began digging, with increasingly frantic but far from effective movements of the steel blade. It was hard work. Harder than she'd anticipated. The ground was considerably firmer than it otherwise would be due to the falling temperature, and within fifteen minutes or so both her hands were blistered and she was sweating profusely, stinking of body odour despite the hardening frost.

She stopped suddenly, resting for a minute or two in the hope of regaining her strength. Much needed strength. Strength she'd undoubtedly require to complete her night's work. Teddy Bear had a lot to answer for. He'd caused nothing but problems in life and now in death. If only he'd never been born at all.

She bent at the waist, rested her upper body on the shovel's handle and looked down at the results of her labour. Shit, shit and shit again! She'd made some progress. That much was true. But, the hole was barely deep or long enough to bury one leg, let alone an entire human body. She looked down again, glancing from left to right and then back again, weighing up her limited options and very close to tears as the full enormity of the task truly dawned. Perhaps she could bury both legs in the one hole. Yes, that made sense. And then achieve as much as she could before dawn's light brought an inevitable end to her night's activities. If it meant leaving some of the remains exactly where they were for another day, so be it. They weren't going to walk off. It was a case of burying what she could tonight and then continuing from there. Exhausted or not, she had to carry on. Come on, Becca. Start digging, girl. Another fifteen minutes and she could prepare the legs.

She took a deep breath, in through her nose and out through her mouth, before intensifying her grip on the shovel's increasingly abrasive handle, raising herself to her full height and getting back to work with a newfound energy, born as much from a growing sense of panic welling up inside her as from stoic determination and reasoned internal argument. So what if it took her two or even three nights to dispose of the entire remains? It would be disappointing, really disappointing. She had to admit that. But she'd get it done in the end. That's what counted. That's what mattered. Yes, admittedly the stink of decay in the house would become something of an issue as the hours passed, as it occasionally had in the past. Air freshener almost certainly wouldn't be up to the task as she'd once hoped. Maybe if she sprayed every single room in the house, impregnating the carpets and curtains, it would do the trick. Yes, that might help. It had to be worth a try. Or perhaps sprinkle generous quantities of essential oil around the place. A splash here and a splash there. Something really pungent like eucalyptus or peppermint. That would probably work. She had some somewhere. Anyway, more of that later. Enough of soul-searching. It was time to redouble her efforts. Time to focus. Time to get on.

She looked down at the shallow hole at her feet,

then at her red-raw blistered hands and then at the hole again. The ice was glistening like a million tiny jewels on the dark earth in the moonlight. The ground was like concrete and seemingly getting harder by the minute. That wasn't good. It wasn't good at all. Just a few inches deeper and it would have to do.

Rebecca chose to ignore the pain in her hands for as long as she possibly could and continued digging for another twenty minutes or more, before finally deciding that she just couldn't go on for a second longer. All that effort and she'd only gone down another inch or two. Her body was aching from a combination of the physical effort and the plunging temperature. She'd never felt lower. She'd never felt so utterly depressed. An already unpleasant night was becoming a nightmare. No, it *had* become a nightmare. Had, had, had! That's what she told herself. It just couldn't have gone any worse.

She looked up into the heavens, threw the shovel to the ground and reached down to lift two heavy stones from the hole's uneven base. Maybe, just maybe, the two legs would fit in there together, nice and snug, if she sliced off as much of the melting flesh as possible. Yes, that may do it. He wasn't the biggest man in the world. Far from it in fact. There was only one way to find out. Just try it, Becca. Just butcher one at a time and drop them in. They'd either fit or they wouldn't. It really was as simple as that.

Rebecca made her way back into the house and sat herself down on the killing room floor in the dim, wavering light of a single candle. As she took the knife in her hand and prodded the tip of the blade into the upper thigh of one of Teddy Bear's gradually defrosting legs, she was reminded of Shakespeare's *The Merchant of Venice* and Shylock's demand for a pound of Antonio's flesh. Words had become actions, her actions, and it was Teddy's time to pay up. There was a strange beauty to it. That's what she thought as she surveyed the scene. A dark beauty that pleased her.

Rebecca used all her weight and strength to force the blade deep into the leg. Not right down to the bone; the deeper flesh was still too frozen for that. But close to it. It wasn't perfect, but time was rushing on. It would have to do.

She stripped off and made a quick but necessary

visit to the upstairs bathroom before continuing her work, utilising a night light to wrap a length of crape bandage around each hand and securing it in place with strips of PVC tape. She looked down, satisfied with her efforts, and decided that the weeks spent studying first aid as a young teenager had finally paid off. Maybe everything happened for a reason. Maybe everything was leading to this precise moment in time. Yes, that was probably it. She was serving her purpose. Fulfilling her destiny.

She glanced in the wall-mounted mirror above the sink before exiting the white-tiled room and decided that she was looking tired. Perhaps work for another couple of hours and leave it at that. She had to think of the day job. She had to be able to function reasonably proficiently to retain her professional credibility. And then it dawned on her. What on earth was she going to say about her hands? What if someone got suspicious? What if that someone started asking questions she couldn't answer? They were the police after all.

She laughed as she descended the stairs, her concerned frown replaced by a beaming smile. What on earth was she worrying about? Yes, they were police officers all right. Detectives even. But most of them couldn't find their own arse with both hands. If they could, she wouldn't be needed. She wouldn't have to spend so much of her time doing what, at the end of the day, was their damned job.

Her erstwhile amused smile was suddenly replaced by a mocking sneer as she re-entered the killing room and sat at Teddy's side with her legs crossed under her. How hard could it be? She managed to track the deviant bastards down easily enough. Tip tap, tip tap, that's all it took. Even the slightest hint of innocence and vulnerability and the salivating, drooling swine came running just as fast as their feet could carry them. It was as easy as shelling peas. Easier. She was ensnaring them. She was making them pay. So why the hell couldn't the police do likewise? It was inexcusable. Utterly inexcusable. An abomination.

She was crying now, the warm tears rolling down her face as her chest heaved and she gasped for breath. The police had the resources, the experience, the training and much else. And they were paid well enough. In direct contrast to her. So why didn't they do more? Why didn't they arrest them all? Surely they could if they really wanted to. If it were any kind of priority. Maybe they lacked the motivation. Maybe children weren't important enough in their eyes. Yes, that must be it. The inept fools. They hadn't been through what she'd experienced. The brutal destruction of self-worth. That may explain it. Yes, yes, that was it. It was just another crime to them. They hadn't lived it. They just weren't her.

Rebecca gripped the knife's shaft tightly with both bandaged hands, lifted it high above her head and brought it crashing down into Teddy's exposed chest with an animalistic screech, before raising herself onto her knees and repeating the process, time and time and time again, before finally slumping exhausted next to his corpse with fresh sweat glistening on her body.

She sat herself upright as her breathing became shallower, and glanced around the room in the pale-yellow light of the flickering flame. Tip tap, tip tap. It was time to cast the net. Time to draw Lover Boy into her trap.

She nodded, pleased to have reached a satisfactory decision.

The slimy rat was as good as dead. If the garden

had to become his final resting place, then so be it. He could keep poor old Teddy Bear company for eternity. How very nice for them both. Two of a kind. Predators who had become prey. "Will you walk into my parlour? Said the spider to the fly. 'Tis the prettiest little parlour that ever you did spy."

25

Gravel had requested a Police National Computer check prior to his visit to Peter Harrington's home, and it seemed that the fifty-four-year-old quantity surveyor did, in fact, have two indecent assault convictions as opposed to the one mentioned by Kesey following her recent discussion with the child protection unit. Grav perused the related case reports with interest, and saw that both offences were against minors. One a boy of just eight years old and another of eleven. Harrington had volunteered as a youth worker in two different church-run youth clubs for several years, no doubt with his own aberrant needs and desires in mind. He'd finally been caught when the younger of his two victims disclosed a series of offences committed by Harrington on the pretext of giving the boy a lift home. The second boy had finally spoken up after seeing a report relating to the conviction of another unrelated sex offender on the front page of a local weekly newspaper. It seemed it had proved to be a seminal moment. A revelation. Suddenly, in that instant, the boy had realised that something could be done despite Harrington's insistence to the contrary.

The authorities would listen to him. They'd act on his statement. And best of all, it would stop.

Grav took a paper hankie from a trouser pocket, blew his nose noisily and hacked up a large globule of green phlegm before discarding the tissue in the waste paper bin to the side of his desk. Two convictions and the dirty bastard had still only served four months in total. Unbelievable. The courts were a joke. A probation order with a sex offender treatment condition on the first occasion and an eight-month custodial sentence on the second, of which he'd served precisely half. It seemed the therapy hadn't worked. No surprises there. Men like Harrington were what they were. They did what they did. What good could therapy do, however well in-tentioned? Could you put a heterosexual man on a course and make him gay? Or a gay man straight? No, you fucking well couldn't. It was a case of experts who weren't very expert at all.

He picked up the phone, dialled, and waited for about thirty seconds before DC Mike Lee eventually answered in an office at the other side of the build-ing. 'Hello, Mike, it's Gareth Gravel. Am I right in thinking you investigated the Harrington case? Kid-welly, a couple of years back. Indecent assault.'

'Hello, boss, how was the holiday?'

Grav coughed, clearing his throat again before responding. 'I haven't got time for that shit now, Mike. We can have a catch-up over a pint sometime. Just answer the fucking question.'

'Some things never change. Impatient as always.'

'So what's the answer?'

'Yeah, I know the case. He's still living in Kidwelly and working in Llanelli as far as I know.'

'What sort of bloke is he?'

'Well, he's a scumbag obviously. That goes without saying. Are you looking for something specific?'

'You know this case I'm working on? Griffiths? The head found in the Tywi? It looks as if he'd been in contact with Harrington shortly before his death. It seems they had a lot in common, both being nonces and all. I'm planning on paying him a visit sometime later today to apply a bit of pressure. Let's see what he's got to say for himself.'

'Okay, makes sense.'

'I'm looking for an angle. Are there any particular vulnerabilities I can play on? Something that will have him on the defensive and keen to please.'

'Ah, okay, I can see where you're coming from. He had a seriously hard time in prison, if that's any good to you?'

'Could be. Tell me more.'

'He had the shit well and truly kicked out of him more than once. Two broken ribs, a fractured nose, loose front teeth. Bottom line, he's a wimp who wouldn't stand up for himself. He rolled over like a pussy from the second he got there, from what I was told. He had other prisoners gobbing in his meals, constantly taking the piss, walking in and nicking his stuff from his cell as and when they felt like it. He finally made an official complaint to the governor and named names after being pinned down and arse-fucked early one morning by three prisoners in the communal showers. He spent the remainder of his sentence in solitary for his own protection after that. Something tells me he won't be too keen on going back anytime soon.'

'Okay, that could prove useful. Am I right in thinking that he's got no history of violence when it comes to adults?'

'No, nothing at all. I can't see him as a suspect for the murders, if that's what you're wondering?'

'No, I'm just covering all the bases... is he married?'

'He was right up to the time of the second conviction, and then she finally saw sense and dumped him. She's a teacher in Haverfordwest. Or at least she was when I last spoke to her. Why it took her so long to kick him into touch is a complete mystery to me.'

'So, he's living alone, yeah? No girlfriend, lodger or the like?'

'Not as far as I know.'

'Is there anything else I should know?'

'Wasn't that enough? I think that's about it to be honest, boss. I can come with you, if that helps. I'm sure he'll remember me. You never know, it may make him more likely to talk.'

Grav shook his head, deciding that was the last thing he wanted or needed. The DC was a bit too much of a follow-the-book merchant for his liking. 'Na, you're all right, thanks, mate. I'm a big boy now. I can handle this one. What's the best sort of time to catch him in?'

'He was usually home by about half six on week-days from what I remember. I've got his home telephone number here somewhere, if that's any good to you?'

'Give me a second, I'll just grab another pen. This one's just died on me... okay, Mike, go ahead. I'm all ears.'

The DC recited the number, waited for Grav to read it back to him and said, 'I've got his work number as well if you want it?'

'Na, why pre-warn the cunt? I'll call on him tonight on my way home and give him a nice surprise.'

'Okay, boss, I'll be in all evening. Give me a bell if you need anything else.'

* * *

Gravel spent the rest of the afternoon ploughing his way through reams of mainly pointless paperwork, and he felt as if a burdensome physical force had been lifted from his chest as he headed down to the police canteen at just before five. He ordered an all-day breakfast and a large mug of milky coffee from the white-clad cook standing at the counter, who glared at him with an expression that left him in no doubt as to her displeasure. 'Oh, bloody hell, Grav, you could have timed it better. I was just about to pull down the shutters and sod off home for the night.'

'Oh, go on, love. I'm gagging here. Just this once, eh? There's a nice drink in it for you.'

She met his eyes and sighed. 'This is the last time. I'm telling you that for nothing. Make sure you're here by no later than half four in future if you want a hot meal. Any later than that and you'll have to make do with a sandwich.'

He grinned as he handed over a large handful of copper coins he was glad to get rid of. 'You say the exact same thing each and every time, love.'

'I'm too soft for my own good and you take advantage.'

'You're an angel, Gloria. The finest cook in Carmarthen. And don't let anyone tell you otherwise.'

She turned away, took the required items from the fridge and began cooking. 'Yeah, yeah, I'm sure. MasterChef standard at the very least. Now, tell me. Have you caught that killer yet?'

'Not as yet, love.'

'Well, get your bloody finger out then. What are you doing here wasting my time when you've got a murderer to catch?'

He chose not to respond this time and sat alone, waiting for his food. She had a point, but a man had to eat.

* * *

Grav sat back in his office chair, picked up the phone, withheld his number and dialled Peter Harrington's home. The phone rang six times before he heard an unfamiliar male voice with a familiar West Wales accent say, 'Hello.' The DI grinned and put the phone back on its cradle. The scrote was in. It was time to make a move.

* * *

It only took him about twenty-five minutes or so to reach Peter Harrington's four-bedroom detached house on the outskirts of Kidwelly, despite a swirling cold grey mist rolling in off the nearby sea and enveloping everything in its path. He parked his hatchback half on and half off the pavement almost directly opposite the house, stubbed out his tenth cigar of the day and stepped out into the clouded darkness of the evening. It seemed Harrington had done all right for himself. Better than all right. A big and expensive house with a nearly new top-of-the-range German sports car parked in the driveway gave the place the misleading persona of monied upper-middle-class respectability. Grav silently observed that on this occasion, first impressions were notoriously unreliable. And just when he'd thought he couldn't like the scrote any less.

Grav could clearly hear a soaring classical aria he recognised but couldn't identify as he knocked the front door again and again with gradually increasing force, until the music suddenly stopped.

Harrington peered out through his velvet curtains and cursed under his breath as his blood pressure began to soar more and more rapidly. Even with the limited visibility, the overweight middle-aged man banging his door so very insistently had pig written all over him in big, bold letters. Harrington couldn't put his finger on exactly what it was about the man that led him to that conclusion, but he'd never been more certain of anything in his entire life. He was a pig. A plain-clothes pig, for sure. But still a pig. An angry snorting pig with a grudge against the world. A pig revelling in his authority. A pig who was out to get him. What the hell did he want? What the hell was it this time? Whatever it was, it wouldn't be good. Shit! Would they ever leave him alone? This particular pig wasn't inclined to give up easily.

Gravel kept knocking, harder, harder and harder, pounding the door with the side of a clenched fist. 'Open up, Harrington. It's the police. I can kick the fucking thing in if you want me to. Open up, nonce! We don't want to upset your posh neighbours, do we?'

Peter Harrington sprinted into the hall just as fast as his legs could carry him, slid to a gradual halt on the parquet flooring, picked up the phone and urgently dialled his solicitor's out-of-hours number. Come on. Come on ... no answer. Please pick up, please pick up. Still no answer!

He stared at the door as Grav turned away, leaned forwards and kicked it mule style with the sole of his shoe, causing it to shudder violently in its oak frame. Answer or don't answer? What to do? What the hell to do?

For a moment or two, Harrington seriously considered making his escape through the patio doors and hiding somewhere in the garden, but the pig would just come back. He knew that only too well. They always came back with their sirens blaring and their blue lights flashing.

Harrington took a deep breath, fastened the top button of his shirt, straightened his silk tie, ran a hand through his short neat hair and slowly approached the door, all the time wishing that the floor would open up and swallow him whole. How to play it? Come on, Peter, back straight, stiff upper lip, bluff and bluster. Look the pig in the eye, hold his gaze, make clear reference to the solicitor and refuse entry. That was the best approach. That was the only approach. Wales was still a relatively civilised country. He had his rights, criminal record or not. Why not make full use of them?

Harrington reached up, paused, and then turned the knob quickly before he could change his mind. He trembled almost uncontrollably as he raised himself to his full height and stared at the detective, feigning indignation surprisingly effectively given the circumstances. 'I assume you've got some form of identification, officer.'

Grav grinned, took his warrant card from the inside pocket of his jacket and held it up at eye level, only inches from Harrington's fast-reddening face. 'My name's Detective Inspector Gareth Gravel, West Wales Police. You're not going to like me very much.'

Harrington swallowed hard and wondered why his mouth felt so very dry. Hold it together, Peter, hold it together. 'I've served my time. I've done nothing wrong since being released. I've got no reason to speak to you. If you want to interview me again for some inexplicable reason, I want my solicitor present. I'm not talking to you without her. I know my rights.'

'Oh, you know your rights. Sure you do. Your sort *always* know their rights. But I don't give a flying fuck. Got it? You ain't got nothing. We can talk here or in the house. But either way we're doing it now.'

'Have you got a warrant?'

Grav laughed hoarsely and stepped forwards, placing his foot in the door as Harrington attempted to slam it shut, banging the detective's right knee hard in the process. Grav yelped and threw himself forwards, colliding with the partially open door and knocking the other man backwards off his feet and onto the floor.

The DI rubbed his knee, stepped into the brightly lit hall and slammed the door behind him. 'Get up, you miserable nonce. I need some information and you're going to give it to me.'

Harrington shuffled backwards, retreating as fast as he could without actually standing. 'You can't talk to me like that. I'm an important man in this town. I know people. I've got contacts.'

Grav walked slowly forwards, reached down, grabbed Harrington tightly by the front of his blue-

and-white-striped shirt and dragged him to his feet, before spinning him forty-five degrees and forcing him backwards into a generously proportioned lounge that screamed affluence and bad taste. 'Oh, I think you'll find I can, Peter. You've got the expensive suit, the slicked-back hair, the big house and the flash car, but you're still just a repugnant little lowlife git. All the money in the world couldn't mask your stink. I can talk to you however the fuck I want to.'

The DI threw Harrington into a conveniently located armchair and loomed over him at touching distance, panting hard as his chest tightened. 'Tell me about Derek Griffiths.'

Harrington looked up at him, pondering his limited options. How much did the pig know? Maybe everything and maybe nothing. Maybe he was on a fishing exercise with very little bait. Denial. Plead ignorance. It had to be worth a try. 'I've got absolutely no idea who you're talking about. The name means nothing to me.'

Grav moved with surprising speed and agility for a man of age and fleshy build. He drew his arm back far behind him and then brought it forward, slapping Harrington hard in the face with an open palm.

'Don't make me ask you again, nonce. I'm not a patient man.'

Harrington hugged his knees to his chest and looked back at the officer with a stunned expression on his face, as memories of prison bullying flooded back. 'You're a police officer, you can't do that!'

Grav shook his head slowly, grinned and slapped him again. Harder this time. 'You snivelling little git. Perhaps now you've got the message. Tell me about your relationship with Derek Griffiths. I won't ask you again.'

Harrington was trembling now, repeatedly flinching, sweating and urgently trying to decide how best to placate the lunatic officer without implicating himself in the process. 'I'll report you. I'll make a formal complaint.'

Grav tilted his head back, laughed hoarsely, cleared his throat and spat in the man's face. 'You invited me into your big flash house and then you attacked me. No warning. No reason. No provocation. And I acted in self-defence. I feared for my life. You were like a wild man. A beast. Are you starting to get the picture, Peter? It would be my word against yours. The word of a well-respected and decorated senior police officer on the one hand, and a convicted nonce on the other. They'll believe whatever the fuck I tell them to believe.'

'Please, I don't know the man. I can't tell you something I don't know the answer to.'

The DI clenched his right hand into a tight first and cupped it with the left. 'You're lying to me, Peter. I'm not a happy man. Any second now you'll resist arrest and I'll have to give you a fucking good hiding. It's something I'm good at. Something in which I excel. How does that sound? It might be a good idea to start cooperating.'

Harrington blinked as a single bead of sweat ran down his forehead. It was time to start sharing information, within reason. Time to say as little as he could get away with and still get the lunatic pig out of there as fast as feasibly possible. 'Okay, so I know who Griffiths is, and I know he's dead. I know he was murdered and dumped in the Tywi. I saw the news reports relating to the case, but I didn't know him personally. That's all I meant. I didn't know the man.'

Grav sat himself down directly facing his interviewee and looked at him with a puzzled expression on his face for a few seconds before speaking again. 'What a crock of shit. What's the denial about, Peter? I know you knew him. I know he came visiting. I know you spent time together doing the things that you dirty little nonces like to do with your time. He was seen here! A trusted witness has given us a written statement to that effect. I want to know what Griffiths was up to. I want to know who else he was in contact with. Adults. Children. The whole picture. That should be clear enough even for you.'

Harrington lowered his knees and leaned forwards in his seat, keen to seem trustworthy and be believed. He was breathing harder now and very close to tears. 'Okay, look, he came to the house once. Just the once. Honestly! He'd heard I'd been inside. He'd heard about the nature of my convictions, but I told him to piss off and stay away. I didn't want him here. I'm trying to avoid reoffending. I don't need his kind of company.'

Grav remained silent for a few seconds, staring at Harrington until he looked away. 'Why do lying gits like you always feel the need to refer to their honesty when you're nothing of the kind?'

'I'm not lying.'

'I hear you didn't particularly enjoy your stay in prison, Peter.'

'They treat animals better than that.'

Grav made a show of looking around the room. 'Weren't the facilities up to your exacting standards? Maybe you were expecting a spa facility, a comfy king-size bed and a butler to tuck you in at night.'

Harrington's face dropped as a stream of urine soaked into his pants. 'Why the hell are you talking about prison? I can't go back. I can never go back. I'd rather die. I'd top myself. Give me a break, *please*! I've done everything that was required of me. I served my time. I'm working. I'm paying my taxes and I haven't touched another boy even once.'

'Like fuck you haven't. You just haven't been caught yet. That's all.' He patted the breast pocket of his jacket and grinned. 'Wouldn't it be a terrible shame if I searched this place and found some kiddie porn hidden somewhere? In your bedroom maybe? That would make sense. You'd be arrested and banged up again before you knew it, with all those hard-case prisoners who can't be at home to protect their kids from scum like you. Imagine it. It would be worse than last time. Much worse. I could tell the guards to look the other way. To abandon you to the pack. Picture it, Peter. Make it big, bright and loud in your mind. They'd hit you a lot harder than I did. You wouldn't last very long, would you?'

He was weeping now, the tears flowing freely. 'Please, n-no, I can't go back. I'm b-begging you, I can't go back there.'

Grav tilted his head sideways, raised a hand to his face and tapped the tip of his nose three times. 'I'm investigating two murders. Just tell me what I need to know and I'm gone from your life forever. You won't hear from me again, guaranteed. It seems like a good deal to me.'

'You'll go? You'll leave me in peace? If I cooperate, you'll leave me alone, yes?'

Grav leaned forwards in his seat, mirroring Harrington and nodding twice. 'That's what I said. Guaranteed. Just tell me the truth and I'm on my way.'

'I have your word?'

The DI reached out and shook Harrington firmly by the hand. 'Help me and I'll help you. That's the way it works. I couldn't give a toss what you've been up to. I just want to catch a murderer.'

This was it. Maybe the pig could be reasoned

with after all. Just give it a go. Just give him what he wanted. There was very little, if anything, to lose. 'Derek came to the house soon after moving here from London. We'd been in contact online. I invited him over. He made use of my internet. He came here twice after that, but that was it. That's the truth.'

'Now, wasn't that better? Finally you're cooperating... was he in contact with anyone else with similar interests as the two of you? Anyone at all?'

Harrington tugged repeatedly at his tie. 'Not that I know of. He was scared. Really scared. That was obvious. He was keeping a low profile.'

'Scared of what exactly?'

'I don't know if there was any truth in it, but he claimed a London gangster was out to get him. He said he'd offered a financial reward to anyone who killed him. I thought he was full of crap at first, but then when he was found dead... well, you know what I'm saying. I wouldn't have allowed him anywhere near this place if I'd thought there was any truth in it.'

'Oh, the threat was real all right. There's no doubting that. Maybe the killer'll come after you next. Have you thought about that?'

Harrington's mouth fell open.

'Had anyone been watching him? Had he seen anything suspicious? Anyone hanging around? Any cars he didn't recognise parked near his house?'

'He was seeing potential assassins anywhere and everywhere when I last saw him. I'd never seen anyone so jumpy. Not even inside. I was beginning to think the poor sod was paranoid.'

'So the scrote was shitting himself right up to the end. Good enough for him. That cheers me up no end.'

Harrington didn't respond.

'But he didn't mention anything specific?'

'Sorry, no, I've got nothing more to offer you.'

'You're certain?'

'If I knew anything, I'd tell you. Honestly I would.'

'What about kids? Was he in contact with any local children that you know of? We're in the process of going through his computer records, so feeding me a load of bullshit would not be a good idea. I can always come back.'

Harrington wrapped his arms around himself

and grimaced, his face twisting and distorting. 'You've found Derek's computer?'

'That's what I said. I don't appreciate having to repeat myself.'

'He was always online: social media, games, carefully chosen chatrooms, self-harm, suicide, eating disorders, that sort of thing. He looked for vulnerable children to target. Boys or girls, it made no difference to him. And he was good at it. He used to boast that he could spot a suitable victim within seconds of reviewing their posts, and isolate them from friends and family almost as quickly. Clever really.'

Grav had never wanted to punch someone so very badly in his life, but he somehow managed to hold himself back. The git was spilling the beans. His time would come. But, for now, his cooperation was enough. 'So, was he in regular contact with any particular children?'

'Oh, yeah, a couple of prepubescent boys in the south of England somewhere that he'd taken a particular shine to, and a local primary school girl who seemed to be something of a favourite. I'm not sure exactly how old she was. Eight or nine maybe.'

Grav took a deep breath and counted slowly to

three inside his head. It would feel so very good to ram his fist down the repugnant scrote's throat. What the fuck was wrong with these people? 'You're saying there was definitely a local girl?'

Harrington nodded. 'Oh, yes, without any doubt. He told me he'd arranged to meet up with her.'

'When exactly?'

He paused before answering, keen to get it right. 'It must have been shortly before he was found dead.'

'You can't be more specific?'

'Sorry, no. I would be if I could. I'm doing my best here.'

Grav moved to the very edge of his seat. 'So, what's this girl's name? I need a name.'

Harrington looked into the far-off distance, focusing on nothing in particular. 'Sorry, I just can't remember. I don't think he ever mentioned it.'

'Oh, for fuck's sake. You really expect me to believe that crap?'

'It's the truth. Nothing but the truth.'

'But she lives locally, yeah? You're certain of that?'

'Oh, yes, somewhere in Carmarthen. I'd bet my life on it.'

'Is there anything else you can tell me about her? Anything at all?'

Harrington shook his head. 'I've told you everything I know. I've answered all your questions. I can't do more. You'll leave me to get on with my life now, yes? Like you said.'

Grav rose stiffly to his feet, looked him in the eye and smiled fleetingly. 'I appreciate your cooperation, Peter. You've got nothing at all to worry about. You won't be hearing from me again. When I make a deal, I honour it.'

* * *

Gravel sat back in the driver's seat with the diesel engine ambling, and only had to wait for a few seconds before Detective Constable Mike Lee swallowed the last mouthful of his homemade lasagne and answered the phone. 'All right, Mike, sorry to disturb your domestic bliss, mate.'

'No problem, boss. How did it go with Harrington?'

Grav turned up the heating and sneered. 'He's one obnoxious git.'

The DC nodded. 'Yeah, that's one way to describe him. So, what can I do for you? I'm guessing this isn't a social call.'

'Harrington was mixing with Griffiths right up to the time he was killed. He'd been at the house more than once. He told me that himself.'

'Okay, so he's still at it then.'

'Oh, he's at it all right. No surprises there. Have a chat with the uniform duty sergeant, and get yourself around to Harrington's place early tomorrow morning with two uniformed constables in tow. Get there when the bastard's still tucked up in bed nice and snug. Say five thirty at the latest. I want you to seize any computers and anything else that's potentially incriminating and bring him to the station. Have a really good look around and put a bit of pressure on. He's in breach of his licence at the very least. Let's get him banged up again.'

'Will do, boss. Do you want to interview him yourself?'

'No, you're all right, Mike. I'll leave it with you. Give me an update later in the day if you come up with anything interesting.'

'Are you in all day?'

'Yeah, I'll be about somewhere... oh, and one last thing before I leave you in peace. Make sure you make a lot of noise when you make the arrest. Drag him to the car, cuffs on. I want all his neighbours woken up and watching. Make it a public event. Put the siren on if you have to.'

'Is that really necessary, boss? Isn't wrecking his life enough?'

'Just follow orders, Mike, there's a good lad.'

26

Rebecca clutched the phone tightly in one hand and pondered whether to dial. The wind had changed direction from east to west, the recent winter weather had become more temperate as a result, and Teddy Bear was dead and buried in the ground. Well, most of him anyway. Some of him was making a final journey through the sewer system.

Rebecca grinned as she pictured herself feeding scraps of Teddy's flesh to a local tomcat who sometimes wandered through the garden. At least he'd served a useful purpose at the end. He'd contributed. He'd finally done something worthwhile. The cat has a full belly. And maybe Teddy was an animal lover.

She stared down at the phone with her finger hovering over the dial. It was important to remember that there were good people in the world. People like her mum. People like her dad. Not everyone was devoid of empathy and virtue. Come on, Becca. Duty calls. Best get it done and dusted. It had been a while. It was time to ring.

* * *

'Hello, Mum, it's Becca. How are you doing?'

Janice forced a brittle smile, closed her eyes momentarily and pictured a smiling five-year-old little girl without a care in the world. 'Hello, cariad, it's good to hear your voice again. It's same old same old here, what with Dad as he is. Are you coming for Christmas? It's almost here. We'd really love to see you again. And you could bring that boyfriend of yours with you if you like. We still haven't met him.'

Rebecca's expression hardened. 'He's back in the States visiting his family. I thought I'd already told you that.'

'Away again? And in America? You said he was in London the last time we spoke.'

'If I say he's in America, that's where he is.'

'Well, that's even more reason for you to come home with us then. You don't want to be on your own on Christmas Day. I'll make a nice turkey dinner with all the trimmings, just like I used to. You'd like that, wouldn't you?'

She gritted her teeth and searched for a response. 'I'd like to, but I've got a friend coming to stay for a couple of days. A lad I met at university. Everyone used to call him Lover Boy.'

Janice Smith wiped away a tear. 'Oh, that's nice, was he a boyfriend?'

Rebecca laughed, struck by the irony. 'No, he doesn't like women that way. We're just friends, nothing more.'

'Oh, a gay friend. That's nice. You could bring him too. There's plenty of room.'

'He wouldn't want to come.'

She took a paper hankie from her pocket and dabbed at her face. 'Is there any point in pleading?'

'None at all.'

'Well, let me come and visit you then. It's only down the road. I could ask Auntie Myra or Olive to watch Dad for me for an hour or two, and pop around for a nice chat. You'd like that, wouldn't you, cariad? I could bring your presents with me. You haven't even had last year's yet.'

Rebecca shook her head vigorously, beginning to doubt the wisdom of calling at all. 'I don't want you to see the house until it's finished. I've told you that before. I want it to be perfect when you come. Surely you can understand that?'

'Always the same response. Always the same rationalisation. You've been saying that for over two years, Becca. I don't care what the house looks like. I just want to see *you*. That's all that matters to me. I've told you that before.'

'I'll tell you when I'm ready. And don't even think about turning up uninvited like you did last year. I won't let you in, even if I'm here, which I probably won't be.'

Janice hung her head and spoke through her tears. 'I just d-don't understand, cariad. We s-see so very little of each other th-these days. You're a virtual s-stranger. We used to be close, didn't we? Once upon a time n-not so very long ago.'

'You're a reminder of the past. A spotlight on a stage. Don't you get it? I've been thinking about

Sheridan. I dreamt about him again last night. He was back living in this area, taunting me, flaunting his freedom, making my life even more of a misery than it already is. It was so real, Mum. So very real. I wish I could delete the memories and start all over again from the very beginning. You know what I'm saying. As if I never met him.'

'Oh no, not this again. Surely not again. It's more of the same. You're so black and white. Up or down in a heartbeat. So ready to embrace despair and wallow in the past. But dreams aren't real. They're not real life. Sheridan's gone. We don't know where to, but he's gone. You're young, you're healthy, you've got a fine job and a boyfriend. Just think of those things and forget him. What happened was awful. Truly awful. It should never have happened. But don't let him destroy the rest of your life. Don't let him win.'

Her face took on an animalistic snarl as she punched the wall. 'What, like you did you mean? Or like Dad did? Did the two of you forget? Did you get on with your lives and walk smiling into the sunset?'

Janice Smith sucked on her asthma pump. 'No, w-we didn't. We let it eat away at us. Particularly

Dad. But where did it get us? Where did it get him? He's lying upstairs in that bed of his like a vegetable and being fed through a plastic tube. That's where it got him. He never forgave himself for what he saw as his failure to protect you. I told him it wasn't his fault time and time again. How c-could he have known? What could he possibly have done differently? Nothing! That's what. I said it and said it again until I was blue in the face. But did it make the slightest difference? A real man would have torn Sheridan a-apart, that's what he told me. A real man would have taken the ultimate revenge and accepted the consequences.'

'Maybe he was right. I'd like to think I would, given the opportunity.'

'Do you really think he didn't want to take revenge? Do you think he didn't think about it? Detective Sergeant Gravel talked him out of it. I talked him out of it. The police let us down, Becca. The CPS let us down. The system failed us all. Not Dad!'

'Then why couldn't he move on with his life? Why couldn't he put it behind him? Why couldn't he forget?'

'Because he's just like you. So very like you. He couldn't let it go any more than you can.'

She didn't reply.

'Look, cariad, all we did was send you for ballet lessons. That's all. You'd been going on about it for ages. We thought we were doing a good thing. A positive thing. How could we possibly have known the type of man Sheridan was? He seemed pleasant enough. He had a good reputation in the town. All the necessary certificates. People even used to say he was great with children. A natural. One of the other mothers at your school recommended him to me personally. What could we possibly have done any differently?'

'Maybe he's still out there somewhere giving ballet lessons and everything that goes with them to another little girl. Another little girl like me. Have you thought about that, Mother? Has it ever crossed that tired mind of yours?'

'Yes it has. Yes it has. More times than I care to remember.'

'Then why aren't you doing something?'

'Now, come on, Becca, it's up to the police to catch men like Sheridan, not the likes of you or me.

We just have to get on with our lives as best we can. It's really time you did that.'

Becca tugged at her hair and began swaying rhythmically. 'But would you like to kill him if you got the chance? I really want to know the answer. I need to know the answer.'

'Okay, if you want to hear me say it. I'd still like Sheridan to be punished. I'd like to see him in court and locked up for ever.'

'Well that's a first. A bit of honesty for a change.'

'You keep pushing.'

'But have you done anything about it? Have you even tried to make it happen?'

Janice slumped onto the floor with the phone's spiralled lead stretched to maximum. 'What could I possibly do? Nothing. Nothing at all. I saw DS Gravel in the supermarket a few months after they dropped the case. He pretended not to recognise me at first, but I was never going to let him get away with that. I walked up behind him and tapped him on the shoulder. He didn't like that. I could see the disappointment in his face when he turned towards me and said something along the lines of, "Oh, hello, Mrs Smith, I didn't see you." I knew he'd seen me. I was certain of it. I'd never been more certain of anything in my life. He'd looked in my direction and met my eyes for a fraction of a second before urgently looking away.'

'So what happened next? What did you do? What did you say for yourself?'

She took a deep intake of breath, sucking the oxygen deep into her lungs before responding. 'I stood right up close to him, almost at touching distance, blocking off his potential escape route, and I glared up at him with accusing eyes. "You let us down, Sergeant! I want you to know that." That's what I told him. Right to his face. Right there in the supermarket where anyone could have heard me scold him like a little boy in primary school.'

'Was that really it?'

'It meant something to me.'

'So did he explain himself? Did he have anything worthwhile to offer you, or me for that matter?'

She was silent for a moment, contemplating the past and picturing events in her mind before speaking again. 'No, not really. He was full of seemingly genuine apologies and regrets. Filled with justified rage at the failure of the system, just like I was.

That's what he had the nerve to tell me. No one regretted the failure to prosecute and convict Sheridan more than he did. No one. Can you imagine my reaction? I accept he was disappointed, angry even, but as much as *me*, as much as *you*, as much as *Dad*? No way! Everything he said just sounded like excuses to me.'

'Was that it? Was that really the pinnacle of your efforts on your only daughter's behalf?'

'I did what I could.'

'And did it make you feel any better about yourself, Mother? Did it alleviate your angst?'

'What are you trying to get at? Do you blame me in some way, even after all these years? Is that the real reason for our alienation? It took me a lot of courage to speak to an authority figure like that. I did my best for you, Becca. Dad did his best. If you blame me and Dad in any way for what happened, you're wrong. I want you to understand that and take it on board this time. You're wrong!'

'Blah de blah de blah. Same old, same old. He's an inspector now. A detective inspector, no less.'

'Who?'

'Isn't it blatantly obvious? Gareth fucking Gravel.

Can you imagine that? He lets an insidious slimeball criminal like Sheridan slip through his hands and slither off to fuck knows where, and what happens? He gets promoted, that's what! The world's gone mad.'

Janice raised a hand to the side of her face and listened as David Smith stirred in his bed. 'It was a long time ago. He'll have dealt with hundreds of cases since then. He must be a good police officer or they wouldn't have made him an inspector, would they?'

'How do you manage to be such a total bitch every single time? Siding with that wanker of all people. Do you know, he doesn't even recognise me? That's how much I mattered.'

'There's no need to become abusive. I don't deserve that.'

'I'm sorry, Mum, I said too much.'

'Have you tried speaking to DI Gravel if it means that much to you?'

'I see him walking around the police station sometimes, thinking he's oh so very important.' She laughed. 'The big man with the even bigger beer gut... he's an absolute disgrace. That's what he is. A complete disgrace. He can't look after himself properly, let alone anyone else.'

'So it seems life has blunted the detective's edges as much as mine. We've had this same conversation so many times, Becca. It never gets us anywhere. I think it upsets you as much as me. Can't we talk about something else for a change?'

'Like anything else matters even in the slightest.'

'All of life is important. Not just the negatives.'

'I'm thinking of asking DI Gravel to find out where Sheridan is for me, if he can get off his fat arse for long enough to actually do something worthwhile for once.'

'Oh, what's the point? What would it achieve?'

'I've tried to find him myself without success.'

'What the hell? Why would you do that?'

'What a ridiculous question. I want him to suffer like I have.'

'Have you thought of talking to Dr Proctor? She may be able to give you something to take the edge off. The antidepressants have worked wonders for me.'

She laughed humourlessly. 'Oh, yeah, you're the life and soul.'

'Well, perhaps not wonders, but they've kept my head above water a few times when I was in danger of drowning. That's fair to say. You're not the only one with troubles. It's not all light and joy for me either.'

'I do realise that. I'm not a complete idiot, whatever you may think. But tablets, that's not for me. I'll find my own way. Perhaps we could kill Sheridan together.'

'You're always on the defensive. Always so ready with the implied criticism or a clever comment. We could get together occasionally and help each other, couldn't we? I could meet you somewhere in town for a coffee and a piece of cake. That vegetarian café in Merlin's Lane is very pleasant. I've been there once or twice. That would be nice, wouldn't it? We could talk about ordinary things. Day-to-day things. It may even cheer us both up a bit.'

She gritted her teeth and screamed inside her head, louder, louder and louder, until she thought her skull may shatter. 'You haven't got the slightest clue. Not a fucking clue. Did you see the report on the news about the body parts found in Ferryside?'

'Not quite the ordinary things I had in mind, but it's a start I suppose.'

'So did you see it, or not?'

'Yes, I did.'

'They've found a leg now. On the beach in Pendine. I overheard one of the detectives say it belonged to the same man as the head.'

'At least you're not talking about Sheridan for once. That's something... hang on, the carers have just arrived. I'll be back with you in a second... okay, Becca, I'm back. They've gone upstairs to give Dad a bit of a wash and change him into some fresh pyjamas. I shaved him this morning before breakfast. I hate to see him with stubble. He was always so proud of his appearance.'

'They were sex offenders.'

'Not again, not again, not again! Who?'

'The dead men. They were sex offenders. Men like Sheridan. Slugs who are better off dead.'

'What on earth can I say to that?'

'Just saying.'

'So, are we going to meet up then? For a coffee? Like I was saying? Olive's a lovely woman. I'm sure she'd keep an eye on Dad. I could ask her now.'

'There's more.'

'More?'

'Focus, woman, focus. Concentrate on what's important, not life's trivialities. Sex offenders. There are more bodies to find.'

'How can you possibly know that? Did one of the police officers say something?'

'Something like that.'

'So, shall I ask her?'

'What? Why would I want to meet up? Why would I ever want to meet up? I haven't got time, Mum. My guest will be arriving and I have to prepare. There's things I need to get. Things I need to do.'

'Well, at least I've tried, even if my efforts fell on predictably deaf ears... I hope you have a wonderful time with your friend. Have you put up a tree?'

'Oh, yeah, and tinsel and fairy lights.'

'There's no need for sarcasm. I was only asking.'

'I decided to plant something in the garden this year rather than decorate the house. It seemed like the right thing to do.'

'How am I going to give you your Christmas presents? They're all wrapped and waiting.'

'Put them in the post. Surely you can manage that much. I received your charity card early yesterday morning. You've got my address.'

'Why so dismissive? Why so very hurtful?'

'I don't know what you're talking about.'

'One's a bit big for posting. I was hoping to give it to you in person.'

'Always the drama queen. You can drop it off at my work, if you must. Just leave it at the front desk with my name on it, and I'll collect it on my way out.'

'Just like before. And nothing in return. Not even a thank you.'

'I'm grateful, really I am, but that's the best I can offer.'

'If you give me your telephone number, I'll ring you on Christmas Day to say hello. It's not in the book. I've mentioned it before.'

'Well, I *know* that, Mother. My number's ex-directory for a very good reason. I thought I'd made that clear enough. You don't ring me, I ring you. That's the deal. That's the way it works. I'll ring you sometime that evening, *if* I get the time.'

'Surely y-you can spare a few m-minutes for your old mum on Christmas Day?'

She stared at the phone with her eyes wide. 'Are you from another planet or something? Are you really that stupid? I'm sure I've already mentioned that I have a guest coming to stay. A guest, Mother, do you hear me? A guest! I think that's rather more important than wasting my valuable time talking to the likes of you, don't you? All my time and effort is going to be focused on *him*. That's who matters. Not you, not Dad, and not me for that matter. *Him*! Get that into your thick head.' And with that, she slammed the phone down. Done. Dusted. Nothing more to say.

27

'Hello, Sarge, it's Sandra on the front desk. Is the boss in?'

Kesey lifted her white chocolate bar to her mouth and bit off a small chunk before responding. 'He's out, will I do?'

'I suppose you'll have to.'

'Bloody charming. So, what can I do for you?'

'I've got a Mr Edward Green here with me, who says he wants to speak to the detective in charge of the murder investigation.'

She couldn't resist nibbling at the bar again before speaking. 'Did he say why?'

'He's come in in response to the press conference.

He reckons he's got some information that could be relevant to the case. He didn't put it in those exact words, but that seems to be the crux of it.'

'Okay, that could be interesting, or not, of course. He took his time. Why didn't he come in any sooner?'

'How on earth am I supposed to know the answer to that? You'll have to ask him yourself, Sarge. I'm not a mind reader.'

'Okay, Sandra, tell him to take a seat in whichever interview room's free and I'll be with him in two minutes maximum. And keep a close eye on him for me. Make sure he doesn't decide to wander off before I speak to him.'

'Why would he want to do that? He came in of his own volition, not kicking and screaming. Edie's a nice guy. I know him pretty well, as it happens. We went to primary school together.'

'It sometimes seems you lot all know each other.'

'You lot?'

'The Welsh.'

'I'll put him in room two.'

Kesey gulped down the remainder of her chocolate bar at breakneck speed, savouring the rich creamy sweetness on her tongue and swirling it around her mouth before finally swallowing. She approached the staircase with a statement form in hand and descended quickly, two steps at a time, until she reached the ground floor. She raised her hand in acknowledgement on spotting Sandra, who was standing with her hands on her hips behind the reception desk, and made her way down the brightly lit corridor leading to interview room two at its far end.

Green rose to his feet as she entered the room, smiled, and nodded in greeting as she approached him. She reciprocated, and observed that the slim and stylish middle-aged man in the smart pinstripe business suit was the last thing she'd expected. 'Take a seat, Mr Green. My name's Detective Sergeant Laura Kesey, good to meet you.'

He sat as instructed. 'Likewise.'

She sat opposite him with her hands resting on the tabletop separating their two chairs. 'So, Sandra tells me you have some information to share with us.'

He nodded twice. 'Yes, I hope I'm not wasting your time. My wife mentioned seeing your Detective Inspector Gravel on the Welsh news, at a dinner party we were attending yesterday evening. I decided I'd better come in and talk to you.'

'You didn't see the report yourself?'

'No, I can't say I did.'

She pushed a single sheet of blank paper and a biro across the table. 'Okay, if you'd write down your full name, date of birth, address and contact number on there for me, that will speed things up a bit.'

He scribbled the required details in hurried, barely decipherable handwriting and handed them to her. 'Sorry about the writing. My secretary's always complaining about it, poor dear.'

She examined the details and decided they were just about readable without explanation. 'Do you work locally?'

'I'm a solicitor based in town. Forsyth and Green in Queen Street.'

'Ah, yeah, I know it... so, what have you got to tell me, Mr Green?'

'I don't know if this is of any relevance, but I thought I'd let you decide that for yourself.'

'Okay, makes sense.'

'I suffer from insomnia. Have done for years.'

'And?'

'I sometimes go for long walks at night. It helps me relax. I think that puts what I have to say within a proper context.'

She nodded but didn't feel the need to verbalise her thoughts.

'On the night in question, I'd parked my car in Quay Street and walked along the riverbank towards the old railway bridge in Johnstown. As I was approaching the bridge, I saw someone kneeling down at the river's edge and putting something in the water. This may seem ridiculous to you, but I thought she may be drowning newborn kittens or puppies. I hear that unscrupulous people do that sometimes. I'm an animal lover. I would have wanted to stop her were she engaged in such a task.'

'You said *she*. *She* may be drowning.'

'Oh, yes, that wasn't a slip of the tongue. It was a woman all right. I've got absolutely no doubt in that regard. She seemed startled when she first saw me, and stood and hurried away in the opposite direction. Increasing her walking pace initially, and then looking back and breaking into a loping trot as she moved away. I looked in the river for a minute or two before turning and walking back towards town, but I couldn't see anything of any note. I can only assume that whatever it was had sunk into the muddy water.'

'But you're sure it was a woman, yes?'

'It was a cold moonlit night, I had my prescription glasses on and I was no more than twenty or thirty feet from her when she took off. She was a young woman in her twenties or thirties. Certainly no older. I could see the line of her breasts under her coat. I'd swear to that in any court in the land.'

'Interesting. And it could be significant. Can you describe her for me?'

'I'd say she was about five foot four or five inches tall and of average build, but she was wearing a padded winter coat with a hood, so she may have been thinner than she appeared.'

'Do you remember the colour of the coat?'

He shook his head and frowned, oblivious to his expression. 'It was dark, dark blue or black possibly, but I couldn't swear to it.'

'What else was she wearing?'

'Blue jeans and white trainers, I think. That's the best I can do, I'm afraid. And I wouldn't bet any money on it.'

'What about her hair? What colour and style of hair did she have?'

'She was wearing a hood, as I said.'

She sighed. 'Okay... did you see her face?'

'Very briefly, just for a fraction of a second when she looked back at me. She was white, young as I said before, but that's about it really.'

'No distinguishing marks?'

'Not that I could see.'

'I know it's a long shot, but would you recognise her if you saw her again?'

He blew the air from his mouth through pursed lips. 'I could give it a go, but I very much doubt it.'

'That's what I thought you'd say. When was this exactly?'

'The twenty-fourth of November at about half past two in the morning.'

Her eyes widened. 'You seem very sure of that.'

'It was my wife's fortieth on the twenty-third. How could I forget? We'd been out for an Italian meal with friends earlier in the evening. We went to bed shortly after midnight and I got up a couple of hours later when I just couldn't nod off.'

She made an unnecessary adjustment to her

spectacles. 'Did you see a vehicle parked anywhere near the river?'

He thought for a moment, casting his mind back to the night in question. 'There was a small hatchback of some description parked near to where I parked the Mercedes.'

'That's somewhat vague for evidential purposes. Can you tell me the make, colour or registration number of the car?'

'Sorry, no. I haven't got the slightest clue. I'm not a car buff. I took no interest.'

'And you didn't actually see what she put in the water? Not even a glimpse?'

'No, I'd have said if I had.'

'You're certain of that?'

'How many times...? I only wish I had. I'm sorry I can't be more helpful.'

She smiled thinly and picked up the statement forms. 'Not at all. I appreciate your assistance, Mr Green. Let's just get a brief statement down on paper and you can be on your way.'

28

Grav knocked on Rebecca's office door and walked in without waiting to be asked. 'Can I have a quick word please, love?'

'What can I do for you, Inspector?'

'You looked at Griffiths' computer for DS Kesey, yes? I think you must have missed something.'

She looked up at him from behind her desk and forced a quickly vanishing smile. Was he onto something or simply responding to instinct and hoping for the response he wanted? 'I was just about to have a cup of herbal tea. Will you join me?'

He shook his head and chose to remain standing despite an available chair. 'I'm all right, thanks, love.

The computer. You told my DS that Griffiths wasn't in contact with any local kids.'

She swivelled in her seat, reached down behind her, and switched on her kettle with wavering fingers. 'That's right. I explored all the conceivable possibilities. He was in contact with several children of different ages in various parts of the country, but nothing in Wales, let alone this area. I can say that with certainty.'

'That doesn't make a lot of sense, love. I've got very good reason to believe that he'd been in regular online contact with a local girl for several weeks. He'd even made arrangements to meet her.'

She dropped her head, allowing her hair to mask her face before picking up the kettle. 'Are you sure you won't have one?'

He rested both his big hands on her desk and leaned towards her. 'How much experience have you got with this stuff?'

She bit the tip of her tongue hard as her face blushed. 'If he'd been in contact with a local girl on that computer, I'd have found out about it. I'm good at my job, Inspector. You can count on me to get it right.'

'This isn't some meaningless university role-play game. You do realise that, don't you, love? We're talking about real people, real victims, and a murderer who needs catching. If you've got any doubts, now's the time to tell me. No one's going to hold it against you.'

She stood to face him. 'I'm very well aware of that, thank you. I take my job seriously. *Very* seriously. I *did not* miss anything. I've told your colleague precisely what's on that computer. I typed it out for her convenience. You can keep asking me the same question for the rest of the day if you really want to, but you won't get a different response. I've told you what I know, and that's not going to change, however much you want it to.'

'Okay, maybe the witness was lying. Or maybe Griffiths had a second computer we haven't found yet. Stranger things have happened... sit down, love. I didn't mean to question your professionalism.'

She sat as requested, breathing shallowly as Grav lowered himself into the room's only other chair. 'Look, love, I'm no computer expert. If he deleted something, it would still be on the hard drive somewhere, yeah?'

'Yes it would be, but it wasn't. I checked. Twice. He wasn't in contact with a local child. Or at least, not on that computer. I can't make it any clearer than that. If you want me to ask my assistant to look at it yet again, I'll happily do so. But the results aren't going to be any different. I can promise you that much.'

He stood to leave. 'No, you're all right, love. Child protection need to go through the rest of the photos and videos. Better them than me, eh. I don't want to hold them up.'

'You don't recognise me, do you?'

Grav looked back on approaching the door and studied her for a second or two. 'I've definitely seen you somewhere. Not around the station, but before. When you were younger. You weren't one of Dewi's old girlfriends, were you?'

She laughed emptily, and then spat her words. 'Rebecca Smith, Becca; I was six. Now do you remember?'

'Oh, for fuck's sake. The Sheridan case. Was it really that long ago?'

'Yeah, I'm a big girl now.'

'It's good to see you again, love. How are your parents doing?'

'Like you care.'

'I asked, didn't I?'

'Dad's bedridden after three strokes. Mum looks after him as best she can, but she's a shadow of her former self. Old before her time.'

He felt a pang of genuine regret. 'Sorry to hear that, love.'

They seemed like nice people. Give them my best for me.'

'You've got no idea, have you? Not the slightest clue.'

'What are you talking about?'

'I blame you.'

He avoided her eyes. 'What exactly are you saying, love?'

'Are you really that stupid? I blame Sheridan primarily, but you played your part.'

Grav closed the office door and returned to his seat. 'It's the system, love. Guilty people sometimes escape justice. I don't like that fact any more than you do, but there it is. Having a go at me isn't going to change it.'

'You promised my father that you'd get Sheridan for something in the end. That his time would come. Dad told me that himself, in the good old days when he could actually speak. You failed us, Inspector. You let us all down.'

'I did what I could, love. The scrote should have paid a heavy price, but you can't win them all.'

'Do you even know where Sheridan is?'

'He left the area for Plymouth years ago. I gave the Devon and Cornwall force a ring and gave them the heads-up at the time, but that must be, what? Fifteen or sixteen years ago.'

'Seventeen years. It was seventeen years.'

'If you say so.'

'So he could be anywhere now, doing God knows what to anyone at all.'

'Yes, he could, but it's some other copper's problem. I can't watch everyone.'

She lifted her cup to her lips and sipped the fast-cooling liquid. 'I want to know where he is. No, I *need* to know where he is for my own sanity. Do you get that? Can you do that much for me?'

'If I found out, if I told you, would it really make any difference to your life?'

'Yes it would, yes it would. It would mean the world to me. Nothing matters more.'

He approached the door, looked back and nodded. 'I'll make a few phone calls, love. If I can track the bastard down, you'll be the first to know.'

29

Rebecca perused the latest digital photos sent by Lover Boy and cringed. Not because they featured his erect penis standing to attention like a soldier on parade, she was well used to such things, but because of his overall build. Lover Boy was fat. Very fat. Disturbingly fat, in fact. And disposing of his body would prove to be something of a challenge. There'd be a great deal of flesh to carve off the bone, and pints of coal-black blood spilling out like a dark geyser in full satanic flow.

Should she abandon her plans and move on to another target? It was an option. No, no, no, what on earth was she thinking? She'd already invested far too much time and effort to let him go at such a late stage of the process. She was the spider and he was the fly. A big fat fly, but a fly nonetheless. A fly in need of swatting. She'd just have to take her time, strip his flesh for however long it took over the Christmas break and resort to the garden again for the skeleton.

Rebecca relaxed back on her bed and smiled. Perhaps in the spring she'd plant some perennials. Something easy to grow. A plant with a seemingly infinite capacity to renew and quickly cover the poisoned ground. Lavender maybe. Yes, that was always easy on the eye. And it had the added advantage of that wonderful scent. Why not spend a few miserable pounds on something beautiful for a change? Something to enhance her memorial garden. Not as any sort of tribute to the dead and buried, but to the survivors. Those were the people who mattered. To all of them. Whoever and wherever they were. It would be as if their abusers never existed at all. As if the will of spiteful fate had passed them by.

She reopened her laptop and glanced down at his most recent communication. He was what she liked to refer to as a complimenter. No less a predator than all the others, but a predator who wrote what on the face of it were nice things, until you realised they were directed at a child for his own twisted Machiavellian reasons. He'd found a method of manipulation that worked for him and appeared to rely on it almost exclusively. She was pretty. That was one he used often. Special. That word again. One of the prettiest girls he'd ever seen. It seemed the stock photos had done their job better than she could have hoped. He was keen to meet up. *Desperate* to meet up. Tip tap, tip tap. The filthy depraved bastard! She gritted her teeth and began typing:

Do you realy think Im prety

He responded within seconds:

Very, very pretty. I really like your eyes.
what do you like about them
They're lovely, just like you are. You could be a model
if you wanted to be. A well-known model with your
photographs in all the glossy magazines.
do you realy think so
Yes, definitely. I can help you become a model if you

want me to. Producers are always looking for pretty
girls like you.
would I be famus
Yes, very famous. You could even be a film star. I
could help with that too. I know the right people.
People who make special films.
OOO yes please
I'll just need to take some sample photos and make a
video of us together so that I can show the producers
how pretty you are.
have you got a camera
Yes, and a video camera. I'll bring them with me when
I come to see you.

She repeated her favourite rhyme in her head:
"Will you walk into my parlour..." and so on, time
and time again, before suddenly stopping and focusing back on the screen:

why dont you come on sunday like we said last time
Only if we'll be on our own in the house. Only if it's
our special secret. You haven't told anybody about
me, have you?
no of corse not

If you tell anyone, anyone at all, you won't be able to be rich and famous. And we wouldn't be friends any more.

why are you cros with me. I dont like it when your cros with me.

I'm not cross. I just want to be sure you understand. It's very, very important.

i wont tell any body

Do you promise? On your mother's life?

i promis

Do you swear to it and hope to die?

Yerrrr

What time does your mum go to work?

she caches the bus at ten o clock

Ten in the morning?

Yer

And you're really sure that you'll be on your own on this coming Sunday? That will be the nineteenth.

yer I told you all day

What time does she come back?

at tea time

Does she ever come back earlier?

No

That's great. I'm really looking forward to meeting you. Now all I need is your address.

She typed the required details with a look of utter disdain on her face.

Will you wear the pretty red-and-white dress you wore in your pictures? I really liked that. Very sexy.
If you want me to and ive got some suprises for you
Oh, that sounds exciting. What surprises?
youll just have to wait and see

She switched her laptop off, closed it, and stared at a spot of mildew on the ceiling, lost in thought. It was time to prepare. Time to get the room ready for Lover Boy's pending arrival. But was it really necessary to replace the tools of her trade after each and every guest? Yes, yes, better safe than sorry. They needed to be at their sharpest. And she was running low on black bags again. It looked as if it was time for another visit to the DIY store.

30

Gravel sauntered into the operations room after a surprisingly satisfying lunch in the police canteen, watered, fed, feeling comfortable in his own skin and very much at home in the investigative world he knew so well. The enquiry wasn't progressing as quickly as he would wish, but it was progressing, and for now he'd have to be satisfied with that.

He looked directly at Kesey as he slowly approached his cluttered desk, and felt a sharp stab of regret for times so recently passed. So much was familiar, unaltered, the world kept turning, and yet so much had changed. Rankin was gone. He wasn't coming back. And this slip of a girl was there in his place. Sitting in what should rightly be his seat, oblivious to the man she'd re-placed. A man she'd never been fortunate enough to meet. Nothing was for ever. Not in this world, as he'd observed more times than he cared to recall. Oh well, such was life. He shouldn't hold it against the girl. It wasn't her fault. He just had to get his head down and get on with it.

'Hello, Laura, a coffee would be appreciated, if you're in the mood to make one.'

She looked up from her paperwork and nodded. 'Yeah, I could do with a break from this lot.'

* * *

'There you go, boss. Are you sure about the five sugars? It seems a tad excessive, don't you think?'

He scratched his nose and smiled. 'If I want to be nagged half to death by a woman, I'll get married again, thank you very much.'

'Okay, it's your funeral.'

Grav sat back in his seat with his feet resting on his desktop and accepted the hot drink gratefully. 'So what did Edward Green want? Sandra told me he's had a chat with you. Anything interesting?'

'The statement's on your desk somewhere, boss. Among all the other stuff. I thought you'd want to read it yourself.'

He glanced at the piles of paper and sighed. 'Just run me through it in your own words, love. I think that's probably best.'

She spent the next few minutes succinctly outlining the relevant information as Grav sipped his coffee and looked on.

'Is that it?'

'Yeah.'

'A woman, who'd have thought it? Was he sure? Could it have been some bloke dressed in women's clothes?'

She shook her head before speaking. 'He seemed pretty certain to me, boss. He told me he could see her breasts under her coat.'

'Well, if anyone would spot her tits, it's that slimy git. He's always been a bit of a hands-on merchant where the women are concerned. My wife used to say he made her skin crawl.'

'Really? He seemed all right to me.'

'Wait until you get to know him a little better, love. Particularly if he's had a drink or two. You'll find out.'

'I'll keep it in mind.'

'So, there's no way he could come up with a better description? Something we could work with?'

'No, I pushed him on it, but it's exactly as I told you. That's as good as it gets.'

He took another swig of coffee. 'I guess anything's got to be better than nothing. Not that our mystery woman's necessarily got anything to do with the case.'

'You've got to admit it's strange though. A woman dumping something in the river in the early hours. It might be worth considering another press release. You know, something asking whoever it was to come forward so we can eliminate her from our enquiries. That sort of thing.'

Grav drained his mug and nodded. 'Yeah, I was thinking much the same thing myself. It can't do any harm... and Green couldn't come up with the details of this car he claimed to see? I've heard better descriptions.'

'It was a hatchback, like I said, but that's about it.

If he could have told me, he would have. He wasn't being deliberately vague. I'm certain of that.'

'I may give him a ring myself. You know, to see if he's remembered anything more.'

'Why would you do that? Don't you trust me to do my job?'

He lowered his feet to the floor. 'Of course I do, love. It's just my way.'

'Anything else?'

'Have a look at the CCTV for the night. There's no cameras in the immediate vicinity, but you may spot the vehicle in the general area. It could be a game changer.'

'Oh, you trust me to do that then?'

'Talk about bloody sensitive.'

'I'll get on to it as soon as we're done.'

'Did I mention I had a chat with my contact at the Met?'

'No, you didn't.'

'They sent someone over to interview Taylor in prison. An experienced DS, from what I was told. He got the distinct impression that he knew nothing of the murder before the visit.'

'That doesn't necessarily mean that Griffiths

wasn't killed as a result of the contract. It could be Taylor just hadn't been informed yet.'

'Yeah, I know what you're saying, but it makes it less likely from what I can see. And we've got this second unidentified victim. Where the fuck does he fit in? I'm beginning to think the Taylor connection is something of a red herring. Griffiths had a lot of potential enemies. Maybe Green's statement is more on the mark. She was putting something in the river. Why not a head?'

'I guess you could be right.'

'I had a quick word with Jane's DS over at child protection. They've checked all possible leads on Griffiths' laptop for a third time for me, but there's still nothing relating to any local kids. They're looking for one final time at my insistence before going through the rest of the photos etcetera, but I'm not holding my breath.'

She raised her mug to her mouth and nodded. 'Makes sense. I'm glad it's them not me.'

'Me too, love. That seems to be becoming something of a theme.'

'Yeah.'

'They've got Griffiths marked down as a prolific

offender. He trawled various chatrooms and the like, looking for kids who meet his victim profile. He was in active contact with at least nine children in various parts of the country during the weeks prior to his death. He'd even arranged to meet a boy of ten in the Bristol area, but nothing local that they can find. Maybe one or more of the photos will tell us something.'

Her eyes narrowed. 'Do we know who the boy is?'

'Yeah, Griffiths was exchanging messages with him right up to the approximate time of his death. It was the usual grooming shit: probing questions, manipulative promises, the sending of sexual images, encouraging him to do likewise. And then he arranged to meet him. He arranged to go to the boy's house when he was home alone. They messaged each other on the day before he planned the meeting, and then the messages stop dead. He didn't send the address.'

'So what happened?'

'The local police had a chat with the parents for me. They went away on a last-minute trip to London just at the right time. Talk about a lucky break. Another twenty-four hours and the boy would have been another of Griffiths' victims. Bet that came as something of a shock. Most people seem blissfully unaware of the risks posed by these people.'

'But no local children? I'm no expert, but that seems highly unlikely to me.'

'Yeah, I thought much the same thing myself. Ease of offending and all that, but like I said, child protection have checked and checked again. They're sick of hearing my voice. And the computer girl said much the same thing fairly insistently when I suggested she may have missed something. It doesn't make a lot of sense, Laura. Why would Harrington lie to me? He had nothing to gain... unless he was telling me what he thought I wanted to hear. Maybe he just wanted to get me off his back and avoid a beating. That wasn't my impression though. My gut's usually pretty reliable when it comes to this stuff. Do you think Griffiths could have had a second computer we don't know about?'

'His missus didn't think so, but she may not know about it if he had.'

'Remind me, did you search his mother's place? He spent a lot of time there.'

She frowned. 'I should have. I really should have.

I was going to, but then I found the laptop, you know what I'm saying.'

'Don't beat yourself up, love. Hindsight tends to make things look a lot clearer than they were at the time.'

'Well, sensitivity and understanding, no less. That was unexpected.'

He laughed. 'I'm the very definition of a new man.'

'So, what do you want me to do first, the search of the mother's place or the CCTV?'

'Tell whoever's free to get themselves over to Griffiths' mother's place, and make a start on the CCTV yourself. It could be crucial. The quicker we see if there's anyone of interest, the happier I'll be.'

'Will do, boss.'

She pushed her empty mug aside and met his eyes. 'Is there anything else, or shall I crack on?'

He smiled again, more warmly this time, and picked up the top file from the pile on his desk. 'Yeah, we're done for now, love. Let me know if you come up with anything useful. No peace for the wicked, eh, whatever the fuck that means.'

31

Grav discovered Sheridan's current location with surprising ease. In his long experience, Social Security records, the electoral roll and the like could be extremely helpful when tracking down a criminal quickly, and they'd proved to be no less reliable on this occasion. Sheridan was unemployed and back living in a rented flat in the Devonport area of Plymouth near to the naval dockyards, after serving half of a two-year stretch for a series of indecent assault offences.

Grav put a cigar in his mouth but didn't light it. At least the law had caught up with him in the end. He'd been banged up. Not for nearly long enough.

But it was a conviction. He was officially a known sex offender. The local agencies were aware of the risks he posed and would keep a close eye on him, as far as that were possible. That was progress of sorts. Hopefully Rebecca Smith would be satisfied with that.

The day passed quickly, as was the norm when he was busy, and Rebecca had long since left for home by the time Grav called at her office with what he hoped was good news later that day. Oh well, she'd waited seventeen years. What harm could another twenty-four hours do? Maybe he should call it a day and spend an hour or so in the rugby club before heading home. There was a pint of bitter with his name on it.

* * *

The DI called in the incident room to collect his keys en route to his car and had reached reception without interruption when Sandra waved at him wildly and called him back with an insistent tone that couldn't be ignored, however tempting it was to try. 'What is it, Sandra? I was just about to go for a pint, love.'

'Don't shoot the messenger, Inspector. Your new DS is on the phone. She needs to speak to you.'

'Oh, for fuck's sake. Can't it wait?'

'She heard what you said, and the answer's no it can't.'

'Bollocks. And just when I had a thirst on.'

Grav leaned against the wooden counter as his chest began to tighten and complain. Maybe it was time to think about cutting down on the cigars once and for all. Heather would be chuffed. One less pleasure in life's rich tapestry of delights. 'All right, Laura, what can I do for you, love? You only just caught me.'

'Yeah, so I heard... I've been going through the CCTV recordings. There's something you need to know about.'

'I'm all ears.'

'You're not going to believe this.'

'Try me.'

'There were only five cars that could possibly be the one seen by Green caught on camera at the relevant time.'

'Spit it out, love. I'm not exactly mesmerised at

this point.'

'Four of the five were being driven by men. I could see that much easily enough.'

'And?'

'I've run PNC checks on all the registered owners. Two have criminal records. One for the use of marijuana years ago when he was a student at Cardiff University, and one for driving while disqualified, but nothing relevant. No history of violence.'

'Couldn't this have waited?'

'It's the fifth car, boss, a red Corsa. It's registered to Rebecca Smith. You know, the computer girl. And she meets the description, when you think about it. Right age, right build, right height.'

'You have got to be kidding me. Can you see the driver on the tape?'

She shook her head as she spoke. 'The quality's not great, to be honest. I can tell there's a woman in the driver's seat, but that's about it really. I haven't seen anything that says it's not her, but it's not possible to identify her with any sort of certainty. It certainly wouldn't stand up in court.'

'So what time was she filmed?'

'The Corsa was being driven in the direction of

the river at one forty-eight a.m. precisely. She could easily have parked the car and walked along the river path to where the woman was seen by Green about forty minutes later, even if she was carrying a heavy load.'

'Surely not? Rebecca? Come on. But I guess she's got some explaining to do, if nothing else. It's not something we can ignore.'

'How are we going to take this forward, boss? Do you want me to call around and have a chat with her this evening? We get on reasonably well. It might make the process a little easier, what with her being a workmate.'

'No, thanks, love. You're all right. This is one I'd better do myself. There's an unrelated matter I need to discuss with her anyway. I can ask her what she was doing in town at that time while I'm there. I'd be amazed if she's got anything to do with the murders, but let's see what she's got to say for herself.

Informally at this point, but I'll bring her in in the unlikely event I think there's anything in it. If she becomes a serious suspect, we'll deal with her like any other criminal. No favours.'

'Do you want me to come with you, boss? My

hubby's out getting pissed on some stag do with his new mates. I could do with an excuse not to go home early.'

'No, you're all right, love. I think I can handle this one. I'll see you in the morning.'

* * *

The light in a front bedroom was the only perceivable sign of life as Grav pulled up outside Rebecca's Carmarthen home. He was already starting to regret his earlier decision to limit his cigar intake as he exited the car, and he wasn't in the best of moods as he pushed open the rusty metal gate and walked up the pathway towards the front door. Grav could clearly hear loud rock music he didn't appreciate as he knocked hard with the side of his fist, and he wasn't in the slightest bit surprised when he didn't receive an answer. If she heard him above the noise, it would be a fucking miracle. She must drive her neighbours around the bend.

The DI knocked for one final time before giving up on any chance of a reply and hurrying around the side of the house with his head bowed low against the drizzle. He pushed open a wooden door forming part of a boundary fence and found himself in Rebecca's back garden, with its alternative access to the house. He considered knocking again, but decided against it almost immediately and tried the back door, which opened, enabling him to step into the kitchen and escape the rain.

Grav took a rubber torch from the pocket of the padded jacket that his subordinates secretly joked made him look like the Michelin Man on steroids, switched it on, and scanned the room for a light switch, which he located within seconds.

Nothing very remarkable: basic units, a large chest freezer, a low-budget cooker. A kitchen typical of someone on a limited public sector salary. Much like his own, the freezer apart. That seemed a bit over the top given she lived alone.

He returned the torch to his pocket and called out, 'Hello, Becca, it's DI Gravel. We need to have a chat, love.' Still no reply, which didn't surprise him given the volume of what he now recognised as a pounding 1960s' Hendrix track emanating from the first floor. He opened the kitchen door and found himself in a dark hallway, devoid of photographs or any other form of adornment. Minimalism, wasn't that what they called it? He'd seen something on some property programme on BBC2. Oh well, each to their own. Heather would have hated it.

He was about to approach the base of the stairs with the intention of calling out again, but instead he opened a door leading off the hall. People's homes could sometimes tell you a lot about them. He had the opportunity. Why not make use of it?

Grav pushed the door open and stared into the empty room in the partial light of the nearby kitchen. He ran the palms of both hands over the wall and flicked the light switch, causing the bare bulb to flood the room with bright light that made him blink. Strange. Every inch of the place was covered in black plastic, secured in place by some form of tape he didn't recognise. What the...? Maybe she was decorating. No, that made no sense. You'd cover the floor maybe, but the walls? You wouldn't cover the walls.

He glanced around the room with darting eyes, spotting a modelling knife on the floor in one corner and a hammer on the windowsill. What the fuck? Could she really be the killer? Rebecca, just a young girl with a grudge. Two men killed and butchered. Cut to pieces in a makeshift bone house.

He walked across the room, bent down stiffly, picked up the knife and examined it for a full ten seconds before taking a clear plastic evidence bag from a trouser pocket and dropping the knife in. It had what looked like dried blood on the shaft. Not a great deal of blood. Someone had done a reasonable job of cleaning it, but it was there. It was definitely there.

Grav left the room on full alert. Nerves taut. Adrenal glands in full production. He approached the staircase as a soaring guitar solo filled the air, and negotiated the first two steps before stopping and clinging onto the wooden banister. 'Hello, Rebecca! It's DI Gravel, police!'

She still didn't respond.

He climbed another step, then another, then another, before stopping again and shouting for a third time, 'Rebecca! I'm coming up, love. We need to talk.'

The music was still blaring, seemingly louder, louder and louder, as he stepped onto the small landing. 'Rebecca! It's DI Gravel. Police!'

The music suddenly stopped, one of four doors

slowly opened and Rebecca appeared, standing immediately in front of him with her hands on her hips. 'What are you doing in my house? You've got no right to be here. None at all. You're a policeman, you should know that. You should work within the law.'

He held his ground. 'I'm here to talk to you about Sheridan, love. I said I'd make a few enquiries for you. You remember that, yeah?'

She took one solitary step forwards and stopped. 'Of course I remember. I'm not a halfwit. Couldn't it have waited until we were both back at work? What's the urgency? You weren't invited here. Why the imposition?'

'I was passing, love. I saw your car parked outside and I thought you'd want to know what I'd found out as soon as possible.'

She stood and stared at him with unblinking eyes.

Grav took a single step backwards, teetering on the very edge of the staircase as she clenched her hands into weapons. 'He spent some time in prison, but he's back living in Plymouth now. Devonport. He's on the radar. That's a good thing. They'll keep an eye on him.'

She took another step towards him and forced a far from persuasive smile. 'So, someone managed to lock him up?'

'That's right, love. They did.'

'Shame you couldn't do the same. If you had, we wouldn't be standing here now.'

'I did my best, love. I can say that with my hand on my heart.'

'But your best wasn't good enough, was it, detective?'

'No, I guess it wasn't. You can't win them all.'

She was glaring now, cold, expressionless. 'You can leave now. You've said what you came here to say. Just go and leave me in peace.'

Grav watched her closely. 'I can't do that, love.'

She moved rapidly, like a sprinter off the blocks, hurling herself forwards in an upwards trajectory and hitting him with her full weight while still in mid-air.

Grav reached out in an instinctive attempt to grab the banister with a flailing hand, but it was never going to be enough. He toppled, as if in slow motion initially, and then dropped quickly, crashing down the wooden staircase, bang, bang, bang, and hitting his head hard on the floor tiles below. He was shaken, bruised, dazed, and too slow to move.

Rebecca rushed after him, squealing as she descended the staircase two or three steps at a time. Within seconds, she was straddling his prone body, sitting on his flabby midriff and raining down blow after blow that stung at first but became gradually less effective as she tired. She kept punching for a time, but then suddenly stopped in mid blow and began crying silent tears that slowly turned to a full-blown torrent that ran down her face as she wheezed and panted. She held both hands to her face and slumped at his side before rolling away, forming her body into the foetal position with her back curved, her head bowed, and her limbs bent and drawn up to her torso. Rebecca lay there, rocking slowly and sucking her thumb like a baby on the nipple. She was done. The inspector didn't deserve to die. He'd failed her, but he was at least on the side of the angels. He understood the difference between good and evil. He tried to do the right thing.

It took Gravel another minute or two to regain his composure as Rebecca lay there sobbing. He struggled slowly upright and sat there for a few seconds, looking down at her with genuine sympathy. She was a young woman in obvious torment. In some ways no less a child than the little six-year-old girl he'd encountered all those years ago. For a second he was back there, at the Smiths' Carmarthen home at the time of their greatest trial. But as he looked around him, taking it all in again, he was instantly back in the present as the past melted away. He lifted himself to his feet, took a pair of handcuffs from a coat pocket, bent down and secured her wrists, taking care not to apply them too tightly. 'What the hell happened to your hands, love?'

'N-nothing major.'

'You don't want to tell me?'

'No, not really.'

'Okay, come on, up you get. There's things we need to talk about.'

Grav assisted her to her feet with a guiding arm and led her towards the open door to the killing room, where he stopped and pointed. 'What happened here, love? Now would be a good time to start talking.'

Rebecca swallowed hard. 'I don't know what you're talking about.'

Grav put a hand on each of her shoulders, turned her gently towards him and looked her in the eye. 'You were seen at the river, love. You were seen throwing the remains in. Got it? A reliable witness made a written statement to that effect. Your car's on CCTV in the area at the relevant time. And then there's this room, the knife, the hammer. It doesn't take a genius to work it out. And it doesn't matter how careful you've been or what precautions you've taken. All the plastic in the world won't be enough to save you. When I get the scenes of crime people to have a good look at this place, they'll find more than enough evidence to link you to the bodies you dumped in the Tywi. There'll be blood, other body fluids, DNA. It only takes a tiny amount. Even the slightest microscopic spot that you've missed when cleaning up. In any nook or cranny. There's always something to find.'

He focused on her face, waiting for a response that didn't materialise as she stood there in silence. 'I don't think it's any coincidence that you carved the word paedo into Griffiths' forehead. The abuse you suffered at Sheridan's hands set you on this path all those years ago. That's mitigation of sorts in my eyes.

I'll help you if I can, love, but you need to start talking. You need to cooperate. Help me and I'll help you.'

She hung her head. 'So it seems further denial is hopeless. A lost cause.'

'That's right, love. It's time to talk.'

'I only killed sexual predators. Slime like Sheridan. Rats like Griffiths. Where's the crime in that?'

'That suggests there were more than two victims.'

She avoided his eyes.

'How many have you killed, love? There's no tape. It's off the record. You can tell me.'

'If you do one thing for me, I'll tell you everything.'

'What's that?'

'Can I trust you?'

'You can't take the law into your own hands, love, however much you want to. Whatever you feel the justification. It doesn't work like that... but I'll help you if I can. Within the confines of the system, you understand. I'm a serving copper at the end of the day. That's the best I can offer.'

'It wasn't what I was hoping for, but I guess it'll have to do. I'm expecting another one to the house this coming Sunday. He thinks he's meeting a child. He sent me photos. Vile photos. Disgusting photos. I was planning to kill him, but I guess that's not going to happen now.'

'No, it's not.'

'I need you to promise me that you'll deal with him. You'll use the evidence I give you to put the rat away for as long as possible. I've done your job for you, Inspector. I need to know you're not going to let me down again.'

'Where are the photos now?'

'You're going to do something? You'll make certain he pays a price?'

He nodded and meant it. 'You have my word.'

'They're on my laptop. All of them. He's been in touch with me for weeks. There should be more than enough to put him away, even for you.'

'Where's the laptop now?'

'It's upstairs on my bed. It'll tell you everything you need to know.'

He turned and guided her back towards the stairs. 'Show me.'

* * *

Grav took what he referred to as the scenic route on the return journey to the police station, and it took almost forty minutes longer than necessary to get there. By the time he drove into the car park, he was fully familiar with both the number of victims and Rebecca's modus operandi. What he didn't know, however, was the extent to which she'd tortured her victims prior to their deaths. She chose to hold back that particular titbit, and he chose not to ask.

The DI parked the car as near to the main entrance as possible and switched off the engine. 'Okay, we're here, but then you know that as well as I do.'

'So what happens now?'

He swivelled in his seat. 'You've killed five men, love. You've told me that yourself. That's a whole life sentence, whatever your reasons. I'm going to take you inside, put you in a cell and contact a duty solicitor for you.'

'I don't want a lawyer. I've already told you that.'

'You need one, love. I'm going to contact one and when they get here, you're going to tell them that you hear voices. Voices telling you to kill. Do you understand what I'm saying to you?'

'I don't hear voices.'

'Look, love, it's a full-life sentence, die in prison, or the chance of being banged up in a secure psychiatric hospital with the opportunity for treatment and eventual release. It's your only chance of ever seeing the outside world again. You'd have some hope, and that matters. I know which I'd prefer.'

'Why are you telling me this? Why would you want to help me, of all people?'

He placed a nicotine-yellowed forefinger under her chin and lifted her head gently from her chest. 'A part of me thinks I owe you, love. Maybe I could have done more all those years ago. Maybe if I'd had more experience I could have nailed that slippery sod despite his denials. If I had, we wouldn't be sitting here now. I'm convinced of that. And you're no risk to the general public from what I can see. It's not like you've been killing any random stranger for the buzz it gives you, like some mindless psychos do... so you're hearing voices, yeah? Agreed?'

'That's right. Voices that tell me to kill. Demanding voices that have dictated everything I've done right from the very start.'

He smiled thinly. 'There you go, love, you're convincing me already. Now all you've got to do is keep it up and convince everyone else.'

She nodded twice. 'Let's see what the voices are telling me.'

'They're telling you that you want a solicitor despite your earlier refusal, yes?'

'Time to cooperate. Time to take your lead. Absolutely. Loud and clear.'

'And you're feeling remorse. Genuine remorse. You're going to stress that, aren't you?'

'The only thing I regret is getting caught, but where would the truth get me now?'

'So, you're sorry?'

'Yes, I am. I'm deeply, deeply sorry. I only wish I could turn the clock back to before any of it happened.'

'That's it, love. Spot on.'

She nodded.

'This conversation never happened, right. If you ever mention it, I'll deny it point blank. I'll say you're making it up. Lying. Got it?'

'Yes, I understand. I won't let you down.'

'Voices, yeah, when you sit down with the duty doctor, voices, when you first speak to your solicitor, voices, when we sit down for the taped interview, voices. I want you to believe it yourself. I need you to be utterly persuasive.'

'I hear things, yeah, I get it. And thank you. I know you didn't have to help me.'

Grav stepped out of the car and opened the front passenger door. 'Okay, love, time to go. Out you get.' And then a joke. A line he'd used before. 'I'll introduce you to the custody sergeant. He's not a bad-looking bloke from a distance if the light's not too bright.'

Rebecca smiled as he took her arm and led her in the direction of the cells. It was time to pay whatever price the system deemed appropriate. Time to face her fate, whatever that may be. It was out of her hands now. Beyond her control and for others to decide. But what she did know with certainty was that she felt no guilt, no contrition and no regret. She was comfortable with her rationale. That's what she told herself. Her conscience was clear. Now all she had to do was focus, put on an award-winning performance and convince the decision-makers that the opposite was true.

32

Gravel and Kesey sat across the interview room table from Rebecca and a young duty solicitor in a sharp charcoal-grey business suit, who'd never felt more out of his depth in his entire life. The principal police surgeon for the county had decided that Rebecca was fit to be interviewed without the assistance of an appropriate adult, despite what he considered her less-than-convincing claim to hear voices, and so the wheels of justice continued to turn.

Grav stared into Rebecca's face and kept staring as she sat there saying nothing at all. 'Switch on the tape, Sergeant. I think it's time we made a start.'

'Will do, sir.'

'Before we begin the interview, Miss Smith, I need to remind you that you're still subject to caution. You do not have to say anything but it may harm your defence if you do not mention when questioned something that you later rely on in court. Anything you do say may be given in evidence. Is that clear?'

Rebecca glanced at her solicitor, holding his gaze for a second or two before suddenly looking away. 'I haven't done anything wrong. Why would I go to court?'

Grav rested his hands on the tabletop and leaned towards her. 'You've been arrested on suspicion of murder, Rebecca. This is your opportunity to respond to the allegations. To give your side of the story in your own words.'

She suddenly jumped up from her seat, swivelled on her heels, and spoke directly to the wall behind her. 'Okay, I hear you! I'll tell him what he needs to know.'

Kesey stood and took the prisoner's arm. 'Sit down please, Miss Smith. All you need to do is answer the inspector's questions. Nothing more.'

Rebecca gave a flamboyant V-sign to the wall and

sat as instructed. 'Okay. If he'll just shut up for a minute, I'll answer your questions.'

Grav felt inclined to applaud her performance, but resisted. She was convincing him, if nobody else. 'A little louder for the tape, please, Miss Smith. I could only just hear you.'

'I said okay! I've got nothing to hide. I'm a good girl. I do everything he tells me. What's wrong with that?'

'You do everything *who* tells you?'

She looked to her left and pointed. 'Him! Him! I don't know his name. Why don't you ask him yourself? See how he likes it.'

'It's you I need to talk to, Rebecca. The scenes of crimes officers have been over every inch of your house. There's a lot of blood spatters: in the lounge, the hall, on the stairs, in the shower. And there was human flesh in the freezer. Plastic bags full of the stuff. We're also in the process of excavating your back garden, and you know what that means. Two bodies have been found so far.'

She glared at him and spat her words. 'That's all there is. He told me to put them there.'

'So you admit to burying the remains of two men in your back garden?'

She glanced behind her again and shook her fist as her solicitor made scribbled notes that served little, if any, useful purpose. 'What are you talking about? They weren't men. I didn't kill men. Just rats and slugs and slime. I did everything he told me to. Every single thing. Why would anyone want to punish me for that?'

'How many? How many did you kill?'

She lowered her head and began to wail like a hungry baby. 'Only f-five. It should have been m-more, but *you* stopped me. He won't like that. He won't like it at all.'

'Who were they, Rebecca?'

She wiped away her tears with the sleeve of her jumper. 'Abominations that had to die. It's all on my computer. Why don't you look for yourself, if you really want to know?'

He nodded. 'We're doing just that. But why? Why did they have to die?'

She stopped crying in an instant and broke into a broad smile as if by magic. 'They were all predators.

Godless creatures who preyed on the innocent without thought or mercy. They destroyed one life after another, and would have continued doing exactly that if allowed the opportunity. Someone had to kill them. Why not me? It became my purpose in life. My reason for living. He told me that time and time again. "You've got to kill them, Rebecca. You've got to make them suffer." I've made the world a better place. Sheridan took my innocence, and I took their lives. That's how it was. I'd do it again if I could.'

Grav sat and silently acknowledged that a small part of him admired her for doing what she believed was right. But nobody could appoint themselves judge, jury and executioner. Not even her. 'What did you do with the other bodies?'

She sat upright in her seat, speaking louder than before. 'You found the two in the garden.'

'Yes, but there were three more. You've said that yourself.'

'Yes there were. Yes there were. That will be something to remember as I wallow in whatever concrete hell you send me to. That'll be something to meditate on in the lonely hours to come. Something to be proud of. But you already knew the answer before asking, didn't you?'

Grav nodded. 'You were seen putting something in the river. I need to hear it from you in your own words. I need the detail.'

She looked behind her again, waved her hands in the air in a whirlwind of activity and shouted, 'Okay, I'll tell him! I'll tell him if you leave me alone for one frigging minute!'

'Come on, Rebecca, look at me. Try to concentrate on what I'm asking you. What did you do with the other three bodies?'

'I cut them up and dumped them in the river, one revolting piece at a time. An arm here, a leg there, a head, until they were gone. And I flushed some into the sewage system. Small chunks I thought wouldn't block the pipes. Bodies are surprisingly heavy to carry, even when dissected. It seemed sensible.'

The increasingly peaky-looking solicitor raised a hand in the air, drawing Grav's attention and annoying him immensely. 'I think now may be an opportune time for a brief break. I'd like to consult with my client privately.'

Grav glowered at him. The ineffectual prat

didn't have a clue. A trained monkey would be more use to her. 'You heard what your solicitor had to say, Rebecca. We can adjourn the interview to allow you time to talk to him, if you so wish?'

She shook her head frantically. 'No, I want to get this finished with.'

'You're sure? It's no problem if you want to stop for a while.'

'I said no and I meant no. Why doesn't anyone ever listen to what I want?'

Grav looked at the lawyer as the young man sank back into his seat. 'You heard her, Mr Gilbert. I'm assuming you're in agreement to continue.'

He made an adjustment to his scarlet necktie as events took an unexpected turn. 'Yes, yes, that seems the most appropriate course of action given Miss Smith's wishes.'

Grav stifled a laugh. 'If you're sure, Mr Gilbert? It's in your very capable hands.'

'Yes, yes, please continue, Inspector. I'm obliged to accede to my client's instructions.'

'Then continue we will. Just as long as you're happy.'

The young solicitor took off his jacket, suddenly aware that he was sweating profusely.

* * *

Gravel spent the next couple of hours going through the specific details of each killing, from the planning stage to the eventual execution. Rebecca was eager to talk. Keen to tell her story, which she told with only occasional interruptions from the imaginary, disembodied voice that so insistently demanded her attention. There was more than enough to charge her. More than enough to put her away for a very long time. It was just a matter of where and what happened when she got there.

Grav pushed up his sleeve and glanced at his watch as his stomach began to rumble. Time for a pie and a few pints of amber nectar. Time to celebrate a good day's work. 'Is there anything else you'd like to say before we bring the interview to a close, Miss Smith? Anything at all?'

'Just that I haven't done anything wrong.'

'That's it?'

'Yes, that's it.'

He tapped the table repeatedly with the yellowed forefinger of his right hand. 'What about you, Mr Gilbert, any final words of legal wisdom to share with us?'

The solicitor's face reddened as he mumbled his response. 'No, thank you, Inspector. I've got nothing to add.'

Grav stood to leave. 'Switch off the tape, Sergeant. Let's get Miss Smith charged and back in her cell for the night. I don't think the CPS are going to have too many problems with this one. We can get her to the magistrates' court and on remand first thing in the morning.'

Kesey swivelled in her seat, looked up at him and left the tape running. 'Can I have a word in private before we finish, boss?'

Grav paused, weighing up his limited options. 'Interview suspended at seven thirty-two p.m. DI Gravel and DS Kesey are leaving the room.'

* * *

'What the hell's this about, Laura?'

The DS frowned. 'What happened to treating her like any other suspect?'

'That's what we're doing, isn't it?'

She shook her head. 'Oh, come on, boss. You've made no mention of the severed ear. It looks as if she's tortured the poor sod, and you're saying nothing at all?'

He was breathing more heavily now, his face reddening. 'She was talking, she's confessed to the killings. What more do we need? Job done.'

'What if she tortured all of them? We need to know. The court needs to know.'

'Just leave it there, Laura, there's a good girl.'

She clenched her teeth together. 'And what about all that voices bullshit? We worked with the woman. There'd have been signs of mental illness. We'd have known.'

'She's a killer. She hid that well enough.'

'She's been in there talking to the wall. We'd have spotted that much. She's putting it on, boss. She's full of crap. That's bloody obvious. Why let her get away with it?'

He took a deep breath and glowered at her. 'Now,

you listen to me, Sergeant. We're going to go back in there, we're going to close the interview without any further questions, you're going to switch the tape off when you're told, and then we're going to charge her with the murders... and that's an order, in case you were in any doubt. I've heard enough. Let's get it done.'

33

Forty-seven-year-old Dr Alistair Gower, a consultant forensic psychiatrist of some repute, had worked in secure units housing some of the UK's most disturbed female offenders for over fifteen years. Rebecca, in his opinion, was no better and no worse than many others he'd met and assessed during that time. It was just a matter of deciding if she was mentally ill or not. Did she really know what she was doing? Prison or hospital? Punishment or treatment? That's what he had to recommend. And then it was up to judge and jury.

The doctor leaned back in his seat, looked into Rebecca's eyes, and noted that her expressionless face appeared strangely devoid of feeling. 'Did you hear me, Rebecca? Or did my comment fall on deaf ears?'

She turned her head towards him and feigned bewilderment surprisingly effectively for an amateur actress. 'Sorry, I was talking to somebody else. Someone much more important than you.'

He nodded and smiled thinly, weighing up her every verbal and non-verbal communication in his analytical mind. 'Ah, yes, the voice in your head. I read the medical report commissioned by your legal team.'

She looked away, choosing to ignore his observation.

'Are your symptoms genuine? That's the question. You wouldn't be the first person to try to pull the wool over my eyes in the hope of an easier life.'

'I've got nothing to hide.'

'I'm sorry not to have been here when you first arrived with us. I was fully committed with other patients.'

'Well, you're here now.'

He opened the green cardboard file on the table

in front of him. 'So, this is day three of your stay with us. How are you settling in?'

'We like it here.'

'*We*, you said *we*.'

'That's right.'

'The staff tell me that you've befriended Sally Deakin. You've been spending a lot of time talking to her. Sharing your food.'

'I like her.'

'Do you know what she did to be here? Has she told you?'

'No.'

'Ah, I thought not. Best not give her too much of your food. She's very easily influenced. We try to restrict her calorie intake as far as possible. She hasn't threatened you, has she? Nothing like that?'

'No. I wouldn't want to be her friend if she had.'

He closed the file and smiled. 'Excellent, that's good to hear. Let one of the staff know immediately if that changes. She has been known to bully other patients on occasions.'

'She seems nice enough to me.'

'Do you know why you're here, Rebecca?'

'I haven't done anything wrong.'

He looked at her quizzically. 'You've admitted to killing five men. It doesn't get any more serious than that.'

She laughed until the tears rolled down her face. 'Are rat-catchers punished? Are they locked up for their service to society? It seems you don't understand. Perhaps what you perceive as the seeming contradiction between my intelligence and behaviour is too difficult for you to comprehend, despite your paper qualifications. They deserved to die. All of them. That's what you need to realise. I did the right thing. A worthy thing. He told me that time and time again. I don't accept society's self-imposed limitations. Why do you find that so difficult to accept?'

'You said *he* told you that time and time again. Who are we talking about?'

'God.'

'You're telling me that God tells you to kill?'

'Yes. And he doesn't like you very much. He told me that himself.'

'And did he tell you to torture your victims? The pathologist was somewhat graphic in that regard.'

She sat there in silence, choosing not to respond.

'You do understand that I'll be preparing a court

report following our assessment sessions, don't you? What you say during your stay with us may well influence your long-term future.'

She smiled without parting her lips. 'Am I mad or bad, eh? That's the question you're trying to answer. You're as misguided as the rest of them. I heard exactly what the judge said. I was there. Don't make the mistake of underestimating me, Doctor. That's never a good idea.'

The doctor nodded once, his glasses slipping to the end of his nose. 'Yes, if you want to put it in those simple terms, I guess that sums it up pretty much. I need to decide if you have a diagnosable mental illness.'

'Governments kill people en masse with impunity and justify it as war, and yet I'm the bad one.'

'We're here to talk about you.'

'So, what do you want to know?'

'Is it really going to be that easy?'

'Why not? I've got nothing to be ashamed of.'

'You've been charged with murdering five men.'

'So you said.'

He reopened the file and referred to his handwritten notes. 'They were torn to pieces.'

She smiled as she recalled events and magnified them in her mind. 'You keep using the word *men*. They weren't men. I don't kill men.'

'Please explain.'

'The things I killed were subhuman. A lower form of life polluting this world of ours.'

He paused before responding. 'You feel your killings were entirely justified?'

'Well, wonders never cease. You've actually got it. I've said that from the beginning. What's so difficult to understand?'

'They were human beings, Rebecca. Men engaged in deviant criminal behaviour, certainly. Flawed men in need of therapy, but human beings nonetheless.'

Her smile became a sneer. 'Do you really think you can change a man's sexual orientation? Are you really that naïve? It's laughable. You can't change a frog into a prince. That's the stuff of fairy tales.'

He looked at her in contemplative silence for a moment or two before finally closing the file. 'We'll talk further in the coming days, Rebecca. We have much to discuss.'

'Oh, that's wonderful. I'll count the minutes.'

'As a remand patient who's fully cooperated with the assessment process up to this point, I've chosen to house you in our medium-security psychiatric unit. You'll still be locked in, of course. There's no avoiding that given the seriousness of your crimes. But you've got your own room, a shower, a communal lounge, television privileges and greater recreational opportunities, such as pool and table tennis. If you continue to cooperate, you'll be able to take full advantage of those facilities. But remember, it's a privilege and not a right. Some of my staff doubt the wisdom of my decision. Any hint of aggression, and I'll have you moved to the maximum-security unit immediately. Do not abuse my trust, Rebecca. Do you understand?'

'I understand perfectly, Doctor, and I'm grateful. You won't have any trouble from me.'

* * *

Rebecca opened the large box of Swiss chocolates sent by her mother, popped a strawberry cream into her mouth, and sucked it in an exaggerated manner, before holding the box out for Sally Deakin to choose with chubby fingers. 'Take two, Sal. Ignore the staff, just enjoy yourself. You deserve a nice treat now and again.'

The thirty-three-year-old serial arsonist took two sweets at random and stuffed them into her mouth. 'Oh, lovely, where did you get them? I haven't had chocolates for ages.'

'My mum sent them.'

'You lucky sod. I never get sent anything. I don't even get visitors.'

'What, never?'

'Nope, nobody wants to know me.'

'Well, we're friends, aren't we? Screw everyone else. You can have the entire box if you do a small favour for me.'

Her eyes lit up as she pictured herself sitting alone in her room and devouring every single one. 'Really, all of them?'

'Take one more now, and then I'll close the box. Do exactly what I say and they're all yours.'

She looked at the box and then at Rebecca. 'Can I have some more now?'

'Just the one. You'll have to wait until tonight for the rest.'

She appeared very close to tears. 'You'd better keep your word. You wouldn't like me when I'm angry.'

'It's a promise. Best friends forever. Now listen carefully. This is what you have to do...'

Rebecca spent the next fifteen minutes or so explaining her plan in simple point-by-point detail she thought Sally couldn't fail to understand. She went over her requirements repeatedly, stressing the importance of each and every action and perfect timing. 'Have you got it, Sal? Are you up for it? The chocolates are yours just as soon as it's done.'

'Yeah, yeah, of course, no probs. Wait until just before the end of the two-till-ten shift and then do it. I'm not stupid.'

'No, of course you're not, Sal. I never thought that for a single second, but the timing is absolutely essential if we're going to succeed. We need some staff to be arriving and others leaving. We need to hit them when they're at their most vulnerable and create as much confusion as possible.'

'And then I get the chocolates, yeah?'

'And then you get the chocolates. And, if our plan works, if I get out of here, I'll send you a big box of your favourite chocolates every week for as long as you're here.'

She looked as excited as an expectant child on Christmas Eve. 'Every week! Oh, I can't wait. It's going to be brilliant.'

'But only if I escape. It's important to remember that. I can't send them if I don't escape.'

'I'll do my bit. You can be sure of that. And then it's up to you.'

* * *

Rebecca waved and winked once as Sally Deakin lifted herself to her feet at precisely ten p.m. and plodded slowly towards the pool table about twenty feet away.

Sally glanced in every direction, confirming that the only two nursing staff in sight were otherwise engaged, before pushing a chair right up against the metal edge of the pool table and using it to clamber onto the purple baize with her pockets stuffed with hard plaster balls. She remained on her hands and knees for a few seconds, catching her breath, before raising herself to her feet with the aid of a wooden cue.

Rebecca jumped to her feet, edged nearer to the exit and began pointing and shouting words of caution as Sally flung the first ball at the back of a nurse's head, missing by a matter of inches. As she threw a second ball, more accurately this time to the cheers of other patients, Rebecca left the room through a door left ajar by a junior nursing assistant rushing through in response to the high-pitched sound of the panic alarm.

Rebecca couldn't believe her luck. Sally's performance was better than she could have hoped. The timing was perfect. The staff members' reactions were just as she'd imagined. Rebecca hurried down a well-lit corridor without looking back, never looking back, and darted into the staff cloakroom she'd noted on the morning of her first arrival. It was empty. Just as she'd hoped. But she had to act quickly. The disturbance wasn't going to last forever.

Rebecca used the end of a stainless steel tablespoon to prise open one inadequately constructed wooden locker after another until she found a grey two-piece nurse's uniform that looked as if it would fit her reasonably well. She smiled on discovering a leather purse in a pocket as she pulled on the cotton trousers over her own, followed by the tunic, which completed the ensemble to her satisfaction. It was almost time to go. Just one final touch and she'd be on her way.

Rebecca took a deep breath, slowly counted to five inside her head, and repeatedly gouged her forehead with the edge of the spoon until the skin broke and warm blood trickled down her face. She was ready to go. Ready to make good the final part of her plan. Come on, Becca, you can do it, girl. She was as good as out of there.

She opened the door, inch by cautious inch, and hurried into the corridor, striding purposefully in the direction of a second door, which was opened with the click of an unseen button as she looked up at the security camera. Rebecca stepped out into reception, sensing freedom, praying for freedom, and stumbled forwards as a buck-toothed security guard wearing a navy jumper and peaked cap approached her. 'Are you all right, nurse? Can I get you some help?'

What to say? What the hell to say? 'It looks a lot

worse than it is, thanks. I just need some fresh air. If you could help me outside, I'd be grateful.'

'Strange. I haven't seen you before. And no wedding ring. I'd have remembered.'

'Just help me outside, please. I'm new.'

'Come on, take my arm. You look ready to keel over.'

She smiled as he took a large bunch of keys attached to a thin chain from his trouser pocket and unlocked the final door between her and freedom. 'One of the patients went totally berserk, but everything's back in control now.'

'Ah, we only deal with the external security. People coming and going. That sort of thing.'

'I don't know your name.'

'Steve, Steve Gibbs, what's yours?'

'Thanks, Steve, I'm feeling a little faint. Perhaps you could help me sit on that low wall over there.'

He supported her weight and walked her into the car park with a view of the road beyond. 'There you go. You sit yourself down and rest right there. You're looking a little better already.'

She lowered herself on top of the wall and held her sleeve to her forehead, pressing hard to restrict the gradually congealing blood. 'You've been an angel. Perhaps I could buy you a drink one night and say thanks properly.'

He felt his penis engorge with blood as she ran a painted nail up and down his right thigh. 'That would be great. How about tonight? I'm just about to finish.'

Think, Becca, think. 'I need to get home urgently. My mum's been taken ill, but I'll be back on Monday. How about then?'

'I can give you a lift. I'll just hand the keys over to my colleague and we can be out of here.'

'It's Plymouth. I need to get to Plymouth.'

'Ah... it's a long way, but what the hell. You'll be grateful. Maybe *very* grateful. How about we make a date of it?'

She laughed. 'You don't hang about, do you? But you never know your luck. I'd make it worth your while.'

He unfastened the hospital keys from his black leather belt and threw them towards a second older guard who'd appeared in the doorway.

'You haven't seen a patient out here, have you, Steve? They're one down on Gower ward.'

He shook his head and reached into a trouser pocket to retrieve his car keys. 'No, nobody. She'll be in there somewhere. They always turn up in the end.'

'Yeah, you're probably right. It's been years since anybody escaped.'

Rebecca stood and blew Steve a kiss as he walked towards her with a seductive smile on his very ordinary face. 'Come on, big boy, let's see how fast you can drive. Plymouth here we come. We need to be on our way.'

34

Kesey switched off her desktop computer, checked the time, and picked up the phone, hoping that an already long day wasn't about to get longer. 'Carmarthen CID.'

'Who's that?'

'Detective Sergeant Laura Kesey. How can I help you?'

'Hello, Laura, I thought I recognised your voice.'

She stiffened. 'Rebecca?'

'I need to speak to DI Gravel. Just get him. I haven't got time for small talk.'

'Where are you?'

She sighed. 'Just put him on the phone, Laura.

And don't bother trying to trace the call. He'll know exactly where I am.'

She stood and stared at Grav with blazing eyes as he approached her with an outstretched hand. 'Hello, Becca, where are you, love?'

'Oh, come on, you're the detective. Isn't it blatantly obvious?'

He rested his weight on the desktop, his chest tightening.

'Devonport?'

She laughed. 'So you're not completely useless then?'

'Have you killed him?'

She paused before replying. 'Not yet. I'm there now. I just wanted you to know it's nearly over. We've gone full circle.'

'Look, I get it, love. I really do. The man hurt you. He hurt your family. But it's time to stop. Five men are already dead. It's time to walk away. You wouldn't have rung if you weren't having doubts.'

'It's amazing who you meet when locked up with the criminally insane. People with contacts. Useful contacts.'

'What are you talking about, love?'

'I've got a gun. A pistol and six bullets. I don't think it's going to be nearly as much fun as a knife, but it's a lot quicker. I'm going to blow the dirty bastard's head off.'

He swallowed hard. 'I helped you, didn't I? When you were arrested. I did what I could, yes?'

'Yeah, you did. I'll give you that much.'

'Well, now I'm helping you again. If you kill him, you'll be locked up for the rest of your life. Just like I said before. You'll die in prison. I want you to take the bullets out of the gun, ring the local police straight after this call, and hand yourself in.'

'Do you remember what you said at the house when I asked you to walk away?'

'I said that I couldn't do that.'

'Well, I'm telling you the same now.'

Grav closed his eyes tight shut. 'I'm begging you, love. Ring the local police. There's been more than enough death and destruction. I was talking to your mother only yesterday. She wouldn't want you to kill him. She told me that herself.'

'Are you done?'

'Just hand yourself in, love. It's the only sensible option.'

Rebecca considered responding with a message for her mum, but decided against it. Actions spoke louder. What was the point of words?

'Are you still there, love? Are you thinking about what I've said?'

And with that, she put the phone down.

* * *

Kesey rose to her feet and glared at her boss as he collected his coat and approached the door. 'Where the hell are you going?'

'I need a drink.'

She rushed after him. 'What the fuck are you talking about? You've got to ring the Devon and Cornwall force. It's urgent. It couldn't be more urgent. She's armed, for fuck's sake. She's a ruthless killer, not some little girl in need of your care and protection.'

'I want to give her the opportunity to hand herself in. I owe her that much.'

She grabbed his sleeve and shook him. 'You're not thinking straight, boss. You've got to ring right now.'

He pulled himself free. 'Ring them yourself if you have to. I'm not stopping you.'

She rushed towards her phone as he fastened his coat and opened the door. 'Where's Sheridan's address?'

'On my desk, blue file. I'll see you in the morning.'

35

The police armed-response unit was ready and waiting by the time Rebecca left Sheridan's apartment building, covered from head to foot in his blood, and with his head in one hand and a black plastic water pistol in the other. She looked up as she negotiated a low metal barrier separating the pavement from the main road, and noted that there were three police cars in all, and at least eight uniformed officers, some with powerful automatic weapons aimed in her direction.

Rebecca held Sheridan's bloody head in the air as she walked slowly towards the guns, and then suddenly flung it along the road in the style of an enthusiastic participant in a tenpin bowling alley.

The officer in charge crouched low behind a convenient car and lifted a megaphone to his mouth. 'Armed police. Drop your weapon. Throw it aside and lie flat down on the road. Do it now!'

She took another step forwards, then another, then another, and then suddenly stopped.

'Drop your weapon!'

Rebecca glanced down, noted several points of intense light moving over her body, and began walking again, picking up her pace towards the armed officers, who were still about twenty yards away.

'Armed police, drop your weapon!'

Rebecca looked at each officer in turn, smiled warmly, and then lifted the water pistol, as if intending to fire.

The first bullet ripped into her exposed chest, ending her life in an instant as a second bullet blew her skull apart, sending fragments of brain tissue and bone spraying high in the air like a red mist that swirled and then slowly settled.

Rebecca's body slumped to the ground and lay twisted and broken just a few inches from Sheridan's head, with its blank, staring eyes that seemed focused on her and only on her as their blood ran and intermingled on the dark tarmac.

MORE FROM JOHN NICHOLL

We hope you enjoyed reading *The Tywi Estuary Killings*. If you did, please leave a review.

If you'd like to gift a copy, this book is also available as a paperback, digital audio download and audiobook CD.

The Castle Beach Murders, the next book in the series, is available to order now.

ABOUT THE AUTHOR

John Nicholl is an award-winning, bestselling author of numerous darkly psychological suspense thrillers, previously published by Bloodhound. These books have a gritty realism born of his real-life experience as an ex-police officer and child protection social worker.

Visit John's website: https://www.johnnicholl.com

Follow John on social media:

 twitter.com/nicholl06

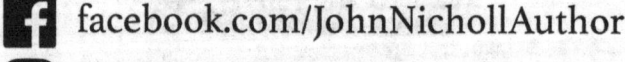 facebook.com/JohnNichollAuthor

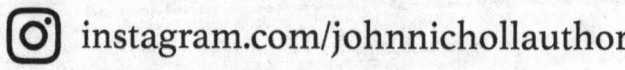 instagram.com/johnnichollauthor

Boldwood

Boldwood Books is an award-winning fiction publishing company seeking out the best stories from around the world.

Find out more at www.boldwoodbooks.com

Join our reader community for brilliant books, competitions and offers!

Follow us
@BoldwoodBooks
@BookandTonic

Sign up to our weekly deals newsletter

https://bit.ly/BoldwoodBNewsletter